1400

Killer on the Court

A *Murder, She Wrote* Mystery

OTHER BOOKS IN THE *Murder, She Wrote* SERIES

Killer on the Court

A *Murder, She Wrote* Mystery

A NOVEL BY JESSICA FLETCHER & TERRIE FARLEY MORAN

Based on the Universal television series created by
Peter S. Fischer, Richard Levinson & William Link

BERKLEY PRIME CRIME
New York

BERKLEY PRIME CRIME
Published by Berkley
An imprint of Penguin Random House LLC
penguinrandomhouse.com

Library of Congress Cataloging-in-Publication Data

Names: Fletcher, Jessica, author. | Moran, Terrie Farley, author.
Title: Killer on the court / a novel by Jessica Fletcher & Terrie Farley Moran.
Description: New York : Berkley Prime Crime, [2022] |
Series: A murder, she wrote mystery
Identifiers: LCCN 2021054446 | ISBN 9780593333655 (hardcover) |
ISBN 9780593333662 (ebook)
Subjects: LCGFT: Novels.
Classification: LCC PS3552.A376 K554 2022 |
DDC 813/.54--dc23/eng/20211105
LC record available at https://lccn.loc.gov/2021054446

Printed in the United States of America
1   3   5   7   9   10   8   6   4   2

Joan Marie Moran,
best daughter ever

Killer on the Court

A *Murder, She Wrote* Mystery

Chapter One

I awoke to the sound of chirping and saw a goldfinch perched on the outside ledge of my bedroom window, his yellow body brightening the gloomy overcast sky that served as his background. I slipped out of bed as carefully as I could, trying not to frighten him away. But it was no use. Birds are sensitive to motion, and he flew off. As soon as I opened the window wider, I could hear his friends and cousins singing in the trees. I began to take deep breaths of the warm, moist air coming in off the ocean. I was sure it would bring rain along with it well before the day's end.

During the summer months, I have an almost childlike expectation that every day will be sunny and cheerful. But if today wasn't going to cooperate, it didn't matter to me. I didn't need sunshine to feel exuberant. At exactly eight thirty-seven last night, I had placed my cursor on SEND and clicked with great determination. That was all it took to propel the manuscript I'd been diligently writing and rewriting for the past several months to my editor's waiting in-box with more than three hours to spare before my deadline.

I stretched my arms far above my head and then touched the floor. In the midst of my second stretch, I made a snap decision. Rain or no rain, I was going for a bicycle ride to shake off the stiffness caused by the long hours I'd been spending hunched over my computer keyboard.

I scrambled into a pair of jeans and a plaid shirt. After I grabbed my faded blue waterproof jacket from the coatrack in the front hall, I headed to the kitchen and poured a glass of orange juice just as the telephone rang.

I glanced at the clock, wondering who would be calling at ten minutes to seven in the morning.

"Jessica, tell me, is it true? Has the world-famous author J. B. Fletcher put another devilishly clever mystery to bed?"

I should have realized it would be my dear friend Seth Hazlitt. Doctors are well-known for being early birds.

I laughed. "Yes, it's true. The manuscript is right where it needs to be—on my editor's desk. I am somewhat surprised that you weren't able to hear me clapping and singing all around the dining room after I sent it off last night."

"Must have been quite a show. Sorry I missed it." Seth laughed. "I had my windows closed in case today's rainstorm came in early. But it's not too late to celebrate. Let's get the revelry started."

"Great idea, Seth. I was about to tour the town on my bike. Do you want to come along?" I teased. Before he could snap at me, I was quick to acknowledge that if Seth was talking about his favorite kind of celebration, it would be one that involved food. "Did I forget we'd made breakfast plans?"

"Woman, with that book taking up every inch of your brain for the past few weeks, do you think you would have remembered if we had?"

He had me there. In recent weeks, I had been so immersed in polishing the final chapters, I could hardly remember to eat three meals a day and to squeeze in enough exercise to keep my heart pumping. Any invitations I might have received were instantly forgotten the minute I agreed to the date and time.

Seth continued. "I will pick you up in, say, ten minutes, and then it's Mara's blueberry pancakes all around."

"I'm more than ready. I'll wait outside." I hung up the phone, put my juice back in the refrigerator, and walked out to wait by my front gate.

My neighbor Maeve O'Bannon was puttering in her garden. She waved at me with a hand wrapped around green-handled pruning shears. "Early morning to you, Jessica—best time of the day. I expect your book is finished?"

She caught me by surprise. "Yes, it is. I sent it to my editor last night. How on earth did you know?"

Maeve laughed and bobbed her head, which set her gray curls bouncing. "Barely seen hide nor hair of you for the better part of more than a week, and now here you are, all smiley and chipper. I said to myself, *Book must be finished.*"

"I can't tell you what a relief it is. This particular story had far more than the usual stumbling blocks. Several times I feared I wouldn't get to send it off to my editor on time." I shivered at the thought.

"Imagine that a former schoolteacher such as yourself would be late with an assignment. Now, that would never do," Maeve said with a broad wink.

"It absolutely would not," I agreed. "Seth and I are headed down to Mara's for a celebratory breakfast. Would you care to join us?"

"I thank you for the invitation, but these roses need caring for." She snipped a tiny branch off her yellow tea rose bush as if to prove the point. "Next time for sure."

Never mind that this was not the first time I had invited her to join a few friends for a meal and definitely not the first time she'd refused. Maeve seemed happiest working in her garden and in her kitchen. Even though she consistently refused my social invitations, I didn't take offense because I knew she considered us good friends. It just was not her way to socialize.

I heard a car roll up to the curb behind me.

"Ah, there's Seth. Good luck with your roses."

Mara's Luncheonette sits directly on the dockside of the cove that gives our town its name. It is a homey restaurant in an old-fashioned sort of way, with a long oak straight-plank counter, Formica tabletops, and vinyl booths and chairs. The wide, high windows along the luncheonette's back wall provide a breathtaking view of the harbor, which I suspected generally had the tourists oohing and aahing as soon as they walked in the door. But for most of Mara's regulars—that is, my Cabot Cove friends and neighbors—the real attraction is that the restaurant is definitely the town's gossip central, rivaled only by Loretta Spiegel's beauty parlor.

Seth held the door open for me, and as I had expected, nearly every booth, table, and counter stool was occupied. The chatter and laughter of friendly conversations filled the air, along with the tempting smells of sausage and bacon sizzling on the grill. No sooner had I entered than I was overcome by an instant automatic yen for coffee and a short stack of Mara's award-winning blueberry pancakes.

"Doc, Mrs. F., over here."

Our town sheriff, Mort Metzger, signaled from a table he was sharing with Mayor Jim Shevlin and, surprisingly, Dan Andrews, a newcomer who'd recently become editor of the *Cabot Cove Gazette* when Evelyn Phillips decided it was time for her to move on. The last I'd heard, she was in Baltimore visiting relatives. I missed her and hoped she'd come to see me soon.

"Are you sure you have room?" Seth looked doubtful. "I have to say that if you three are having some kind of confab about town business, we'd just as soon not interrupt."

We all knew Seth meant that, as always, he didn't want to listen to any kind of serious talk while enjoying his pancakes.

Dan Andrews immediately stood, looked around, and pulled a chair from a nearby table so that there were now two empty seats between his chair and Mort's. "Plenty of room, Doctor. Please join us."

Jim looked at me over the wire-framed eyeglasses perched low on his nose. "Susan told me she met you in the Fruit and Veg last week and you seemed stressed. Something about a deadline. Since you are here, am I correct in assuming everything is now fine? Deadline met?"

Jim Shevlin's wife, Susan, and I served on several committees together and she was my favorite travel agent. I'd been planning a beach getaway for as soon as I was done working on my latest book, so we'd had several conversations. Seeing Jim reminded me to check with Susan to make sure my plans were set.

"You can report that everything is back to normal. I sent my manuscript off to my editor and now I can relax. Tell Susan I'll call her later today."

Mara appeared with a coffeepot before we'd even settled in our chairs. After she poured coffee for Seth and me, she moved to top off the other cups. Jim and Mort accepted gratefully but Dan held his hand above his cup, indicating that he'd had his fill.

Seth and I ordered our pancakes, and when he asked for extra butter, Mara tut-tutted. "As if I didn't know your standard order by now: short stack, maple syrup, extra butter."

"Ayuh, you got that exactly right." Seth was practically salivating. "And since Jessica is celebrating, I believe I'll have a couple of strips of bacon."

"So the book is finished, eh, Jessica?" Mara asked.

"I am happy to report that it is." I couldn't help beaming with a smile that I am sure stretched from ear to ear.

"Well, even though my blueberry pancakes are the best you'll ever taste, I hope you are planning more than a pancake breakfast as your reward for a job well done." Mara laughed as she headed to the pass-through to place our orders.

"As a matter of fact, I am," I said.

"What are you going to do, Mrs. F.?" Mort crinkled his brow and I noticed his face was beginning to develop its usual summer tan line across his nose and cheeks where the shade from the brim of his uniform hat ended.

"Are you heading off to buy yourself something special at Charles Department Store? According to Maureen, their summer sale is loaded with terrific bargains. Just yesterday she bought me some snazzy swimming trunks. She's been complaining that she's embarrassed to be seen with me in public because the ones I have are what she calls 'raggy and baggy.' I suppose you could say she eliminated that problem. Last night I saw both pairs of my old swimming trunks in the garbage bin. She didn't even try to hide the fact that she'd tossed them."

"Now, Mort." Seth looked indignant. "Celebration doesn't mean 'go on a spending spree.' Why, I can think of a dozen ways—"

"I'm sure you can." I cut Seth off before he started spouting a long list of his penny-pinching ideas. "But I already know exactly what I am going to do. In fact, Jim, that's why I am going to call Susan later today."

"Planning a trip, are you?" Jim asked.

"Well, I didn't want the summer to get away from me without spending time with Grady, Donna, and young Frank, who is almost eleven and will be off on his own before you can say Jiminy Cricket. I want to spend as much time with him as possible before he is grown and forgets all about old Aunt Jessica." I laughed although I was only partially joking. "And now with the book turned in, I have a window of opportunity."

"So then you'll be off to New York City. Might be a bit too hot for my taste this time of year. And stuffy with all those tall buildings blocking the breeze." Seth huffed. "I suppose you'll want me to keep an eye on your house while you're gone."

"Oh, I don't think it will be too hot where I'm going."

I'm sure I had a twinkle in my eye. Because he could be such a fussbudget sometimes, I did enjoy teasing Seth, perhaps a little more than I should.

Seth raised his coffee cup to his lips and stubbornly refused to ask about my plans.

Dan Andrews said, "Before I came to Cabot Cove, I lived in New York City for my entire life. Jessica, it sounds like you are planning to stay somewhere close to the water."

I nodded and he turned to Seth. "Dr. Hazlitt, many people don't realize that four of New York's boroughs are situated on islands, and the Bronx, which is the fifth borough, is considered by many to be a peninsula, since only its northern tip is connected to the mainland. All through the city, there are dozens of rivers, creeks, and bays where folks can cool off on a summer's day, not to mention that New York City borders on a good chunk of the Atlantic Ocean."

I clapped my hands. "Dan, you got it exactly right. I've been invited to stay in a beach bungalow that my nephew Grady assures me is set right on the edge of the Atlantic."

Jim Shevlin looked surprised. "Surely not in the city proper. I can't imagine beach bungalows actually in the city. More likely the suburbs." He smiled as if he had answered his own question.

But I noticed Mort give Dan Andrews a wink. "Should I tell him or do you want to?"

Dan blushed slightly, his colorless cheeks turning ruddy. Clearly, as the newest editor of the *Gazette*, he didn't want to go up against the mayor unless he had to, and since this wasn't Cabot Cove news, he most certainly didn't have to.

He nodded to Mort. "You go right ahead, Sheriff."

If Mort had been standing, I am sure he would have hitched his gun belt as he automatically does when he is positive that he has his facts straight and is about to surprise everyone with what he has to say.

"Let me tell you, New York City has miles and miles of sandy beaches," Mort said, in a voice that barred any challenge. Then he turned to me. "Which dazzling New York City beach are you going to visit?"

"Are you familiar with Rockaway Beach?" I asked. "Grady told me it's in the borough of Queens."

"Am I familiar?" Mort chortled. "Mrs. F., I spent my very first summer as a rookie officer in the New York Police Department on a foot post in the Rockaways. Owen Collins and I walked our regular beat along the boardwalk from Beach Eighty-seventh Street to Beach One Hundred First Street. All day long we patrolled back and forth in the broiling sun. We loved it when we rolled into the night tours—you know, four p.m. to midnight. By that time of day, folks might have been rowdier if they'd had a beer or two, but soon enough that blazing sun was setting and the ocean breeze would come along to cool us down."

Dan Andrews laughed. "I'm surprised we didn't cross paths. My friends and I used to spread our blankets to the left of the lifeguard station on Beach One Hundred Third."

"Ahh, took the subway to Beach One Hundred Fifth and

then walked a couple of blocks east to avoid the crowd that marched straight from the subway stairs to the sand. Smart move." Mort turned to me. "So, Mrs. F., how did Grady score a place at the beach? They sure are hard to come by this time of year."

"Actually, when Grady invited me, he said that the vacation had something to do with Donna's new promotion at work. To be honest, my brain was still wrapped up in my book, so I didn't pay all that much attention. He, Donna, and Frank will be staying there for the entire month. When he invited me to join them, I had my book to finish, so he made me promise that the minute I submitted the manuscript to my editor, I would fly down to New York."

"And yet here you sit in Cabot Cove with us. I can't believe you didn't jump on Jed Richardson's plane and head south at the crack of dawn." Seth chuckled.

"That is exactly what I plan to do—tomorrow." I looked at Jim. "I spoke to Susan the other day and she assured me that I wouldn't have to worry about a thing. She would arrange my transportation and be sure my travel connections were in order. I gather she didn't mention that to you."

Jim shook his head. "No, she didn't. Telling me that when she ran into you in the Fruit and Veg you appeared frazzled about your deadline is merely chitchat. Divulging your travel plans would be a violation of Susan's sense of ethics."

I nodded, not the least bit surprised at Susan's standards of professionalism.

Dan said, "Rockaway is a terrific beach. When I lived on the west side of Manhattan, as soon as ten o'clock mass ended on summer Sunday mornings, my friends and I would hop on the A train and ride straight to the beach. That first tickle of the ocean lapping at your feet—there's nothing like it."

Mort broke in. "I am still curious, Mrs. F. How did Donna nail a bungalow through her job?"

"I am sorry to disappoint you, but I'm not sure. Other than Grady mentioning that Donna's company owns a number of bungalows and that Donna . . . Well, Grady said she won a month at the beach, which sounds like a raffle of sorts, but I am sure it is more likely that Donna received the opportunity as a bonus for a job well done. I promise that I will bring back the answers to your questions when I return home."

Chapter Two

As always, Susan Shevlin had arranged my travel schedule perfectly, right down to the minutest detail. Demetri, who with his cousin, Nick, has owned our local cab service for many years, was waiting in front of my house exactly ten minutes before I expected him. As soon as I opened my front door, he came along the walkway and took my suitcase.

"Good morning, Jessica. Your book is finally written, I see. Now you will have a little R and R, I hope. No more work for a while. Am I correct?"

"You are very correct," I said as I climbed into the backseat of his car. "I am going to swim in the ocean, play in the sand with my grandnephew, and catch up on my reading. I need to recharge my batteries."

And that was exactly what I repeated to Jed Richardson as he flew me in his Cessna 210 from Cabot Cove's airstrip into

Boston's Logan Airport, where I would catch my flight to John F. Kennedy Airport in New York.

"Might be so, Jessica. But everyone knows that trouble follows you like day follows night." Jed chuckled.

I stayed silent rather than tell him that I didn't find his observation to be the least bit amusing.

The flight from Boston to New York was less than an hour and a half. I drank a cup of black coffee and read a few of the short stories in the latest Malice Domestic anthology. As always, the stories were entertaining and mysterious in a deliciously cozy way. I looked forward to reading the rest of them during long, lazy afternoons while I sat in a beach chair and gazed out over the ocean from time to time.

I'd flown into and out of both New York City's Kennedy Airport and LaGuardia Airport many times, but I never tired of looking at the city from the air. This particular flight didn't give me a view of the Statue of Liberty, but I was able to see exactly what Dan Andrews had described yesterday: a city of islands separated by waterways large and small that were all crossed by bridges, lots of bridges.

I was on the down escalator heading to the baggage claim area in search of carousel four when I heard my name shouted with massive enthusiasm.

"Aunt Jess, Aunt Jess!" My grandnephew, Frank, named for my late husband, had one hand tucked behind his back and was waving wildly with his other arm. He was standing directly at the foot of the escalator while his father, my nephew Grady, tried, to no avail, to pull him out of the way of exiting passengers.

The other travelers were delighted to see such excitement

in the fair-haired young boy wearing denim shorts and a yellow shirt proclaiming ROCKAWAY BEACH in bright blue letters. One woman patted Frank on his head as she passed by. A balding middle-aged man with a golf bag slung over his shoulder turned to see who Frank was greeting, and when he saw me returning Frank's wave, the golfer gave me a thumbs-up and a smile.

As soon as I stepped off the escalator, Frank drew his hand from behind his back, presented me with a sweet bouquet of pretty pink flowers, and said, "Guess what these are called, Aunt Jess. They have a weird name."

"Why, I have no idea, but they are quite lovely. If I say 'I give up,' will you tell me the name?" I smiled.

"Swamp milkweed!" Frank was close to shouting again. "Isn't that a weird name for such a beautiful flower? Do you want to know why it has that name?"

Before I could answer, my nephew Grady gave me a kiss on the cheek and deftly slid my carry-on bag off my shoulder. "Frank, let's get Aunt Jessica's luggage and you can tell her all about the flowers on the ride home."

Then Grady turned to me. "We're so happy you're here, Aunt Jess. I can't wait to show you our bungalow. It's the perfect spot for you to relax. As dusk settles in, we sit on the front porch, gazing over a wide expanse of the sand and surf. Heavenly! And the bungalow is very modern. We even have a dishwasher."

Frank interrupted. "You even have your own room, right next to mine. We can tap secret code messages on the wall that connects us! I'm learning Morse code. 'F' for 'Frank' is dot, dot, dash, dot. When Dad said you were coming, I memorized the letter 'J,' which is dot, dash, dash, dash. That's all I learned so far, but we can memorize the rest of the alphabet together." He crowed with delight and then turned toward carousel four. "Which bag is yours, Aunt Jess?"

Luggage had begun drifting along the conveyor belt, and I was pleased to see my suitcase heading our way. I pointed. "It's the brown tweed right behind that extra-large black case with the green plaid ribbon."

Frank started to lean across the silver rail and reach toward my suitcase but Grady grabbed him by the back of his T-shirt. "Sport, I think that's too heavy for you. I'll get it."

Disappointed, Frank moved closer to me and frowned. "I bet I could have lifted it."

I changed the subject by tapping the tip of his nose with my index finger. "Why, I believe you have even more freckles than the last time I saw you. How did you manage that?"

But I had apparently landed on another "parents are always interfering" subject.

Frank scrunched his nose. "Mom says I am not using sunscreen often enough. She wants me to rub it all over myself every two hours. I'm busy all the time. How am I supposed to remember to keep redoing my sunscreen?"

I was secretly pleased that my suitcase contained a small gift that would remedy Frank's problem but I merely said, "You know the only reason your mother is concerned about your sun exposure is that she wants you to be healthy."

Frank nodded. "I know that, Aunt Jess. I really do, but sometimes parents just get in the way."

I had to smother a chuckle.

Grady held my suitcase high and asked, "Is this all you have?"

When I assured him we had everything I'd brought, he said, "Well, let's head for the beach. The parking garage is this way, Aunt Jessica."

I reminded Frank that I was anxious to know all about the swamp milkweed and he immediately flipped from disgruntled child to the bright happy boy I was used to visiting.

"Did you ever go to the Jamaica Bay Wildlife Refuge? It is an amazing place, and it's right near the beach. You wouldn't believe the different kinds of birds and animals that live in the refuge. Right here in New York City. And it is not even a zoo! There are animals roaming free. Who would think?" he asked.

"Certainly not me." I took his hand as we crossed the street to the parking garage. "Please tell me more about it."

"Dad took me there yesterday and a park ranger named Tariq showed us around. When we came to an area where the ground was covered with bushes of pink flowers as high as my elbow, they smelled so nice I had to stop for a minute. I said, 'I bet my aunt would love those flowers,' and Tariq told us they're called swamp milkweed. 'Swamp' because they only grow where the soil is really, really wet, and then he snapped a stem and showed us the milky liquid that flowed out, which is how it got the 'milkweed' part of the name. He let me pick a few flowers to take home to give to you and then we went to see the horseshoe crabs."

"Well, it sounds like you had quite an adventure. Maybe we can spend a few hours at the wildlife refuge while I am here. What do you think, Grady?"

Grady said, "I'm sure we can. That's our car over there. I did tell you we bought a new Chevy Blazer, didn't I?"

Frank asked, "Can I run, Dad?"

And when Grady gave him the go-ahead, the boy looked both ways carefully, then ran ahead to the car. He pointed to the dark blue SUV and called, "It's this one, Aunt Jess."

As we followed immediately behind him, Grady said, "I guess you can tell Frank is really happy to have you visit."

I laughed. "I think his eagerness is caused more by the adventure of showing off Rockaway Beach, Jamaica Bay, and the Atlantic Ocean. We've explored Manhattan dozens of times but this is a completely new experience for him and for me."

"True," Grady said as he popped the trunk and loaded my luggage inside. "And there are plenty of children spending the summer in the bungalows. I'm sure he'll tell you all about his new friends."

We were out of the garage and on our way, with Frank chattering nonstop. He described the ocean in vivid detail and finished with a warning. "Those waves can knock you right over if you aren't careful, Aunt Jess. Even Dad took a big tumble just the other day."

Grady nodded sheepishly. "True enough. Sometimes the waves are stronger than they look. And everyone has to be aware of the occasional riptide."

"That's why the only time we're allowed in the water is when the lifeguards are on duty. When we get home, I'll be sure to show you the lifeguard station. That way you can always know when it's safe to swim," Frank said, his enthusiasm wrapped in authority.

"Hey, Sport, Aunt Jess has been traveling since early this morning. She might want to unpack and relax for a few minutes before you take her off gallivanting," Grady said.

"You're right, Dad. Sorry, Aunt Jess. I didn't mean to push," Frank answered. "It's just that I'm so excited you're here."

I reached into the backseat and ruffled his hair. "Don't be silly. I am as excited as you are. However, your father is correct. We have an entire week to explore the beach and everything else you've mentioned. During that time I intend to have you teach me everything there is to know about Rockaway Beach."

"I will, Aunt Jess. I promise. And I can introduce you to all my friends. There are an awful lot of children here. A couple of the girls are a bother, always wanting me to help them build sandcastles when I'd rather build bridges and tunnels, but the other girls are great and so are all the boys I've met."

In a few minutes we were driving over a bridge and Frank said, "Aunt Jess, the water we are crossing is Jamaica Bay."

"Do you mean we are now riding above the famous Jamaica Bay, where horseshoe crabs roam free?" I teased.

"Yes, we are, and when we get home, I can show you the horseshoe crab I painted. Reggie taught me," Frank said.

"Is Reggie a friend of yours?" I asked.

"No, he's one of the art teachers. The other teacher is Carissa. She teaches us to make things out of clay. They both hold classes at the community center farther down the beach. Mr. Courtland hires teachers to keep us kids busy. We have plenty to do playing on the beach and swimming in the ocean, but since Mr. Courtland decided to hire teachers, I am glad he likes art because so do I," Frank said.

"Mr. Courtland? Grady, is he Donna's boss?" I asked.

Grady guided the car off the bridge ramp and onto a local street. "Jason Courtland is the chief executive officer of the company and the reason we are here. When Donna got her promotion at Courtland Finance and Investments, she was put in charge of a challenging project involving international mergers and tax liabilities. Apparently she did a bang-up job because a month at this beach bungalow was her reward."

"Lucky us!" Frank clapped his hands. "We all get to share it. Aunt Jess, I am having so much fun here. Wait and see. You will, too."

I laughed. "Well, if your enthusiasm is anything to go by, I'm sure I will."

Grady made a left turn into a parking lot and pulled into a space by a picket fence that looked to be made from natural wood. "Here we are, Aunt Jess."

I got out of the car and looked around. On the far side of the fence was the parking lot, which surrounded a six-story terraced apartment building topped by what appeared to be a penthouse apartment with a well-tended garden terrace.

Frank tugged my sleeve. "Look, Aunt Jess, the Atlantic Ocean."

I turned and looked in the direction he pointed. The landscape was dotted with at least half a dozen beach bungalows of different sizes surrounded by ornamental grasses and plants. When I peered between the houses, I saw waves coming in from the ocean onto a wide stretch of sand.

"Looks like low tide," I said.

"How did you know?" Frank asked. "Dad had to explain it to me. This month it's low tide at lunchtime. High tide in the morning and the evening. Did he tell you?"

"The sand in front of the waves is wet, which tells me that other waves have already covered that area. And since these waves don't reach the dry sand, well, the waves must be going out, not coming in."

"That's genius. I'll have to tell my friends. It is a safety thing. When it is high tide, the water is coming in and getting deeper. No one wants to get caught in water over their head."

"Frank, where were you? We painted starfish on seashells today."

Two small girls with neatly braided sun-streaked hair had run into the parking lot from between the houses. Their unbuttoned beach robes showed matching green bathing suits splattered with goldfish. The older one stopped in front of us, dropped the pail she was carrying, and planted her fists resolutely on her hips.

"You missed a lot of fun."

"Madeline, I had a better time going to the airport. Aunt Jessica, this is Madeline and Juliet. They like to build sandcastles."

He rolled his eyes and I had to laugh at Frank's way of letting me know that these were the two girls he thought were a bother.

Then he said to the girls, "My aunt's name is Mrs. Fletcher."

Madeline said, "How do you do, Mrs. Fletcher? Frank's mother is Mrs. Fletcher, too. Your family is like our family. We have lots of Mrs. Courtlands."

Juliet interrupted. "Except for Aunt Edwina. She is Mrs. Courtland-Young because she married Uncle Tyler. I think that's an awfully long name."

As if on cue, a tall woman dressed in black shorts and a

matching tank top came across the parking lot. Her tan was so deep that I wondered if she spent her winter evenings at a tanning salon. She appeared to be approximately sixty years old but I did wonder if all that tanning had aged her face beyond her years. She looked directly at Madeline and Juliet.

"Young ladies, your mother is looking for you. March on home."

"Yes, Aunt Edwina."

And the girls ran toward the bungalows, pigtails flying behind them.

Edwina held out her hand to me. "You must be Donna's aunt. I am delighted to meet you."

Grady stepped forward. "Aunt Jessica, may I introduce Edwina Courtland-Young, who is a member of the board of directors of the company Donna works for, Courtland Finance and Investments."

I must admit that I was disconcerted when Edwina waved the title away and began to rant. "According to my brother Jason, the exalted CEO of the company, we directors are superfluous. He claims he keeps us around only to make the company look good to our clients and investors. And I am sure he is correct, because he certainly doesn't give us any opportunity for real input."

I was at a loss for a response but Grady rescued me by ignoring everything Edwina had said. He gave her a wide smile and assured her that we would all have lunch together one day during my visit. Then he purposefully hoisted my suitcase and told Frank to carry my tote bag, signaling that we were on our way.

Edwina said she would love to get together and walked off

toward the street while we headed to the houses. When she was out of earshot, I thanked Grady for his quick thinking.

"I was surprised that Edwina was so open about her annoyance with her brother regarding how the company is run. It's one thing to speak in front of you, but I'm a complete stranger."

"Don't mind her, Aunt Jess. Donna thinks it's sibling rivalry. Edwina carps about Jason nonstop. She avoids the negative talk only if either he or her mother is present. In those cases she is sweet as pie, unless she has already drunk one too many margaritas or whatever is her preferred indulgence."

We followed a path between the two largest houses and then the garden opened up to a view of the white-capped ocean under a nearly cloudless sky. Grady led me to the front porch of a white clapboard cottage. Donna must have heard us as we clambered up the porch steps because she pushed open the screen door and greeted me with outstretched arms.

"Aunt Jessica, I can't tell you how happy I am that you could make time to share our good fortune." She enveloped me in a big bear hug, her blond curls tickling my nose.

"Oh, Donna, I was delighted when you called. This last book was . . . Well, let's say I had tremendous difficulty wrestling it into shape. Your call was the exact push I needed to get the manuscript finished so I could spend time with my three most favorite people in the world."

Donna gave me an extra squeeze. "Now, you go unpack and relax. Grady will barbecue a few burgers tonight and then we can have a restful evening sitting on the porch, listening to the waves hit the sand. There is not a more peaceful sound anywhere."

Frank grabbed my hand. "Let me show you where your bedroom is."

My room was cozily arranged. The coverlet on the double bed was a bright pink chintz spread, which matched the pink-and-white-striped curtains decorating the high, wide windows. There was a comfortable brown leather chair that looked like a rocker/recliner, and a few magazines were piled on the night table next to a pitcher of water and a stack of paper cups. When I opened what I thought was a door to a second closet, I was delighted to find a small bathroom with a walk-in shower.

I took my time unpacking. After I washed up, I changed into black shorts and a gray golf shirt. Totally comfortable for a family meal on the porch.

When I came into the living room, Donna looked dismayed. "Oh, Aunt Jess, I am so sorry. Mrs. Courtland just called. She insisted that we come to her house for dinner promptly at seven. I tried to dissuade her but . . ."

"Oh, Donna, I understand. I take it that Mrs. Courtland is your CEO's wife. Duty calls. We must answer."

Tired as I was due to spending much of the day traveling, I consoled myself that getting to the Courtland house would involve only a few minutes' walk.

"Oh, no, Aunt Jess, it's not that simple. The invitation was extended by Matilda Courtland, the family matriarch. Jason Courtland, the CEO, is her eldest child. Matilda is the reason we are all here at Rockaway Beach. She owns the bungalows and she rules the family with an iron fist. Believe me, she spares no expense to keep the family together and available at her beck and call. Last year Matilda commanded them all to travel through Europe together to celebrate her eighty-fifth birthday. From what I heard, there wasn't a lot of enthusiasm but not one family member dared refuse."

"Well, I suppose she who controls the purse strings has the most to say," I answered.

"In any event, Jason's wife's name is Linda. And I will introduce you to her tomorrow. She is an avid tennis player and always looking for a partner. In fact, I am scheduled to play with her in the morning. I can tell you right now that she will beat me in straight sets and be absolutely delighted to do so."

"I take it she's a highly competitive person," I said. "I've noticed that corporate wives often are, if only to hold up an image that matches their husband's."

"'Competitive' suits Linda to a T. In fact, from what I've heard, she is the only family member ever to go up against Matilda and win. Linda wanted a private tennis court here on the property so she could practice without driving to the tennis club or, heaven forbid, playing on the local public courts."

"And I take it Matilda Courtland complied."

"Did she ever! Wait until you see Linda's tennis court. It could easily be mistaken for Wimbledon's Centre Court, except that Linda required a hard court surface to keep her competitive on the country club circuit. The only thing missing is the stands, but there are lovely wooden benches with filigree wrought iron arms. We can walk over there tomorrow. It's right behind the other guest cottage. For now, we'd better get dressed for dinner."

Chapter Three

I was not surprised that Matilda Courtland lived in the largest house in the complex. Her wraparound porch was fully screened and seemed to have enough rocking chairs, lounges, and porch swings to host the entire Courtland family along with plenty of visitors besides.

A tall sepia-complexioned woman wearing a long white apron over her red blouse and black slacks opened the door and greeted us warmly. She had a Caribbean lilt to her voice. "I'm so glad you could come for a visit." She turned to me. "Tilly can't rest until she meets everyone who is staying in any of these beach houses. You must be Aunt Jessica. Young Frank could not hold on to his excitement. He's been counting the days until you came. Welcome. I'm Anya Wiggins."

We settled in a living room furnished in white wicker with green-and-blue-pastel cushions. The walls were painted a barely there powder blue and decorated with collections of what looked like family pictures taken on the beach over dozens of years.

Anya brought in a tray holding a pitcher of lemonade and glasses. She set it on the coffee table and said, "Please help yourselves. Tilly will be with you shortly. I've got to get back to the kitchen and tend to dinner."

I thought it was odd that we were being left alone in someone else's house but Grady and Donna seemed comfortable, so I relaxed and we began planning our adventures for the week.

I said, "I confess I have one bit of business I would like to accomplish. I'm not sure how to get there from here but I'd like to have lunch in Manhattan with my new publicist. We've never met, and I—"

"The ferry is probably your best bet. It's a quick trip, about forty-five minutes or so from the dock on Beach Hundred Eighth Street to Wall Street." A rotund, wizened, gray-haired woman leaning on a silver-tipped black cane stood in the arched doorway that led to the dining room. She continued. "You must be the aunt. I'm Matilda Courtland. I hear you're a famous writer. Have I read anything you've written?"

People using words like "famous" when talking about my writing always makes me uncomfortable, and it's worse still when they ask me if they've read any of my books.

Anya came up behind Matilda and poked her arm.

"Tilly, stop your teasing. All along, you've been so excited to learn that J. B. Fletcher, one of your favorite authors, would be spending some time here at the beach. Why, Mrs. Fletcher, Tilly has a stack of books she's hoping you will sign. Her favorite is *The Corpse That Wasn't There*."

I was relieved to find that Mrs. Courtland was merely teasing me. It would have been awkward to spend the evening explaining who I am and what I write. "Of course I'd be happy to sign whatever books you would like me to, and please call me Jessica."

"We can save the signing for after dinner. Right now, please, everyone, let's be seated," Anya said.

Mrs. Courtland led the way to the dining room. She took a seat in the armchair at the head of the rectangular mahogany table, which appeared much too heavy for a beach house. She signaled me to sit at her right-hand side. As I took my seat, I noticed the chairs had deep brown tapestry seat covers. Again, not beachlike at all. It seemed odd for the living room to be so beachy and the dining room to be so opposite.

Donna sat at Mrs. Courtland's left, with Grady next to her. Frank took the chair by my side. Anya came back into the room, carrying a tray covered with salad bowls. She served us each a fine array of greens, cucumbers, and tomatoes and then sat in the armchair at the foot of the table. She pointed to three small crystal bowls in the center of the table and said, "Help yourself to whatever dressing you choose. Donna, please pass the green goddess to Tilly. It's her favorite."

Matilda asked Frank if he was enjoying his time at the beach and he regaled her with stories of all he'd been doing. She seemed genuinely pleased that he was having fun during his family's stay as her guests and said, "I am glad that you are enjoying the art program. I do think that is the nicest of the amenities here at the beach."

As Anya served the main course, a delicious mango

salmon on a bed of jasmine rice, Matilda asked Grady and Donna if they had any interest in boating.

"I don't know if anyone has mentioned it but we have several smallish motorboats docked on the bay side. You are welcome to use them whenever you like," Matilda said.

"The bay side," Frank practically squealed. "You have boats in Jamaica Bay?"

I had to smile. I was fairly certain I knew where this was leading.

"I do indeed. I take it you have a special interest in Jamaica Bay, young man?" Matilda seemed pleased that her offer had generated such enthusiasm.

"Dad and I were at the Jamaica Bay Wildlife Refuge in Gateway National Park yesterday. It was awesome. We promised to take Aunt Jess to visit the refuge. Imagine if we could see it all from the water view."

"That won't be a problem. Our boats are moored in the Moonbeam Gateway Marina off Flatbush Avenue and we have an experienced captain available. Anya will make the arrangements for you. Won't you, Anya?"

Anya reached over, patted Frank's hand, and gave him a big toothy grin. "It would be my pleasure. I'll call your parents in the morning after I have a chance to check Captain Craddock's schedule."

Frank could barely contain himself. "Did you hear that, Dad? We're going to ride in a boat on Jamaica Bay!"

A deep male voice said, "Don't forget to take a rod and reel. There's great fishing on the bay."

A tall man, wearing navy blue slacks and a beige golf shirt, was lounging against the doorjamb between the kitchen and the dining room. His dark bushy eyebrows contrasted with his light skin and threw shadowy circles beneath his blue eyes. He walked directly to Matilda and she presented her cheek, which he dutifully kissed.

"Jessica, this is my son Jason."

Ah, I thought, *the company CEO. No wonder Donna began fidgeting at the sound of his voice.*

An awkward silence enveloped the room. Anya stood and began clearing the table. Finally Matilda said, "Well, don't hover, Jason. Either take a seat or go about your business. Anya is getting ready to bring out dessert."

Jason slipped into Anya's vacant seat and said, "Mrs. Fletcher, I can't tell you how pleased we all are with your niece's performance at our company. Not only is she diligent and meticulous, but she manages to inspire those same traits in her subordinates. She is a team leader without equal. You should be very proud."

While I was assuring him that I was not the least bit surprised to hear of Donna's excellent performance, Anya began to serve chocolate parfaits garnished with strawberries. Jason signaled to Anya to come and reclaim her seat.

"No need for you to get up," Anya said between tightened lips. "Enjoy dessert with your mother and her guests. I have work to do in the kitchen. Does anyone care for a cup of coffee? No? Tea, then?"

Matilda and Donna both opted for tea. And Anya disappeared into the kitchen once more.

"Mr. Courtland," Frank asked, "what kind of fish do you think we can catch in Jamaica Bay?"

"Well, this time of year, I'd say you'd find striped bass and bluefish jumping right onto your hook," Jason said. "Either one will make a delicious dinner."

By the look on Frank's face, I could tell the thought of eating his catch had never entered his mind. I'd have to remember to tell him stories of the many times I'd gone fishing in Cabot Cove and thrown back what I caught. The fun was in the catching, not in the keeping.

Grady quickly changed the topic to his recent visit with Frank to the wildlife refuge. He stressed how extraordinary the wildlife and foliage were, especially to city dwellers.

Jason asked Frank, "Did you see any diamondback terrapins while you were there?"

"Yes, we did. Tariq, the ranger who showed us around, said we were lucky. Some days the turtles stay in the water, but yesterday we saw a group of diamondbacks sunning themselves on the grass. We also saw two really huge horseshoe crabs. Did you know those crabs have been around since the dinosaurs were still alive?" Frank stopped long enough to taste a spoonful of parfait.

Jason looked deeply interested. "I did indeed. And what did the ranger tell you to do if you ever come across a horseshoe crab that's been flipped by the waves and is stranded on its back?"

"Tariq said that I should flip the crab over very carefully by only touching the edge of its shell. I might have thought grabbing its tail would be an easier way to flip it, but Tariq said the tail is very sensitive and pulling on it could cause serious damage to the crab."

I noticed that while Frank was talking, Jason nodded as if he were following every word, but in reality his eyes never left his mother. As soon as Matilda pushed her parfait dish away and placed her napkin on the table, Jason stood up.

"Mother, I was wondering . . . I hate to take you away from your guests but might I have a small word?" Jason gave Matilda a tight smile, expecting her to return it.

Instead I heard Matilda draw a sharp breath and she didn't answer her son.

Jason repeated with a touch of impatience. "Mother? A word?"

Matilda sighed. "I suppose if we must."

She leaned heavily on her cane and rose from her chair. Jason offered her his arm and they left the room. The rest of us sat silently until we heard the front door open and close.

Grady started to ask, "What do you think . . ." but went quiet when Anya came in from the kitchen, carrying a white china teapot.

She stopped dead when she saw that Matilda and Jason were gone. Then she set the teapot down between Donna and Matilda's empty chair and shook her head. "That rascal. No matter how many times I tell him not to bother his mother with business, he doesn't listen."

She sank down into Matilda's chair and turned to me as though we were old friends and she had a secret to confide.

"I joined the family many years ago. I was nanny to the children. First Jason, then Edwina, and finally Dennis. They were all strong-willed, each in their own way, but only Jason learned to pester his mother for everything and anything he wanted. Didn't matter what I said. Didn't even matter what his father—may he rest in peace—said. Whether it was a new bicycle when he was ten or a fancy new car when he was twenty, it was never important who said no because Jason could magically talk Matilda into turning no to yes."

Donna began toying with her napkin. I could only imagine how difficult listening to these intimate details about the Courtland family must have been for her. We all sat wordlessly, waiting for Anya to finish, but she was far from done.

"All these years later, he still uses her. I can tell you that Tilly lost interest in running the business many long years ago. But whenever he feels the need, Jason comes in and hounds her about something or other to do with the company. Her words have no real meaning except that he uses them against the rest of the family. When he wants to do something that the others don't support, he spends twenty minutes with Tilly and then he announces, 'Mother thinks it would be best if we do it my way.'" Her shoulders slumped. "He is her son. I can't protect her from him. But someday, you mark my words, he will cause her to have a stroke."

I looked at Donna, who was practically cringing, so I came up with a distraction. "Anya, perhaps Donna and I could clear the dinner table."

Relieved to have a way to end the conversation, Donna jumped up so quickly that her chair wobbled on its hind legs but finally settled without falling back. Donna never noticed. She busied herself and began removing parfait cups and spoons.

I asked if Anya wanted a cup of tea and she nodded mutely. Donna stepped into the kitchen and brought back a clean cup that she filled from the teapot and placed in front of Anya. I moved the sugar bowl and creamer near her cup but she waved them away.

She took a deep swallow of tea and said, "Thank you. I need the strength to take care of Tilly in case he really upsets her with whatever scheme he is trying to get her to be party to right now."

Grady said, "Perhaps it would be best if we leave." Which I thought was a fine idea.

"Well, unless you want to sneak out the back door, there is no way you can get past the two of them out there on the front porch. You'll have to wait until Tilly finally says, 'Do as you please,' and then Jason will go away and Tilly will go to bed with a migraine that may last a day or two. In the meantime Edwina, Dennis, and Tyler will all come sniffing around, trying to find out if Tilly really supports whatever Jason's latest plan may be," Anya said, "and there will be harsh words."

At that very second, we heard the screen door open and slam shut, followed by the sound of Matilda's cane and footsteps echoing across the living room. When she came into the dining room, her face was pale and drawn. Grady instinctively offered his arm, which she took gratefully. Frank jumped up and pulled out the chair that Anya and then Jason had been using. Matilda sat down and looked around as if wondering what she should do with us all.

Grady reached out his hand and said, "Thank you for having us, Mrs. Courtland. It was a delicious dinner. We enjoyed our evening very much."

Matilda took his hand and her eyes softened with gratitude, I supposed because Grady's words made the end of our visit appear natural and seamless and removed the burden of being the hostess from her shoulders.

I said good night and promised to come back within a day

or two to sign Matilda's books. Thankful as we all were to leave, I am sure Matilda and Anya were far more grateful to see us go.

The sky was clear and filled with stars, and a nearly full moon reflected repeatedly as the ocean's waves came ashore and retreated.

Donna asked if I would like to walk down to the water's edge. Before I could answer, Frank said, "Please, Aunt Jess."

I laughed. "Grady, would you like to make it unanimous?"

Grady was hesitant. "Well, if you are not too tired. It is a beautiful night."

"Tired?" I replied. "Even if I was tied up in knots, the sound of the waves and the vision of sky and sea would untie me instantly." I took Frank by the hand. "Lead on."

We walked silently to the very edge of the ocean. Grady and Frank slipped out of their footwear and rolled up their pants legs. They ran to meet the very top of each wave as it rolled in.

Donna put her arm around me. "Aunt Jess, I am so happy you are here. You have no idea how strange it feels to spend my leisure time among the family who owns the company where I work. There is not one moment of relaxation for me. I am constantly on my guard. Now that you are here, I have someone I can talk to without worrying about every word that comes out of my mouth."

"I am glad you feel that way about me. You know I feel the same about you. As to the Courtlands, you must remember that families do have their ups and downs and misunderstandings."

"I suppose you're right, but the Courtlands seem to have more than their fair share of drama," Donna said.

"Oh, yes, I can see that. To be honest, I do have a question or two about the family dramas that seem to occupy them. I am curious about Jason's siblings. I wonder how they feel about his special relationship with their mother."

A wave knocked Frank to one side and he landed in a small puddle of ocean water. Grady picked him up and that led to both of them being soaked. At that point Donna decreed it was time for us all to head back to the bungalow and turn in for the night.

It had been a very long travel day and going to bed seemed like a wonderful idea. My questions about the Courtland family could wait until the morning.

Chapter Four

I woke the next morning with boundless renewed energy. Sunlight poured through my bedroom window, signaling we were going to have a wonderful beach day. It was barely past six thirty a.m., so I decided that a walk along the shore would be the perfect way to entertain myself and get to know my surroundings. I pulled on the shorts and golf shirt I'd started with the night before and slid my feet into a pair of slip-on sandals. I filled my water bottle and left a note by the coffeepot in the kitchen to let Grady and Donna know I'd be wandering around the beach.

I opened the front door and was surprised to see Frank sitting on the porch swing. He put down the book he'd been reading.

"Good morning, Aunt Jess. I remembered you are an early bird, so I hoped you'd be the first one awake. Do you want to go to the water's edge with me and we can build bridges and dig tunnels?"

He pointed to what, at first glance, I thought was a wagon filled with shovels and pails of various sizes. Then I took a closer look.

"That sounds like a fine idea," I said, "but first, tell me, is that a sled you have to haul your equipment around the beach?"

"Yes, it is. They call it a pull sled. The double slats that run around the top side are supposed to prevent little kids from falling out when their parents pull them through the snow. Dad found it in the garden shed behind Mrs. Courtland's house and she said I could use it. Lots of kids here have them. And some of the grown-ups use them to carry beach chairs or coolers. Dad said, 'If it works on snow, it should work on sand,' and he was right. It does."

"What a dandy idea that is. If you'll give me a minute, I will be back and ready for action." I went inside to add that Frank was with me to the note I left for his parents and was back in a flash. "Now, my fine young man, let's see what we can create with all this wonderful sand."

Frank grabbed the sled handle and gave it a pull, and we headed toward the ocean. A couple of early-morning surfers on colorful boards were riding the waves in and paddling out again.

Frank stopped a few feet from the water's edge. "This looks like a good place to work."

He pointed about five yards to our left. There were multiple footprints heading to and from the ocean. "The surfers are coming and going over there. If we stay here, we won't be in their way."

"You can be the construction supervisor. I don't know much about building bridges and tunnels, so you'll have to tell me what to do," I said.

Frank stood with his hands on his hips and said, "Well, the most important rule for building anything in the sand is to use plenty of water. The wetter the sand, the better it sticks together. That's why we build close to the water's edge. That is where the wet sand is and where we can easily get more water if we need it."

Frank looked so serious that I had to resist calling him "boss" when I replied, "Got it. Should we start by filling buckets with water so we have it at the ready?"

Frank picked up a large blue pail and passed a slightly smaller one to me. "Good idea. And you can decide what we should build first, a bridge or a tunnel."

I wondered which one was easier but decided not to ask. "How about a bridge? Will I be able to manage that?"

"I'm really good at bridges," Frank said with great confidence. "We won't have a problem."

Each time I had a chance to visit Grady's family, I marveled at how self-assured Frank was becoming. In the blink of an eye, he was growing from a little boy into a young man.

We walked into the ocean until the water was just below my knees and we scooped up buckets full of water. Back at our construction site, Frank emptied his pail onto the sand. He told me to put my pail back on the sled.

"It will be our reserve. Now take this."

He handed me a green shovel with a long wooden handle.

"We need to pile the wet sand into a really big mound. When the mound is tight, we'll use your bucket of water to saturate it and tamp it down. That will make it superstrong. Then we'll dig out the underside and shape the bridge."

I was tempted to salute and say, *Aye, aye, Captain.*

Instead, I dutifully followed Frank's directions. We were making progress when Frank noticed a woman who was running along the water's edge. He waved and called out, "Miss Carissa, come meet my aunt Jessica."

A red-haired woman, probably in her early forties, wearing a long-sleeved T-shirt, running shorts, and top-of-the-line Nike ZoomX running shoes, waved back. She slowed to a half jog as she got closer to us and stopped when she saw we were working in the sand.

"That's my star student, Frank Fletcher, practicing even when we are not in class." She smiled at me. "I'm Carissa Potter. I teach sculpture at the community center art project, and Frank is one of my most talented students. You must be the mystery writer Frank told me was coming to visit."

"I am happy to meet you. I'm Jessica Fletcher." I reached out my hand, but she shrank back.

"I've been running for more than an hour, so I'm far too sweaty to touch. I'd better get home to shower and change and get ready for the day. Mrs. Fletcher, it was lovely to meet you. Please feel free to come to class with Frank anytime. We are very informal here."

"Thank you. I think I would enjoy—"

A loud shriek pierced the air, startling us all.

Frank straightened immediately and said, "Oh, no. That's my mom. She must be hurt."

He ran at top speed toward the bungalows. I called to him to wait for me but he kept going. Carissa and I exchanged a look and we both tore after him. The wailing sound continued. Frank followed the noise, running around the corner of first one house and then another. We were not that far behind him but couldn't quite catch up.

When we turned the second corner, I stopped. Ahead of me Grady was holding Frank and smothering him into his chest. On a bench a few feet away Donna was clutching her knees and crying pitifully.

Behind them was a tennis court, and over the sound of Donna's sobbing I could hear a repetitive *whomp, whomp, whomp.*

I began to walk forward, but Grady said, "Aunt Jess, please don't. I've already called nine-one-one. Someone will be here soon."

Then I saw the cause for his concern. The sound was coming from a machine that was pitching tennis balls over the net at lightning speed. And the balls were landing on someone lying on the ground. The person didn't look as though they'd moved for quite a while.

I couldn't let this go on until the authorities arrived. I had to try to help.

"Carissa, do you know anything about this machine?"

She shrugged her shoulders and shook her head.

"Well, I think we should try," I said.

She looked extremely hesitant but finally nodded her agreement.

Grady started to object but I cut him off.

"Grady, why don't you take Donna and Frank home? Carissa and I will wait here for the police." I used my sternest schoolteacher voice, hoping for immediate compliance.

"But, Aunt Jess, shouldn't someone tell the family?"

That was when I realized I didn't even know who the person lying on the ground was.

"Yes, someone should, but it needn't be us. Take care of your family first. Carissa and I will see to the rest."

Grady was reluctant to leave Carissa and me alone at the scene of whatever tragedy had happened, but slowly he realized it would be best for Donna and Frank if he did as I asked. With one arm around his wife and the other around his son, he led his family to their bungalow.

As soon as they were out of sight, I hurried to the chain-link door that was the entrance to the tennis court, with Carissa right behind me.

She gave a soft yelp and said, "Oh, my goodness, it's Mr. Courtland."

I saw she was correct. Jason Courtland was lying on his back, completely immobile, while the machine continued to hurl tennis balls that ricocheted off his body. How could this possibly have happened?

"I think the first thing we should do is try to turn off the machine," I said. "I'll open the door and then we can slide along the chain-link fence until we are able to get behind the machine. We'll figure out the rest once we are in a safe spot. We have to keep an eye on the machine. For all we know it is on a timer set to move left, right, and center."

Carissa agreed. "You are clever. I never even thought of the machine doing anything other than what it is doing right now. I guess mystery writers think that way."

At that moment I was not thinking about a plot for a story but rather of my own safety. We eased around the edge of the tennis court until we were positioned behind the machine, which didn't stop flinging bright yellow tennis balls across the net. We crept closer, slowing down with each step almost as if we were afraid the machine could turn on us at any moment, and for the little I knew about that kind of machine, perhaps it could. Finally we were close enough that I could see the dashboard. It had model number 1184 stamped on a small silver plate at the very top. The velocity of the balls was turned to the highest setting and there were still a fair amount of tennis balls in the bin ready to be served.

Carissa looked over my shoulder. "Try that big white button on the end. It looks like the power button."

I pushed it and the machine became silent and motionless. Carissa and I ran to the opposite side of the net, where Jason Courtland remained ever so still. His tennis racket was on the ground a few inches from his right hand. I checked for a pulse but couldn't find one. As soon as I lifted his wrist, several tennis balls began to roll across his chest to his shoulder and fell to the ground. I picked one up. Although I wasn't a keen tennis player, it looked odd to me. I looked at another and saw the same oddity.

"Here comes help," Carissa said, and pointed to a red-and-white ambulance with large letters emblazoned on the side, FDNY, pulling onto the grass directly outside the tennis court fence.

It had barely come to a stop when both doors flew open and blue-uniformed paramedics jumped out. They saw us waving and ran in our direction just as a white police car with blue markings parked behind the ambulance. It seemed as though our nice quiet corner of the beach was about to get the full attention of the government of the City of New York.

The paramedics asked us to move away from the space they'd quickly carved out as their work area and they knelt, one on each side of Jason. They cleared the tennis balls from his body and each of them felt for a pulse, one trying his wrist, the other pressing her fingers on his neck. They apparently had the same negative result I had, because when the police officers came through the gate and one asked, "Anything?" the female paramedic shook her head, causing her braided ponytail to fall over her shoulder. She pushed it behind her before bending once again over Jason's body.

While his partner returned to their car, the elder of the police officers turned his attention to Carissa and me. He opened a small black memo book and asked, "Ladies, do you know what happened here?"

"Apparently the tennis ball machine malfunctioned. I've heard they do that once in a while," Carissa said, as if death by tennis ball was a common occurrence.

"Were you both here when it happened?" the officer asked.

His name tag read LASKY, and I noticed that the numerals on his collar were a one followed by two zeros, which led me to believe we were in the confines of the NYPD's Hundredth Precinct.

"Goodness gracious, no," I said. "My niece came to the court, perhaps to play or practice, and when she saw Mr. Courtland lying there, she began screaming. Carissa and I heard her and ran up from the beach. My nephew, who also heard her, arrived before we did and he'd already called nine-one-one by the time we got here."

Lasky shooed a fly that had been buzzing between us. "Seems to me an awful lot of people were here and gone in a short space of time."

His partner leaned through the open gate and called, "Squad's on the way."

"Good." Officer Lasky nodded while he continued talking to us. "The detectives will be here in a few minutes. I'd like you to wait so they can speak to you. Perhaps you'd be comfortable sitting on one of those benches outside the fence?"

I hoped that Carissa realized, since I certainly did, that Officer Lasky's mannerly "I'd like" and "perhaps you'd be comfortable" weren't suggestions. They were orders.

He escorted us to a wooden bench with curved wrought iron arms that had an excellent view of the entire tennis court. Once we were seated, he turned away and began conferring with his partner and the paramedics.

Carissa fretted. "Do you think they'll let us leave soon, Mrs. Fletcher? I have to get ready for my class."

I shook my head. "I'm afraid your class will probably have to be canceled. We are in for a very long day."

"But once they remove Mr. Courtland and notify the family, what is left to be done? For the sake of the Courtland children, isn't it best to keep their day as normal as possible?"

Before I could answer, there was a disturbance behind us. I'd never met Linda Courtland but I instantly realized that the willowy blond dressed in tennis whites who dropped her racket and began running to the court entrance, moaning, "Oh, no. Oh, please no," had to be Jason Courtland's wife.

Carissa confirmed it when she leaned into my side and said, "That's Mr. Courtland's wife. Poor woman."

The younger police officer caught Linda and put his arm around her waist, holding her firmly, clearly intent on preventing her from entering the tennis court. The female paramedic hurried to assist. The two of them led Linda to the police car and settled her in the backseat with the door open. The paramedic opened the side door of the ambulance, reached in, brought out a bottle of water, and gave it to Linda, encouraging her to drink. They spoke for a few minutes. Then the paramedic checked Linda's blood pressure and, I suppose, her pulse.

The police officers and paramedics were comparing notes when a silver car with a dented front fender squeezed in beside the marked radio car. I suspected the detectives had arrived and now the investigation would begin in earnest.

A middle-aged man whose pale face was mottled with large brown spots, probably from too much sun, got out of the front passenger seat and waved to the uniformed officers. His necktie hung loosely below his open shirt collar and he had a sports coat draped over one arm. His partner, a younger woman with russet brown skin, wore a bright yellow cotton wrap dress that seemed suited to the weather and the location.

Officer Lasky walked over to them and, I assumed, gave them a fast rundown of the morning's events. At one point both detectives looked over at the police car where Linda Courtland still sat sipping water. A few minutes later their eyes slewed to the bench where Carissa and I sat, not so patiently, waiting to be dismissed.

Both detectives walked onto the tennis court and spent time looking at Jason Courtland's body. They paid special attention to the tennis balls that were now strewn all around the body.

The male detective called, "Lasky, all these were covering the, er, Mr. Courtland when you got here?"

"Sure were, Vinny," Lasky answered.

Detective Vinny nodded. Then he and his partner walked around the net and peered carefully at the ball machine. I wondered if they would turn it on, but instead they walked back to the gate. They spoke briefly to Lasky and his partner; then the female detective and Lasky's partner spoke to Linda Courtland. They helped her from the car and then walked with her toward the houses. I assumed they were taking her home. Detective Vinny walked purposefully toward Carissa and me.

"Good morning, ladies. Tough day all around. I'm Detective Vincent Tieri. My partner, Detective Aisha Kelly, and I will be handling this investigation. May I ask your names?" He opened a small notepad, his pen poised at the ready. "And I'd appreciate readily accessible phone numbers. Maybe your cells would be best."

Once we complied he moved right into the events of the day. Since we'd seen him consult with Officer Lasky, I was surprised at his next question.

"I understand that you ladies were the first to discover Mr. Courtland. Is that correct?"

Carissa began, "We ran up from the beach—"

"No," I interrupted. "That is not correct. My niece Donna

Fletcher was the first to see Mr. Courtland lying there inca-pacitated. We heard her screams, and by the time we got here, Donna's husband, my nephew Grady, had arrived. He as-sessed the situation and called nine-one-one."

Detective Tieri turned back to Carissa. "So you were at the beach together? Little early in the morning, wasn't it?"

Carissa merely nodded, but I thought he was pointedly looking for inconsistencies, so I felt it best to explain how we happened to be together when we heard Donna.

After I finished, the detective asked, "So this niece, nephew, and grandnephew, where are they now?"

"Donna was so upset, I thought it was wisest to send them home," I said.

"You thought it wise, did you, Mrs."—he looked at his pad—"Fletcher? Didn't it occur to you that we might want to speak to her? Now, offhand, do you know her address or will you have to call someone and get it for me?"

As much as I didn't like his sarcasm—technically he was correct that I had no idea what the address was—I was confi-dent I could one-up him, so I stood, turned, and pointed.

"Do you see that green bungalow? Walk past it and make a right, and Donna and Grady are in the second bungalow along the path."

He nodded but didn't acknowledge that sending Donna home likely wasn't the massive error he'd assumed it to be. He simply continued with his questions.

"When you got here, was everything exactly the way it is now? I know the tennis balls that are on the ground now were on top of Mr. Courtland, but is everything else exactly the same?"

Carissa remained silent, so I responded. "Well, no, it isn't. When Carissa and I arrived, that machine"—I pointed to it—"was flinging balls rapidly across the net. Mr. Courtland was on the ground and not moving. Donna was on this bench and my nephew Grady was standing by that bush, shielding his son from the scene."

"And when did the machine stop tossing the tennis balls?" he asked.

"When I shut it off," I said.

It wouldn't have surprised me if the detective's sharp exhale could be heard all the way back in Cabot Cove.

"What possessed you to turn it off? Don't you know tampering with evidence is a crime?"

Chapter Five

Now I was getting as exasperated as he seemed to be. "I couldn't be one hundred percent certain that Mr. Courtland was dead without getting closer to his body, and there was no chance of getting near him as long as those tennis balls were flying through the air. The only practical thing I could conceive of doing was to get behind the machine and shut it off."

Detective Tieri rolled his eyes. I could almost hear the phrase "meddling civilian" rattling around in his brain. He took a moment to measure his response, but when he spoke, I could hear definite frustration in his voice.

"*Okay, then.* Now tell me, Ms. Potter, did *you* touch the machine?"

Carissa shrugged. "I honestly don't know. I may have. Everything happened so fast. We were trying to save Jason's— that is, Mr. Courtland's—life. I pointed out what I thought was the power button to Mrs. Fletcher and she shut it down, but regarding whatever I may have touched"—she shook her head—"I just don't know."

"Well, our technicians will be arriving momentarily. Once they have taken your fingerprints—"

"Fingerprints!" Carissa became alarmed. "Why do you need my fingerprints?"

"It's nothing to worry about," Detective Tieri assured her. "We need to eliminate your prints and sort them out from any others we might find on the machine. As I was saying, once we have your prints, you will be free to go. I have your contact information. If we need to speak again, I'll be in touch. Thank you for your cooperation."

He turned on his heel and walked away. I stood and followed him.

"Excuse me, Detective, but I noticed something that you might find useful."

He stopped and, with forced patience, asked, "What is that, Mrs. Fletcher?"

"Well, it's the tennis balls. Some of them aren't fuzzy."

I hoped that didn't sound as foolish to him as it did to me.

"Fuzzy?"

"When I looked for Jason Courtland's pulse, some of the tennis balls fell off his chest, and I noticed that they appeared to have been, well, shaved."

"Shaved? You mean, with a razor?" Tieri looked incredulous.

"I know it sounds bizarre but the felt covering of a tennis ball is . . . I can't think of another word, so I'll stick with fuzzy. I once read that the fuzzy texture helps the player put a spin on the ball when he hits it with the racket. I would imagine that if someone shaved the ball, that would make it travel without any spin; plus, of course, without that tiny bit of cushiony felt wrapping, the ball might land a little harder."

Convinced I had explained my thoughts perfectly well, I spread my hands as if I had presented him with a gift.

He reached up and scratched his neck behind and below his right ear as if he was giving himself time to think of an appropriate response. But his answer was not what I'd hoped to hear.

"Well, thank you, Mrs. Fletcher, but my guess is that you happened across some old worn tennis balls that should have been discarded long ago. They could have been in the basket of that machine for months. Now, if you'll excuse me . . ." He tipped an imaginary hat and walked away.

I walked back to the bench, sat down, and began to study the crime scene. I knew that besides the shaved tennis balls, there was something else out of whack, but I couldn't quite figure out what it was.

Carissa broke into my train of thought. "Mrs. Fletcher, I am so sorry I took a long run this morning. If only I had stayed in bed, I could have avoided being at the scene of this terrible tragedy entirely."

I decided not to mention that Jason Courtland was the benefactor who paid for her summer employment, so she might well be impacted by his death regardless of where she'd been this morning.

Officer Lasky brought us each a bottle of water, which we accepted appreciatively.

Then he said, "The techs are in the parking lot. As soon as

they unload their gear, the print man will do the two of you first so you can get out of here. I'm sure Vinny will be in touch over the next day or so."

Carissa said, "Are they ever going to take the body away? I'd hate for Mrs. Courtland to see him like that."

"Didn't you see her? She was here a while ago. Took it real hard, like any wife would," Lasky said.

"Oh, I meant his mother. The elder Mrs. Courtland," Carissa replied.

Lasky looked incredulous. "His mother? You mean, she's around here somewhere? Ouch. Gonna be difficult for Vinny to interview her. He probably should let Aisha do it. She has a softer touch."

I could see him making a mental note to pass this information on to the detectives, so I gave him another tidbit.

"The older Mrs. Courtland lives in the big house over there with the wraparound porch."

Having my fingerprints taken was speedier and far less messy than it had been decades ago when I first got my teaching certificate. Officer Lasky was kind enough to inquire if either of us felt that we needed an escort home. When we both declined, he said we were free to go.

As Carissa and I walked to the bungalows, I asked if she lived nearby.

She indicated a three-story building farther along the beach and said, "The community center where I teach is on the main floor of that stucco building. Mr. Courtland rents small apartments on the upper floors for his teachers each summer. I think the building manager gives him a break on the rent because the classes are open to all the children in the neighborhood, and I suspect the rent for the community center is a large slice of the owner's income. Over the years I've noticed the building has been turning into a regular artist colony. Some of the full-time tenants are painters and one is a really talented fellow who creates metal art. His work is extraordinary. You must visit his studio one day."

"That sounds delightful. Perhaps the tenants could organize an art show for the neighborhood," I said.

"Now, there's an idea. I'll have to talk it up among my neighbors. The community center would be the perfect venue."

I stopped at Donna's front steps. "This is my niece's bungalow. Would you care to come in for a few minutes? I am sure we have coffee and perhaps Donna or Grady made breakfast."

"Oh, that's so nice of you, but I have to head home. I really need to take a shower." Carissa reached across her torso and rubbed her hands up and down her arms. "I feel so grungy."

She started to walk away and then turned back and said, "I hope Frank isn't too traumatized. And his poor mom." She shook her head and then started a slow jog toward home.

Frank was sitting on the couch reading. When I opened the front door, he looked up and asked, "Do you want to sit with me for a while, Aunt Jess?"

"I can't think of anything I'd rather do, unless it would be going down to the ocean and bringing the sled filled with your pails and shovels back to the house before the tide takes them out to sea."

"You don't have to worry. Dad and I got them first thing. The sled is around the side of the house all packed with equipment and ready for our next construction project. It's too bad we couldn't finish the bridge we were working on. It had a great start."

"Well, for now I'd love to sit with you. And I'm wondering about the book you are reading. Would you care to tell me what it's about?"

He held the book up so I could see the cover. *Hazardous Tales* was written across the top in a yellow banner, and a very dapper-looking eighteenth-century general was smiling at us while crossing swords with a redcoat. The book title *Lafayette!* was splashed across the illustration.

"The Marquis de Lafayette! I seem to remember hearing about him. Didn't he come over from France to help America win our independence from Great Britain?" I said.

"He did!" Frank was enthusiastic. "This book is part of a great series of history books written by Nathan Hale."

"Nathan Hale? Oh, come on. Really?" I gave Frank my "stop teasing Aunt Jessica" look.

"Honestly, Aunt Jess, that is his real name. Nathan James Hale. I looked it up. And wait until you see inside. There are some great pictures."

Frank opened the graphic novel and showed me several pages.

I was impressed and said so. "Mr. Hale is a very talented man. He can write and draw. I'm a good writer, but I've tried my hand at painting several times and I confess that, although I enjoy it, my artistic talent is limited."

Just then Grady walked into the room, carrying a ceramic

mug. "I heard you come in, Aunt Jess. I thought you might like a cup of coffee. How about you, Frank? Can I get you a glass of juice?"

"That would be great, Dad. I am just about to tell Aunt Jessica all about Lafayette and the American Revolution." Frank opened the book and pointed. "This was the marquis's father, who was killed by the British in the Battle of Minden in some place called Westphalia long before our American Revolution. It seems to me that could be the reason Lafayette was so interested in helping the colonists with their rebellion. He didn't like the British very much."

"That may well be," I said.

Grady came back and handed Frank a glass of apple juice. "Here you go. While you are teaching Aunt Jess all about the American Revolution, I'm going to go check on your mom."

As soon as we heard Grady open and then close the bedroom door, Frank looked at me. "Mr. Courtland is dead, isn't he? When I got to the tennis court, Mom was sitting on the bench crying. Dad told me that he called for an ambulance because Mr. Courtland was injured. Then he kept blocking me from looking into the tennis court. I knew if Mr. Courtland was only hurt, both my dad and my mom would have tried to help him, and . . . they didn't." Frank shrugged. "So I knew he must be dead."

"Yes, he is dead." I knew I had to tread carefully. "There appears to have been some sort of accident with the . . . I guess you'd call it the practice machine. When the ambulance came, the paramedics couldn't revive him."

"So many of my new friends will be very sad," Frank said quite matter-of-factly. "You met Madeline and Juliet. He was their uncle in the same way you are my aunt. But you didn't meet Shane, Billy, and Katie. They are his grandchildren. And there are cousins I haven't met."

Frank reached over and gave me a fierce hug. "I love you, Aunt Jess."

"I love you, too." We hugged for a silent minute and then I said, "Right now I am filled with curiosity. Please tell me more about the Marquis de Lafayette."

Frank explained all the reasons he thought Lafayette was a great favorite of General George Washington.

"Lafayette was interested in being a real soldier and was willing to learn, and did you know that he was a loyal man and managed to foil a plot that would have cost George Washington his command?"

A short while later, we heard the bedroom door open.

Although her eyes were red from crying, Donna managed a big smile as she came into the living room. "Is anyone as hungry as I am? I've talked Grady into making his famous French toast."

Frank jumped up. "Aunt Jess, can we finish this later? We found a handheld eggbeater in this kitchen, and Dad says he's never seen anyone turn that crank as fast as I can."

At my nod, he was off to the kitchen.

Donna sat in the sea-green upholstered chair opposite the couch. "Aunt Jess, I am so sorry about all of this. Here Grady and I were trying to give you a restful vacation at the beach, and, well, look what happened."

I assured her that I was happy to be with my family whatever the circumstances. "I am truly sorry that you were the one to discover the body. Had you gone to the tennis court to meet Linda Courtland for the game you mentioned yesterday?"

Donna shook her head and sighed. "I wish I had waited until I was supposed to meet Linda. Then maybe someone else would have found Jason. I think I will have nightmares about him lying on the ground half-buried under tennis balls until the day I die. No, I went to the court early because I wanted to practice with the TeachTennis machine. I mean, I know I can't beat Linda at tennis, but I hoped to at least be a challenging opponent."

Grady was wiping his hands on a dish towel when he entered the room. "Breakfast in ten minutes, ladies. Time to wash up. Donna, I know how terrible you feel, but I will be eternally grateful that Jason got to the tennis court before you did. Otherwise you might have been the one"—he jerked his head toward the kitchen, where their son was practicing to become a master chef, and lowered his voice—"when the machine went crazy. You know what I mean."

Donna sighed. "I guess you're right."

"No, Donna, Grady is wrong." I couldn't help but correct them. "The machine didn't go crazy. Someone tampered with it. I am not sure how. But the one thing I *am* sure of is that Jason Courtland was murdered."

"Dad, the eggs are bubbly," Frank called from the kitchen.

"Be right there," Grady answered. Then he looked at me. "Can we talk about this later? Now is not the time. In fact, why don't you both come and sit in the kitchen while Frank and I cook?"

I was sure that was his way of ending any conversation about the morning's events. Donna set the table and I went to wash up. By the time I returned, Grady and Frank were ready to serve us French toast with blackberries and orange slices on the side.

"What do you think, Aunt Jess?" Frank was practically jumping out of his seat. "I can't wait to hear how you think I did beating the eggs."

I made quite a production of slicing a bite-sized piece of French toast and putting it into my mouth. As soon as I swallowed it, I said, "Frank, I have never, ever tasted a fluffier piece of French toast. Why, even my friend Mara, who owns her own restaurant and serves dozens of breakfasts every day, would be hard-pressed to say she has ever tasted anything so delicious."

Frank beamed. And we sat and talked and laughed as if this was a usual breakfast on an ordinary day. When we'd all finished eating, Donna and I shooed Grady and Frank out of the kitchen, insisting that such talented chefs should not have to partake in cleaning up after they'd created such a scrumptious meal.

As we were clearing away the dishes, I asked Donna about the family leadership team at the firm. "I've already met Edwina. Grady told me she is a member of the board of directors. I understand there are other family members who serve the company as well. Jason's death must be a terrible blow to them all."

Donna paused for a few seconds, looked down at the bowl she was holding in her hand, and then continued loading the dishwasher.

"I'm sure it is. I suppose any death in a close-knit family-run firm is bound to lead to massive disruption to the company. I dread having to deal with that. Jason and Edwina have a younger brother, Dennis, who is the chief financial officer. He and Edwina often resented Jason's authority but I always took that as a sibling-rivalry thing. I mean, they are all adults, but who knows what childhood resentments lurk in the back of their minds?"

"I know that does happen, but seriously, at their age? I mean, Jason is a grandfather. How long can his siblings take umbrage because he was allowed a later bedtime when they were in grammar school?" I shook my head.

Donna pressed the start button on the dishwasher and we stood there, both lost in our own thoughts, listening to the water fill.

Finally she said, "Well, there are other issues. My boss, Tyler Young, is married to Edwina. He handles the global division and he doesn't like any of his staff talking to Jason for any reason. As a matter of fact, ever since I was awarded this month at the bungalow, Tyler has reminded me more than once to keep my business activities, as he called it, 'off the beach.'"

"That is odd," I agreed. "After all, Jason is in charge of every aspect of company business. You would think keeping him informed would be a requirement."

The doorbell rang and I must admit the jangle startled me. I followed Donna into the living room just as Grady opened the door.

A tall, distinguished-looking gray-haired man with a well-trimmed mustache said, "I hope I'm not intruding but I wanted to be sure that, after this morning's trauma, you are all doing well."

Chapter Six

Grady looked uncertain, which seemed odd to me, but then he opened the door wider. "That's very kind of you. Please come in."

The man stepped into the living room, his eyes searching. As soon as he spotted Donna, he walked directly to her and stood so close that, if I were her, I would have felt distinctly uncomfortable. He took both of Donna's hands in his.

"There you are, my dear. I'm delighted to see you looking so well. I understand you've had quite a shock."

Donna became flustered and pulled her hands away. As I was nearest, she immediately reached out and took me by the arm. She stepped back, widening the space between them, and thrust me front and center.

"Dennis, I'd like you to meet my aunt Jessica Fletcher. Aunt Jess, this is Dennis Courtland."

"Mr. Courtland, I am sorry to meet you under such tragic

circumstances. How is your mother? I had the pleasure of dining with her last night. I can't imagine how distraught she is. Your entire family must be . . ."

I trailed off when I noticed that he didn't seem to hear a word I said. Instead he was still looking at Donna, and as soon as I finished speaking, he asked her once again how she was managing.

Grady stepped forward and put his arm firmly around Donna's shoulders, which seemed to give Donna the resolve to speak.

"Dennis, I am fortunate to have my family with me. Rest assured, I'll be fine." She looked toward the couch. "I don't recall . . . Have you met my son? Frank, please come and say hello."

As soon as Frank was near, Donna pulled him in front of her, which actually forced Dennis Courtland to take a few steps backward. We must have presented quite a tableau: Donna standing with me on one side, Grady on the other, and Frank directly in front of her.

After shaking hands with Frank, Dennis looked at me, Grady, and finally Donna. "Well, I can see your family is ready to give you all the support you might need. I'll be off now. There is so much company business I must attend to."

He turned on his heel and walked out the door.

Donna heaved a long sigh of relief.

I was sure there was a story to be told, but I doubted that Donna would tell it.

Grady glanced out the window as if to be sure Dennis Courtland wasn't lingering on the porch and then said, "He's a strange man. He doesn't seem to be the least bit broken up about his brother's death. He didn't even respond when Aunt Jess mentioned his mother. I mean, the woman lost her other son, his very own brother, and Dennis just . . . I don't get it."

"Jealousy, sibling rivalry—call it what you will, but I can assure you of one thing," Donna said. "From the first day I met him, Dennis Courtland has always envied his brother's position as CEO of Courtland Finance and I think that gnawing envy has superseded any familial grief."

And Grady, who always tries to see the good in everyone, replied, "I guess. Probably when the shock wears off, he'll realize what he's lost."

I was the only one who noticed when Donna shook her head.

Grady made a valiant effort at livening up the atmosphere. He took out his telephone and began hitting keys.

"I'm checking to see what movies are playing nearby. Anyone interested?"

Frank was quick to raise his hand, so I said, "That sounds like a great idea."

Donna begged off, saying she had a headache that just wouldn't quit. "If you don't mind, I think I will stay home and take a nap. I could use some peace and quiet."

No sooner were the words out of her mouth than there was a knock at the door. Grady raised his eyebrows and looked at me as if to say, *What now?*

He opened the door and none of us should have been surprised to see Detectives Tieri and Kelly standing on the porch.

"Hello. I assume you are Mr. Fletcher." Tieri introduced himself and his partner. "We are sorry to barge in like this, but I am afraid we are going to have to speak to you and your wife."

"Come on in." Grady sounded resigned.

Detective Tieri gave me a curt nod and then said they would first like to speak to Donna, who blanched at the idea but recovered swiftly. She asked Frank to go to his room and offered the detectives a seat on the couch.

Tieri cleared his throat. "Actually, Mrs. Fletcher, we'd like to speak to you privately and someplace where we won't be interrupted. We'd like you to come to the precinct with us."

Before I could ask if that was really necessary, Donna burst into tears while Grady started waving his arms, saying, "Absolutely not."

Tieri reared back like a stallion whose rider was pushing him in a direction he didn't want to go. I was sure he was going to snap back at Grady, but then I noticed Detective Kelly unobtrusively place her hand on Tieri's arm.

She said softly, "I understand your concerns, but we need to speak in a place where we cannot be overheard or interrupted. Clearly this house is small and is occupied by several other people. I don't see a space where we would be able to have a private conversation."

"I have a suggestion, if I may," I started, and when no one objected, I continued. "Why don't Frank, Grady, and I leave the house? We can take a few chairs off the porch and settle them in front of the house facing the ocean. That way we won't be able to overhear your conversation, and should anyone come along who wants to see Donna, we can explain she is indisposed."

The detectives exchanged a glance and Detective Tieri said, "I suppose that could work." He tapped Grady on the arm. "C'mon, I'll help you move the chairs."

Grady called Frank, who came bounding out of his room so quickly that I suspected he'd been listening at the door. He followed his father outside. I went to my room to get my iPad and then picked up *Lafayette!* from the coffee table. I noticed a newspaper folded next to the book and took that as well. By the time I got outside, we had a cozy seating arrangement at the bottom of the porch steps.

Frank was delighted that I'd thought to bring out his book. He immediately opened it to the page he had bookmarked and began to read. I tried to hand Grady the newspaper but evidently he thought I should look through it.

"The *Rockaway Times* is an amusing community paper, Aunt Jess. All the local news and information. I thought you might like to take a look," Grady said.

"Not right now, thanks. I have my iPad and there are a few things I want to look up. But don't recycle that paper when you're done. I definitely want to read it while I'm here. Dan Andrews, who is the new editor of the *Cabot Cove Gazette*, used to come to Rockaway Beach quite often when he lived in New York. I'd like to bring the paper home to him if you don't want to keep it," I said.

"That's so thoughtful. I'm sure he'd love to see it," Grady said as he opened the newspaper and was promptly immersed in the local news.

I leaned back in my chair and watched father and son enjoying their reading material. A gentle breeze of moist, salty air blew across us straight from the ocean. The sun was high with nary a cloud to hide behind. I watched the ocean waves gently lapping against the shore. The surfers had been replaced by children, many younger than Frank, whose parents were protecting them carefully with sunscreen and umbrellas on the beach or standing within arm's reach of every child in the water. I sighed at the serenity of it all.

After a few minutes, I opened my iPad. The joy of being a writer is that whenever my curiosity gets the best of me and I decide to delve into any topic for more information, everyone, my family included, assumes I am doing research for my next book. I typed Courtland Finance and Investments into the search bar, and within a second or two, I had dozens of articles and websites to examine.

I started on the company's own web page, where I didn't find much information that I didn't already have. On the history page, there was an old-fashioned formal picture of a man with a receding hairline and a dark handlebar mustache. He also had the same bushy eyebrows I'd seen on Jason Courtland. Underneath the picture it read Everett Courtland, Founder. Matilda's husband. There was no indication of when he had died, and when I looked at Jason's write-up as CEO, there was no mention of a start date, so I had no idea how long ago Matilda had been widowed.

The bungalow door opened and Detective Kelly came out. "We have finished speaking to Mrs. Fletcher and would like to speak to Mr. Fletcher next. We'll take a five-minute break. If anyone would like to go inside to get a drink or use the facilities, please feel free."

Donna came through the doorway behind the detective and Grady jumped up from his chair. He took her hand as she came down the stairs and he began murmuring too softly for anyone but Donna to hear. His genuine concern brought back many memories of his uncle Frank, my late husband, who was the most considerate person I have ever known. Grady clearly inherited that gene, as had young Frank, who popped out of his chair and said, "Here, Mom, sit down."

Donna smiled. "I am fine. Really." She kissed the top of Frank's head. "Why don't you run inside and get yourself a snack? And please bring me a glass of water, plenty of ice."

"Sure thing." Frank hurried away.

As soon as he was out of earshot, Donna said to Grady and me, "Really, the interview was easy. The questions seemed to be routine and I answered truthfully. I'm guessing that once they speak to both of you, we'll be out of the loop even before the police decide this was a dreadful accident and no further investigation is required."

Obviously Donna felt far more optimistic than I did.

Detective Kelly called Grady inside just as Frank came out with Donna's water and a package of chocolate chip cookies, which he offered to share with all of us.

While I munched on a cookie, I chided myself for not being able to accept Donna's notion that Jason Courtland's death was an accident, a total quirk of mechanical failure.

I opened my iPad again, this time to search for information about the TeachTennis machine. I found several links, including one to its manufacturer. I clicked and found a row of pictures of the training machines in various sizes and shapes. I looked for model number 1184. Compared to some of the others, it was certainly a powerhouse, capable of sending a tennis ball every second at speeds up to one hundred miles an hour. I remembered that when I turned the power off, I saw the velocity dial set at the highest level. So it was likely that every second the TeachTennis was running, it was hurtling a tennis ball directly at Jason Courtland.

I noted that model 1184 could be set to change direction, at least vertically. The elevation-control function could stay steady at one height or move up and down at irregular intervals so that the machine would throw the balls at a half dozen levels, from ground strokes to lobs. I imagined that Jason tried to duck, maybe even thought he could run around the net and turn the machine off, but I suspected he became seriously injured rather quickly. Then I realized what had been bothering me at the tennis court. Why wasn't there a remote control?

I looked at the advertisement and, sure enough, there was a remote sitting in a holder on the right side of the control panel. I didn't recall seeing any gadget that looked like the remote anywhere on the court near Jason's body. If he hadn't used the remote to start the TeachTennis shooting balls over the net so he could slam them back, I had to wonder who had.

I was about to ask Donna if she'd seen or used a remote at the tennis court when I was distracted by the bungalow door opening.

Grady came out as though he had not a care in the world. "Who is ready for the movies? I hear there is a great one playing just across the bridge."

Frank jumped up from his chair, nearly dropping *Lafayette!* on the ground. "I'm ready. It's not too late? We still have time to catch the beginning?" And he whooped when Grady nodded.

Donna said, "I'm afraid I have to bail. My head is still splitting. I think I need a cup of tea, followed by a nap. What about you, Aunt Jess?"

"Well, actually, I expect the detectives will have more questions—"

"Not at all, Mrs. Fletcher," Detective Tieri said from the doorway. "We pretty much covered everything earlier today. I don't see that you have more to contribute."

"I am very curious about the TeachTennis machine, as I am sure you are—"

He cut me off. "Our police technicians will find out all we'll need to know about that machine, believe you me. I am sure some salesman will be happy to satisfy your curiosity."

"Really, Detective, I must insist that you allow me a few minutes," I said.

Instead of responding, he changed the topic entirely. "Your nephew said that you are visiting his family for a brief vacation and that you actually live in Cabot Cove, Maine. Is that correct?"

"Yes, I live in Cabot Cove, but I do come to New York frequently both for business and to visit my family. Why do you ask?" How could my residence possibly relate to his case?

"Well, it happens I have an old buddy I worked with for years here in the NYPD, name of Mort Metzger. He's the sheriff now in your neck of the woods. By any chance, have you ever run across him?"

"You're correct. Mort is the sheriff of my hometown, and we are very good friends as well." I put a special emphasis on the word "friends" and hoped Detective Tieri picked up on it.

He didn't appear to, so I tried again. "Mort told me that he once worked here in Rockaway and patrolled the boardwalk. Is that when you and he met?"

The fact that Mort would have shared personal information with me didn't soften up Detective Tieri at all. He said, "Nah, I met him years later when we both worked in the eight-four in Brooklyn. When you get home, be sure and tell him Vinny said hello. Thank you all for your cooperation."

And he and Detective Kelly stepped off the porch and turned toward the tennis court.

Grady could tell by the look on my face that I was irritated by Detective Tieri's lack of interest in any further conversation with me.

"C'mon, Aunt Jess, don't let him upset you. I know where we can find a great movie filled with furry animals and all sorts of fun. As a bonus, I can predict there's a bag of popcorn with your name on it."

Frank looked at me with pleading eyes. "I heard the bulldog is a really strong character. He leads the pack. I think you'd like him, Aunt Jess."

"Well, there's only one way to find out. Let's go to the movies."

As I ran to my room for a sweater to ward off the air-conditioning that flooded most movie theaters this time of year, I decided to put the day's misadventures behind me and focus on what I'd come to the Rockaways for—family fun.

Chapter Seven

*D*ogs' *Night Out* was wonderfully entertaining and quickly pushed the morning's tragedy to the back of my mind. As Grady was driving us back to the bungalow, I realized that so much had happened in such a short period of time that I hadn't remembered to give Frank the present I'd brought him. That was definitely at the top of my to-do list. I also hoped to have a long walk on the beach to sort out the ideas that were flitting around in my head. How did the TeachTennis machine attack Jason Courtland? Surely it didn't turn itself on, and since I hadn't seen any remote control, I didn't understand how Jason could have started it from his side of the net. It seemed ridiculous to even consider that he would have turned on the TeachTennis at maximum speed and then raced around to the other side of the net. He was bound to realize that he would have been bashed by ball after ball before he had a chance to get in position to swat the tennis balls back across the net.

In case Donna was still resting, we entered the house quietly, but we found her bustling around in the kitchen, humming tunelessly. She came into the living room and placed a bowl of fruit on the coffee table, saying, "I thought you might want some healthy snacks for energy. I can only imagine what you ate at the movies." She laughed and then asked, "How was the picture?"

While Frank went into great detail about the adventures of Boxer the bulldog and his companions, I slipped into my room and came out with a small package.

Donna turned to me and asked, "What did you think, Aunt Jess?"

"I certainly agree with Frank that Boxer was a strong, creative leader of his pack, but my favorite character was Darnell the dachshund. It's true he was old and slow, but when the dogs were about to be trapped in that warehouse, it was Darnell who figured a way out, and not one of them was caught by Mr. Catcherman."

Grady laughed. "Leave it to you to notice the characters in the background, the ones who cause things to happen. I suppose that is your writer's mind at work."

"Well, my mind wasn't working too clearly when I got here yesterday, because I completely forgot that I brought a very special present for my grandnephew."

I held out the small box gaily wrapped with dark blue paper and a sparkling light blue ribbon.

"Thank you, Aunt Jessica." Frank removed the ribbon with

one yank and quickly tore the paper off. Then he whooped. "A smart watch! Best present ever! Dad, look."

Grady began a quick once-over of the directions booklet. "Games, music, a camera, flashlight, video recorder, and whoa, look at this, Sport. It even tells time."

"Very funny, Dad," Frank said, and then grinned at Donna. "Mom, did you know these smart watches have alarms? Whenever I'm outdoors, I can set it to go off every two hours and then reapply my sunscreen. I know that will make you happy!"

Donna laughed. "It certainly will. Aunt Jess, you come up with the best presents. Thank you so much."

"Well, I have been hearing about these smart watches for the longest time, and when I stopped in Charles Department Store to see what I could find to surprise my favorite grand-nephew, they had quite a large display right near the front entrance."

Frank jumped up and gave me a big hug. "Aunt Jessica, you always get me the most terrific gifts. I can't figure out how to thank you. Hugs and words aren't enough."

He looked so dejected that I replied with the first thing that popped into my head. "I may have thought of a way. Perhaps you could teach me to make a solid bridge out of sand and water. When I go home, I will be the star of Cabot Cove and can show off to all my friends."

Frank giggled and his right hand shot toward me. "Done." We shook on it. I noticed his grip was getting stronger.

Grady and Frank took the smart watch out to the porch, determined to decipher every function the watch had to offer.

I was sure they'd both be experts in an hour or less. Donna went back to puttering in the kitchen. When I asked if I could help, she shooed me away.

"I find that when my brain is scrambled, the simple pleasure of following the clear directions of a recipe and using measuring cups and spoons helps me reorder my thoughts and relax," she said. "So tonight we will be dining on creamy scallops with pasta and a side of baked avocado fries. How does that sound?"

"Delicious. And if I can't help out here in the kitchen, I think I will take a walk and get to know this beautiful community."

Donna's face clouded over. "Aunt Jessica, you're not going to begin investigating, are you? I worry about your safety when bad things happen and you get too involved. You did say you believe Jason was murdered, but I think you should let the detectives decide if that's the case."

"Donna, I assure you, I am only going for a walk. And I'm looking forward to a delicious dinner when I return."

I gave her shoulder a quick squeeze and headed out the door. After stopping on the porch long enough for Frank to take my picture with his new watch, I waved good-bye and intentionally walked in the opposite direction from the tennis court.

As soon as I was out of sight, I doubled back behind the bungalows and walked directly to the tennis court. When I got there, I was pleased that not a soul was in view. The fence door was secured with yellow crime scene tape, but I didn't feel any need to go inside. I could see the entire court from where I was standing. There were chalk marks outlining where Jason Courtland's body had lain. Even his tennis racket had been chalked before it was removed. On the far side of the tennis net, another set of chalk marks outlined the location of the TeachTennis machine, which, as I'd expected, the police had removed. I was absolutely sure that when I'd turned off the TeachTennis, there was no remote control on any part of the dashboard. And I hadn't seen anything that looked like a remote on or near Jason's body when I tried to find his pulse.

I studied the scene in front of me diligently. There was no small rectangle drawn in chalk to mark the place where the police technicians had found the remote control. Because it wasn't on-site, I was sure someone had removed it and then used it to deliberately set the machine to pummel Jason Courtland. Or could he have been an accidental victim and the killer meant to attack someone else? Perhaps the victim was supposed to be Linda Courtland, who played and practiced frequently. I wondered if the TeachTennis had a timer setting. I'd have to double-check the website.

I was so lost in what-ifs that I didn't hear someone come up behind me. Then a man cleared his throat and said, "Excuse me, missus. I don't want to disturb, but could you tell me what happened here earlier today? I saw the ambulance and the police cars."

I turned to find a short, elderly man dressed in a tan leisure suit from days gone by. He was wearing a straw hat with a red-and-black band that I knew from research for one of my books was called a straw boater. I really couldn't remember that I'd ever seen anyone other than the members of our local

Cabot Cove barbershop quartet wear a boater. That kind of hat had been out of style for decades except for musical theatrical events or, I would imagine, some sailing or rowing festivities.

I hadn't been visiting the beach community long enough to know if the man was a nosy neighbor or a member of the Courtland family who'd recently arrived and hadn't yet heard about the tragedy.

I decided to introduce myself and see how he responded. "Hello. My name is Jessica Fletcher. I am visiting my niece and nephew, who are staying in a cottage just down there."

I waved vaguely toward the Courtland bungalows.

"Forgive my manners." The man removed his hat, revealing a sparse growth of white hair. "My name is Julius Machelli. I live up there."

He pointed to the top floors of the apartment building I'd first noticed when Grady parked his car next to a fence that separated the building's parking lot from the Courtland property.

"I know this is where the Courtland family lives in the summer. And I have a long history with, ah, the firm. So I ask again: Can you tell me what happened?"

I was surprised that living so nearby he hadn't already heard. I saw no harm in telling him that there'd been an "accident" and Jason Courtland had been killed.

I was shocked when the color drained from his face and he leaned forward, clutched my arm, and asked, "Dead? You're sure?"

"Unfortunately, I am," I said gently. "I saw his body myself."

"Thank you. Thank you so much for letting me know." He pushed his boater onto his head. "I must go to Matilda. I need to be sure she is all right."

He started to hobble toward Matilda Courtland's house, then stopped and looked back at me. "You have done me a great service, Mrs. Fletcher. I will not forget you."

Clearly Julius Machelli had more of a personal relationship with the Courtland family than he had with the firm. And it appeared that the relationship had begun many decades ago.

When I got back to the bungalow, Grady and Frank were nowhere to be seen but I could hear Donna still feverishly at work in the kitchen. I heard her exclaim, "Darn!" So I waited for about ninety seconds before I stepped into the doorway and said, "Oh, my, something smells delicious."

"I hope the scallops taste as good as the sauce smells. I nearly forgot the red pepper flakes, so I am hoping I added them in time. Grady took Frank to the bakery to buy a loaf of semolina bread. When they get back, dinner will be ready."

I washed my hands at the kitchen sink and offered to help.

Donna assured me that she had dinner well under control and offered me a seat and a glass of iced tea, saying, "I'd love the company while I finish up here. So how was your walk?"

"Quite enjoyable. This is certainly a charming beach community."

"It really is," Donna agreed as she stirred a pot on the stove. "I was so excited when Jason invited me to bring the family here for the month. Then Grady's boss agreed to allow him to take his entire three weeks of vacation at the same time. We decided that he would go back to Manhattan for the final week that Frank and I are here and then come to bring us home on the weekend. I had visions of happy family times, but then, who could have predicted such a tragedy?"

I took her comments as my chance to ask exactly how her opportunity had come about.

"Oh, Aunt Jessica, it was really unexpected. Anthony Barlowe suddenly retired. He was barely sixty and no one expected him to leave the company for many more years. In fact, our office is on Pine Street and Anthony had recently bought a condo in the old Cocoa Exchange building only a few blocks from the office. He could literally walk to work, which of course gave everyone the impression that he planned on staying at Courtland Finance well into his golden years. Then a few months later, he suddenly retired. Said he had a change of plans."

"I can understand. As they age, many people find themselves wondering how they really want to spend however many years they have left, and they often make decisions that surprise even themselves." I stopped to take a sip of tea, hoping to hear more.

"Anthony had been in charge of the company's financial dealings with Asian nations, and his division had really grown in the past five years. When he announced his retirement, the office was awash with speculation as to who would replace him. There were several front-runners, and I'm certain that my boss, Tyler Young, who is the vice president in charge of the company's global division, had his eye on someone else, a fellow he brought over from Goldman Sachs a couple of years ago named Rodney Miles. Everyone assumed Rodney was being groomed to become Anthony's top assistant and eventual replacement."

"But it didn't work out that way. So tell me, how did the best possible candidate"—I pointed directly at Donna, causing her to blush—"get chosen?"

"Honestly, Grady and I spent months mulling over how my selection came to be. I have a stellar work record but my experience was primarily in domestic finance. I did help to fill in for a colleague in the South America division when she was out on maternity leave, but all I did was sit in on meetings, entertain clients—the parts of the job where great knowledge of the market wasn't necessary. And I had absolutely no decision-making responsibility. So I was shocked, as was everyone in the company, when Jason called me into his office and offered me the position. The one person I can guarantee was more shocked than me was Tyler Young. I heard through the grapevine that he objected strenuously to having me . . . I believe the phrase was 'foisted upon him.' But Jason stood firm. Would you hand me the dish towel hanging on that hook?"

I passed her the towel and said, "I can't even imagine how stressful all this must have been for you."

Donna opened the oven door, slid the rack partway out, and began flipping the avocado fries with a spatula. "Awkward, stressful, nerve-racking, and a million other feelings. At first Tyler gave my team menial jobs. It didn't take long for the team members to begin grumbling. They'd been with Anthony for years and knew how things should run, so I'm sure they were wondering if I was the cause of this turnaround. But after a few months, Tyler started, little by little, to give my unit the kind of assignments I'd been expecting. The team seemed happier and we all pulled together. Life at work got immeasurably better—that is, until the company picnic."

She slid an avocado fry onto a saucer and set it and a fork down on the table in front of me. "There you go, Aunt Jess. You can be my taste tester. Let it cool for a minute."

I was bubbling over with curiosity and couldn't help but say, "Don't stop your story now. What happened at the picnic?"

"In the middle of his 'thanks to all of you, we've had a booming year' speech, Jason announced that, as an award for my exemplary hard work and leadership, my family and I were being invited to spend a month at Courtland Beach, which is what he likes, er, he liked, to call this group of bungalows."

Donna shook her head.

"I suppose that caused trouble at the office?" I prompted.

"You have no idea. First of all, invitations to the bungalow generally go to people who are far senior to me in terms of time at the company. But the absolute worst was Tyler. At the office, he immediately slipped back to being wary and terribly critical, questioning everything I did. And as I told you this morning, he is neurotic about my being here. He keeps reminding me in ways subtle and not so subtle not to speak to Jason about anything regarding my work."

The front door flew open and slammed shut. Frank came running into the kitchen. The ends of two loaves of bread were peeking out of the long white paper bag he was holding.

"Mom, Aunt Jess, wait until you smell this bread. And it is still warm from the oven. Isn't it, Dad?"

He turned to Grady, who had come into the kitchen behind him.

"It does smell delicious. I'm surprised you and Dad didn't eat an entire loaf on the way home from the bakery," Donna teased as she took the package from his hands.

"We were lucky on that score," Grady said. The woman behind the counter said that she is always happy when a nice young man comes into her store and waits his turn politely, without touching and squeezing the bread and rolls.

"She meant me," Frank said, glowing. "Tell them the rest, Dad. Wait. Can I tell them what she did?"

Frank was practically dancing around the kitchen. At Grady's nod, Frank blurted, "She gave us each a roll to eat on the way home. She said that way she was sure the bread would get to the chef. That means you, Mom."

Donna said, "How nice. I hope you'll both still have an appetite for dinner."

Frank laughed. "Dad knew you'd say that, so we split one roll and saved the other for you and Aunt Jess. It's in the bottom of the bag."

"That's terrific. Now go wash up. Dinner will be on the table in a minute," Donna said.

As Frank spun out of the room, Grady's phone rang and he stepped into the living room to answer it. When he came to the kitchen, his face looked pinched and drawn.

"That was Detective Kelly. She and Detective Tieri will be by to talk to us again sometime tomorrow. They would like everyone to stay in place until the investigation of Jason Courtland's death is complete."

Donna said, "I was sort of hoping that the Courtlands would ask us to leave. Being here is so uncomfortable."

Grady shook his head. "Donna, the Courtlands will have nothing to say about who stays and who goes. This phone call from the detectives is their way of saying we are all suspects."

I had nothing to add because there was a strong possibility Grady was right on target.

Chapter Eight

I was half-awake when I became conscious of the noise. Sunlight was shining through my window, promising another perfect beach day. I could hear nonstop tapping but wasn't sure of the source. I sat up in bed and focused on my surroundings. It took me a while before I understood exactly what I was hearing.

A short tap, followed by three slightly longer taps. The sound was repeated. And repeated again. I realized it was Frank tapping the letter "J" in Morse code and undoubtedly waiting impatiently for my reply. What was the code he had told me for the letter "F"? I searched my brain until I was fairly certain he'd said it was dot, dot, dash, dot. Hoping I remembered it correctly, I tapped two shorts, a long, and a short on our common wall. Instantly I heard a muffled "Yay" from the other side, and seconds later, there was a knock on my bedroom door. When I opened the door, Frank was standing there, fully dressed.

"Good morning, Aunt Jess. Are you ready to learn how to make a sand bridge? We have to get an early start because I have my art classes in a couple hours, and by the time school is finished, there will be a lot of people on the beach, and they could get in our way. We need an awful lot of room and sand and water to make a bridge, you know."

Frank spoke with the authority of a structural engineer with a master's degree. Then he switched topics.

"Don't forget you're invited to come to my art classes. Remember Miss Carissa said so before . . . well, before what happened at the tennis court yesterday. And I'd really love for you to come. I know we'll have a lot of fun. I promise it's always interesting."

Then he switched to a third subject and held up a small cooler bag. "I packed breakfast. Two strawberry yogurts, two bottles of water, and an orange that we can split. And I remembered napkins and spoons."

In spite of the early hour, Frank had the energy of a frantically spinning top.

I said, "Oh, my, you have been busy this morning. While I get dressed, why don't you write a note to your parents telling them they can find us at the water's edge? I will meet you on the porch in five minutes."

"Will do," Frank said, and he was off like a shot.

There were no surfers on the beach this morning. The only activity was in the deep water, where a blue boat with a white cabin and NYPD emblazoned on the side had several wet-suited divers tumbling over the side. I naturally supposed there was a connection to Jason Courtland's murder. Of course, it could be something else entirely, but in this quiet community, I didn't think that was likely.

I was impressed with how seriously Frank took his sand-construction project. He calculated every step before deciding what to do. I followed his concise directions and it wasn't long before we were making exceptional progress on the bridge. A number of early-morning walkers stopped by to admire our handiwork. I reveled in Frank's delight when people commented, "Good job," "That looks like the Brooklyn Bridge," or "I'm sure this young man has a future as an architect."

Finally Frank declared the bridge complete and decided we should celebrate our success by enjoying our orange slices. He was unzipping the cooler when my cell phone rang. I looked at the screen. Mort Metzger.

Before I could say so much as hello, Mort heard the line open and said, "It's me, Mrs. F., and Doc Hazlitt is with me. We're both wondering how you are doing. You happen to run into any excitement down there at the beach?"

I could hear Seth in the background. "Stop your banter, Mort, and get to the point. For all we know, Jess could be in grave danger."

Since Seth was the person who looked after my house when I traveled, his words sent a shiver of alarm through me. "Mort, what is Seth implying? Is my house all right?"

Mort reassured me. "Absolutely. I drove past on my way to work this morning and Doc will check it tonight like he always does. He'll make sure everything is locked up tight and the timer on your living room lamp is working the way it should be." Mort hesitated. "Um, I got a call last night from a voice from my NYPD past. My old friend Vinny Tieri mentioned that he ran into you."

"Get to the point, will you?" Seth was losing patience but he needn't have done so for my sake.

As soon as I heard Detective Tieri's name, I knew exactly why they were calling. They'd heard about Jason Courtland's death and wanted to be certain that I was not in harm's way. Seth, of course, always worried that I would put my nosy-body hat on and become too involved in trying to sort out the puzzle pieces of whatever tragedy had occurred and that could put me in danger.

"Mort, please tell Seth I am fine. In fact, right now I am sitting on the beach with my grandnephew, Frank. We have just finished building a spectacular replica of the Brooklyn Bridge. So perhaps we could have this discussion later? I can call you back in, say, half an hour."

"Okay, Mrs. F. I get it," Mort said. "You don't want to talk about the grisly murder in front of the kid. No need to call me back. Just listen. I wanted to let you know that Vinny called me because he wanted to check you out suspect-wise. I told him he was on the wrong track and that you are one of the good guys. I pushed him to trust your instincts and I said it wouldn't be a bad idea for him to follow up on any hunches or notions you might offer. And, Mrs. F., I guarantee you can trust Vinny. I worked with him for years. He's a straight-up cop."

Once again Seth interrupted. "Ayuh, well, if you don't want to talk to her later, she can certainly call me back." I suspected Seth had moved closer to Mort's phone, because his voice got louder. "You can call *me* later, Jess, anytime outside of my office hours, even during office hours if it's an emergency."

While I thanked them for calling and said I would be in touch with Seth later, I watched Frank taking lots of pictures of our bridge with his smart watch. I decided to follow his lead. As soon as our call was finished, I took a picture of Frank proudly kneeling by his bridge and texted it to both Mort and Seth.

Frank handed me a few orange slices wrapped in a napkin and continued his picture taking. As I munched, my mind was scrambling. Mort had used the phrase "grisly murder" in referring to Jason Courtland's death. Detective Tieri must have confirmed that Jason had been murdered and passed that information on to Mort while he was inquiring about me. Grady's supposition that the detectives considered us all to be suspects had turned out to be an extremely likely scenario after all.

Frank scrolled through the bridge pictures on his watch face, and after I'd admired them with appropriate enthusiasm, he looked at the time and said, "We have to pack our tools. Mom will be looking for me. Art school starts in less than an hour. You can finish your orange. I'll clean up."

I watched him dip his pails and shovels in the ocean to rid them of sand and stack everything neatly in the sled. I couldn't help but notice how much he reminded me of Grady at that age. That same determined look while working and then a satisfied smile when the project was complete.

When my husband's brother and his wife died in a tragic car accident many decades ago and Grady came to live with us, it never occurred to me that all these years later I would be building sand bridges on the beach with a boy I loved as though he were my grandson. I only wished my husband had been able to get to know this little boy who bears his name. I shook my head before the memories took hold.

When Frank asked if I was ready to go back to the bungalow, I ruffled his hair and said, "You lead. I'll follow."

By the time I showered and changed, Donna and Grady were seated at the kitchen table, eating bowls of cereal. Donna asked if I would like her to stir up a pot of oatmeal, but I told her that Frank had fed me a healthy breakfast, so all I needed was a cup of coffee.

Donna poured my coffee and sighed. "I know it is a good thing that Frank is so capable and self-confident, but sometimes I get a bit misty-eyed at the thought of my little boy growing up too fast."

"Just this morning I was remembering when I felt the same way about Grady when he was Frank's age, but I have to confess that all these years later the joy has only increased. Grady brought you and then Frank into my life." I patted her hand. "For that, I am forever grateful."

Grady's cell phone rang and he went into the living room to answer it. I wondered if it was Detective Tieri but got distracted when Frank came bounding into the kitchen. He was wearing denim shorts and another Rockaway Beach T-shirt. This one was black with white letters.

"Mom, guess what. Aunt Jess is going to come to art school

with me this morning." Then he amended, "If that is okay with you."

"Of course it is," Donna replied. "I'm sure you'll both have a terrific time."

Grady came into the kitchen. "Art school? Aunt Jess, you will love it. Last week I went to the painting class and learned how to make different colors and had great fun. I do have a little bit of annoying news. That was my office. Mr. Hargreaves wants to see me, something about an audit. I am probably going to have to go into Manhattan for a few hours some day this week. Not sure when. And I hate to have to work while you are staying with us."

"Don't worry, Grady. That may fit in with my plan to have lunch with my publicist. Perhaps once you know your schedule, I can check if Nancy is available, and you and I can travel together, maybe on the ferry Mrs. Courtland mentioned," I said.

Perhaps I should have held my tongue, because my mentioning the ferry nudged Frank to ask, "What about our boat ride in Jamaica Bay? Remember Mrs. Courtland said we could. Miss Anya said she would call a captain—I forget his name—and make the arrangements."

"Sport, this isn't really the best time to bring that up," Grady said. "Mrs. Courtland has a lot on her mind right now, don't you think?"

Frank looked crestfallen but nodded dutifully, then brightened. "You're right. And Miss Anya did say she would take care of it, so maybe we will still get the chance." He looked at me and began to sing, "Heigh-ho, heigh-ho, it's to art school we go."

I laughed and said, "I can take a hint. Let me get my purse."

*   *   *

Portable beige accordion-style room dividers separated the gymnasium of the community center into a reception area and two larger rooms, each identified by a sign: one read WATER-COLOR, the other SCULPTURE. Children were laughing and talking while greeting one another or scurrying around looking for other friends. Frank introduced me to a middle-aged woman whose jet-black hair was streaked with gray and framed her extremely fair face. She was wearing white shorts topped by a navy blue T-shirt that read LIFE IS BETTER AT THE BEACH.

"Aunt Jessica, this is Mrs. Ingram. She keeps the whole community center organized. If you have any kind of problem, you can come to Mrs. Ingram and she will fix it one, two, three."

"I am happy to meet you," I said.

"Not nearly as happy as I am. And please call me Jamie. I'm a big fan of J. B. Fletcher, so it is a joy for me to meet you in person."

She brushed a lock of hair away from the frame of her oversized square-lensed eyeglasses. "I am hoping you will be able to find a few minutes to sign my copies of your books before you go home to Maine. Not today, of course."

"I'd be delighted. I am sure we can arrange a time," I said.

Jamie Ingram thanked me as she turned to the business at hand, picking up a clipboard from the table at her side. She glanced at it, pulled a pencil from behind her ear, and drew a check with a bit of a flourish.

"Frank, today you are in watercolor for the first session and sculpture after the break. Enjoy your art."

She turned from us and greeted two youngsters coming into the building.

Frank took me by the hand and led me into the watercolor area. "You are going to like Mr. Reggie. He knows all about color and he tells us lots of jokes."

Mr. Reggie was a tall young Black man with a popular hairstyle I'd heard my younger friends call a high fade. His khaki shorts were knee-length and his tank top seemed very patriotic, with wide red, white, and blue stripes crossing his chest. He was distributing art supplies to each student as they took their seat.

He welcomed me graciously. "Good morning, Mrs. Fletcher. I'm Reggie Masterson. Frank was very excited when he told me that he would be bringing a special guest to class this week. I am so pleased to have you join us."

He set some paintbrushes along with two small pie tins in front of me and placed a pad of art paper, a jar of water, and a stack of paper plates between my supplies and Frank's.

Frank said, "Mr. Reggie, when we were walking over here, I told Aunt Jess you tell the best jokes. I hope you have one for us today."

Reggie gave me a crafty wink. "As it happens, I heard on the radio this morning that a red ship and a blue ship crashed into each other in the middle of the Atlantic Ocean. The radio announcer said that the survivors are marooned."

Frank looked puzzled, so I stifled my laugh until his face lit up. "I get it," Frank said gleefully. "Maroon is a shade of purple. Red and blue make all the purples! Good one, Mr. Reggie."

Class began with Reggie teaching us how to mix yellow and blue to create all the shades of green represented by the leaves and stalks he'd brought to class. Our job was to mix the paint and then copy the greenery with as close a color match as we could manage. The next hour flew by.

I was actually startled when Reggie said, "That's it for today. You've all done very well. Light greens, dark greens, pale greens, bright greens. I thought I'd have to be in a garden to see so many greens. Now let's leave the room as clean as we found it."

Frank immediately began tidying up our work space, separating trash from supplies that would be used in a future class and putting our best efforts off to the side so we could take them home to show Grady and Donna.

Reggie stood in front of me. "So what did you think, Mrs. Fletcher? I do wonder if, as a writer, you see art as a worthwhile endeavor."

"I most certainly do. But I must confess, as much as I enjoy it, it's not something for which I have a real talent. Some years ago, I stayed in the Hamptons with my dear friend and publisher Vaughn Buckley and his wife, Olga. I had the intention of taking some painting lessons while I was there, but unfortunately a major calamity interfered with my lessons. Afterward I did manage to go to Montauk for three glorious days of acrylic painting on my own."

I sighed at the memory.

Reggie and I both noticed that Frank had finished stowing

our gear and was shuffling from one foot to the other, clearly indicating there was someplace he was hoping to go.

Reggie said, "It was a pleasure to meet you, Mrs. Fletcher, and I hope you will stop in again before you leave the beach. Right now I think Frank is anxious to show you where you can find the snacks and juice."

Frank didn't skip a beat. "It's right over here, Aunt Jess."

He took me by the hand and led me to a long table in the reception area where the children had gathered. "You can take any two bags of cookies or crackers and either a bottle of water or a bottle of juice. It looks like the juice today is apple."

"Well, this is an unexpected treat. Thank you, Frank. I will greatly enjoy a bottle of water."

Frank reached across the table and passed me a bottle of water just as I heard someone call my name.

"Mrs. Fletcher, are you here to join us for sculpture class?" Carissa Potter was wearing a dark green artist smock and had a pale green scarf around her neck.

Before I could respond, Frank said, "In watercolor today we learned how to mix different amounts of blue and yellow to make lots of greens. Too bad you didn't come in during class. I bet we could have matched your greens."

Carissa laughed. "I'm sure you could have, Frank. Why don't you go talk to the other children? I have something I'd like to ask your aunt."

Frank looked at me, and when I nodded, he scampered toward the far end of the table, happily picking up a bag of chocolate chip cookies in the process.

Carissa grabbed my arm and leaned in, whispering, "I'm having difficulty eating. Looking at the cookies and juice is turning my stomach right now. And last night, I can honestly say that the nightmares just would not stop. I would toss and turn, finally get to sleep, and then I would dream of Mrs. Courtland throwing herself on her son's grave and I would wake up in a cold sweat. I'd calm myself down and then the tossing and turning would start again. I don't think I had two hours of sleep during the entire night. How are you coping, Mrs. Fletcher?"

I hadn't had any of the issues that Carissa described, but I didn't want her to feel alone, so I took a moment to sort out my response. Finally I said, "These situations are impossibly difficult. I think everyone involved will be going through some sort of personal trauma."

"True. Especially Mrs. Courtland. You know, Jason's mother. I imagine it is tough enough to lose a husband . . ."

I can assure you it is difficult passed through my mind. That was a loss I knew well.

Carissa continued. "I can't even imagine what it would be like to lose a child, even a child who is well into his adult years. And at her age, I am sure Mrs. Courtland must have depended on him for so many things."

Of course, based on what I'd observed at our dinner with Matilda Courtland, I could dispute Carissa's assumption, but I decided there was no reason for me to reveal what amounted to gossip.

"And Mr. Courtland's grandchildren. I notice they aren't here today. What a distressing time this must be for them. I should know," Carissa said. "My father died in a car accident when I was four years old. I barely remember what it was like to live with him but I can never forget that he went out and didn't come home again. Every year on the anniversary, I go to Riverhead, where the North and South Forks meet. I sit on the side of the road and look at the spot where my dad disappeared from my life forever."

I was searching for words of comfort when she abruptly turned, clapped her hands, and began herding the children into the sculpture class and me along with them. I never had a chance to tell her that the detectives had stopped by our bungalow. I wondered if she'd had a visit as well.

Chapter Nine

As we walked home, Frank asked, "So what did you think of art school, Aunt Jess? Will you go back with me again?"

He was carrying a paper shopping bag that contained our paintings of grass, leaves, and stems as well as the clay flowerpots we'd crafted in Carissa's class.

"I certainly hope to. I enjoyed myself and it's always fun for me to spend time with you. Oh, it looks like your parents have company."

I could see Detectives Tieri and Kelly standing on the porch talking to Grady, who spotted us and waved.

Frank took my hand and slowed his pace so that he was a few steps behind me, as if he was trying to hide. "Aunt Jess, are they ever going to stop coming around?"

"They have to ask questions so that they can find answers. That's the way law enforcement works. I'm sure they won't be here too much longer," I said, although I was sure of nothing of the sort. But with what Frank had seen at the tennis court, I was not surprised that any reminders, including the detectives, would unnerve a ten-year-old boy.

As we reached the bottom of the steps, Detective Tieri said, "Good morning, Mrs. Fletcher. Mort Metzger told me to say hello. He wanted me to mention that he hopes you are having a fine time on your family vacation. In fact, his exact words were 'Tell Mrs. F. I said hello and have fun.'"

I replied, "Mort happened to call this morning and he mentioned that you two had spoken."

My response relaxed Tieri and he said, "So maybe we could take a walk to the tennis courts. Kelly and I only need a few minutes of your time."

"Donna is fixing lunch, Aunt Jess." Grady was giving me a way out if I didn't want to talk to the detectives, but the fact was, I very much did.

The tennis court looked much the same. Although the sea wind had blown away some of the police chalk, the outlines were still visible. Detective Kelly and I sat on the bench facing the court while Detective Tieri leaned against the fence. He nodded to Kelly, who asked me some easy questions, including how long I'd known Mort. Once she'd warmed me up, Tieri took over.

"As it turns out, Mrs. Fletcher, our technicians agree with you. None of the tennis balls were worn out, but many of them had been shaved."

I contented myself with a brief nod and a satisfied smile, although I was tempted to say, *I told you so!*

"Which," Tieri continued, "is what led me to call Mort.

You said you knew him, and so I wanted his opinion of you. To be honest, your strong insistence that the tennis balls were shaved moved you high up on the suspect list once we found out that was true."

I bristled, which Detective Kelly noticed, so she quickly said, "We were following routine procedure, that's all. You seemed to have more information than we get from the average witness, so we decided to look more carefully into your background."

Tieri agreed. "You can understand. We had to check. Sometimes killers trip themselves up by bragging about how smart they are. Anyway, Mort didn't just give you a clean bill. He suggested that we pay strict attention to any of your questions or hunches. He thinks you have a knack for this sort of thing."

"Well, I wouldn't call it a knack; it's more that my mind doesn't like inconsistencies. Unanswered questions challenge me to search for answers," I said.

"So tell me, do you have any unanswered questions about Jason Courtland's death?" Detective Tieri asked.

"I have several," I said. "The most pressing question is, who turned on the TeachTennis machine? The next question is, where is the remote control that I am sure belongs with the machine?"

For the first time since we met, Detective Tieri grinned. "Mort said you were sharp. It does seem that the easiest way for a killer to start the tennis balls flying would have been to use a remote control. For this model, the remote is only two and a half inches wide and five inches long. It could easily be hidden in someone's pocket or even in the outside compartment of a tennis racket bag. And where do you think the perp would dispose of the weapon?" He gestured between the bungalows toward the Atlantic Ocean.

"Figuring the tides would be similar, we sent divers into the ocean this morning close to the same time that the medical examiner estimates Courtland died yesterday. They searched, but only in the twenty yards on either side of the direct line from here to the water. We have neither the time nor the resources to search miles and miles of coastline. I suspect the remote is out there somewhere. By now it might be in the belly of the whale that folks have reported seeing off the beach up by Fort Tilden."

Detective Kelly pulled a pair of sunglasses from her purse, and as she put them on, asked, "So tell me, what do you think happened here, Mrs. Fletcher?"

"Well, it is possible that Jason Courtland came for an early-morning practice session and his killer happened to be nearby, saw an opportunity to set the TeachTennis, and then slipped away as Jason was being pummeled by tennis balls."

Tieri said, "Could have been that way, but—"

I finished his sentence. "But highly unlikely. This murder was planned very carefully by someone who is not only familiar with the Courtland complex but with the comings and goings of the family themselves. Surely the killer would take care not to be seen as she or he filled a bag or two with tennis balls from the practice machine, brought them home, shaved them, and then came back and swapped them out for another batch. That had to have been done multiple times.

"And another thing, the tennis player who uses this court regularly is Linda Courtland. Did she always schedule her practices and her games at specific times? Those times would be off-limits for a methodical killer who had a murderous setup to prepare. And how would the murderer arrange to get Jason Courtland alone on the opposite side of the tennis court from the TeachTennis machine?" I finished, completely satisfied that I had made my points clear.

Detective Kelly grew excited. "That's exactly the track we're on. This was a premeditated murder committed by someone who knew the family well. Do you have any idea who that might be, Mrs. Fletcher?"

I shook my head. "I arrived only the day before the murder. There are some Courtland family members I still have not met, never mind any friends or acquaintances. Although, in this situation, I have to admit that family does seem most likely."

Tieri pursed his lips and nodded slightly. "The family is at the top of my list, but we have to remember there are other people staying here in the bungalows."

I held up my hand like a crossing guard with a stop sign. "Just a minute. If you are talking about Grady and Donna, I can assure you that they may be on your suspect list but they are most certainly not on mine. You will be wasting your time if you investigate them."

I stood. "If there is nothing more, I'd like to go home for my lunch. Have a good afternoon."

As I walked toward the bungalows, I heard Aisha Kelly throw a sarcastic "Well, that went well" to her partner and I couldn't help but smirk.

As soon as I got back to the bungalow, I found Grady and Donna in the kitchen. Grady was setting the table and Donna had prepared a light lunch of cold chicken and vegetables. I quickly whispered that Jason Courtland had definitely been murdered. Before we could say anything else, Frank came bounding into the room.

"Aunt Jess, Mom and Dad were very impressed with our artwork," Frank said, "especially our flowerpots."

"They really are pretty. And Frank made a yellow one and you made a blue one—sort of a reflection of the 'yellow and blue make green' lesson from your watercolor class," Donna said.

"Yes, that was our intention." I winked at Frank, who grinned back.

"Can we put real plants in them or are they only for display?" Donna asked.

"Miss Carissa said that we should let the pots sit for a few days until we are sure the clay is hard. Then we can add dirt and a pretty plant. She suggested, er, succulents. That's the kind of plant, right, Aunt Jess?"

I nodded and Frank went on.

"Miss Carissa said that we are such busy children, she thinks succulents would be easiest for us to take care of. Something like a cactus. They are hard to kill."

"Miss Carissa is right," Donna said. "I am glad we have a few days to take our time looking for the perfect plants."

As soon as lunch was finished, Frank went to find his Lafayette book and Donna began clearing the kitchen table. Grady jumped up to help her. He picked up the glass pitcher and offered me more iced tea before he put it in the refrigerator.

After Donna started the dishwasher, she turned to me.

"Grady drove over to the florist in Belle Harbor and bought two stunning floral arrangements. I'd like to bring a spray of flowers to Linda Courtland and another to Jason's mother." She looked at Grady. "I know you said you would come with me for the condolence calls but I thought, that is, if Aunt Jessica wouldn't mind—"

"I'd be happy to accompany you," I said before she finished asking.

Grady said, "Are you sure, Aunt Jess? It could be gruesome."

"I'm quite sure. Donna is going to have to deal with the results of Jason Courtland's death for some time to come." I lowered my voice. "Especially now that we know the cause. I am sure she'll need your support while her company goes through all sorts of turbulence. Since I am here, let me do this small chore. Save your energy for when it's needed. For a time when Donna needs support and I'm not around."

Both bouquets that Grady brought home were gorgeous and fragrant mixes of white hydrangeas, scarlet peonies, and pastel roses in fluted glass vases decorated with white bows.

Donna thought it best that we take a bouquet to Linda Courtland first. "After all, I was supposed to be her tennis partner yesterday, and then I found her husband's body . . . I feel almost as though I should apologize, and now to find out that Jason was murdered . . . I don't know how she can bear it. Do you know if the detectives have told the family yet?"

"I'm sorry. That's one question I did not think to ask. I am sure we will find out sooner or later. Now, do you want to carry the vase or shall I?"

I was somewhat surprised when Edwina Courtland-Young opened Linda's front door. I would have expected her to be comforting her mother. But who is to say what arrangements had been made within the family? In hushed tones, Edwina told us that she and her husband, Tyler, were there to watch over Linda, who was napping.

"Dr. Milstein sent a prescription to the pharmacy and Tyler rushed right over to bring the pills home. Two pills knocked Linda out within a few minutes," Edwina confided as she seized the vase and pulled it right out of Donna's hand. "These flowers are absolutely lovely. I will be sure to tell Linda that you ladies were kind enough to stop by."

And before we could respond, she shut the door firmly but quietly.

We walked back to the bungalow and Donna went inside to get Matilda's flowers, and when she came out, she said, "Grady left a note. He and Frank have gone crabbing on Jamaica Bay."

"Crab soup for dinner tonight?" I asked.

"Probably not." Donna laughed. "This is the third time the boys have gone, and whenever they pull up their traps, if there are any crabs inside, my softhearted son insists they drop the cage again so the crabs can go home to their families."

"Donna," I said, "these are the times he reminds me of Grady as a boy."

We stood on Matilda's screened-in porch and Donna tapped lightly on the front door. There was no response, so Donna tapped with a bit more pressure. After a while, Anya opened the door and stepped out onto the porch.

"The two Mrs. Fletchers. How kind of you to stop by. Tilly will be sorry to have missed you but she is resting right now.

An old friend dropped in, and talking with him about Jason . . . well, it tired her to the point of exhaustion."

"Would that old friend happen to be a man named Julius Machelli?" I asked.

My question startled Anya and caused her to look quite guarded. "Why, yes. Julius was here. How do you know him?"

"I don't really. I met him yesterday near the tennis court and he mentioned that he had quite a long history with Mrs. Courtland. I had no reason not to take him at his word."

Anya relaxed once more. "Julius and Tilly have been friends since they were youngsters. He's probably the only person alive who's known Tilly longer than I have."

Donna held out the flowers.

Anya brought the bouquet to her face and took a deep breath. "Ah, these are so fragrant. Peonies always sweeten up the smell of roses. You have outdone yourselves, ladies. As I said, Tilly will be sorry to have missed you. Now, if you'll excuse me, I want to put these lovelies where Tilly can see them."

Just as she turned, we all heard a knock on the edge of the porch screen door. A husky blond man, dressed in a tan golf shirt and navy blue shorts, was standing on the steps.

"Excuse me, ladies. My name is Lawrence Torsney and I've come to pay my respects to Mrs. Courtland."

Anya got the same guarded look I'd noticed earlier. "I'm sorry, Mr. Torsney, but Mrs. Courtland is not up to receiving company just now."

The man smiled easily. "I completely understand. I am a longtime client of Courtland Finance and I recently moved into the Tides at Arverne by the Sea. Since we are now practically neighbors, when I heard about the accident, I thought I would stop by and offer whatever assistance I can render."

"That's very kind. I'll let Mrs. Courtland know you were here," Anya said.

"I'll just leave my card." He pulled a business card out of his pocket and slipped it between the screen door and its frame. "Good day, ladies."

We waited until he was out of sight and then I opened the door, snatching the card before it fell. As I passed it to Anya, I noticed that it contained nothing more than his name and a phone number. The area code confirmed he was local.

While we walked back to the bungalow, I asked Donna if she knew who Lawrence Torsney was, but she said she'd never heard of him.

"That's odd," I said. "You would think that a client who, upon hearing of Jason Courtland's death, knew exactly where to find Jason's mother would be a client that had a long and very lucrative relationship with the firm. You might never have worked with him but you would certainly know who he is."

Donna's eyes widened. "We have dozens of clients exactly as you describe. The staff calls them the bread and butters, reliable big investors who keep our business at full throttle. I can recite the names for you right now."

"And Mr. Torsney is not on the list?"

"He most certainly is not." Donna was emphatic.

Chapter Ten

Donna told me she was going to walk to the bay to find Grady and Frank, but I had a few chores I needed to get done. First, I sent a text to Mort Metzger.

I met with Detective Tieri. He speaks highly of you and seems to have removed me from the suspect list.

I ended with a smiley emoji.

Then I opened my iPad and searched for Lawrence Torsney. There were dozens of men by that name. About half of them had pictures associated with their profiles, but none of those were of the man I had met on Matilda Courtland's front porch. I knew so little about him that without a picture, I was at a loss. I decided to look for another man who'd aroused my curiosity. It turns out that Julius Machelli was a vintner on the North Fork of Long Island, and a very successful one at that.

I was so immersed in reading about him that I never heard Grady come home.

"Hi, Aunt Jessica. Would you like a glass of iced tea? Donna took Frank to the library. He's afraid he is going to finish *Lafayette!* and not have anything to read."

"Iced tea sounds perfect." I followed him into the kitchen. "Because I'm both a writer and a teacher, it warms my heart to see any child who loves books so much, especially when it's my favorite child."

Grady poured the tea into two glasses loaded with ice and we sat at the table. He took a long drink. "Ah, now that feels good. So what have you been up to? I saw you were on your faithful iPad when I came home."

"Actually, I was researching a man named Julius Machelli, who has been a lifelong friend of Matilda Courtland and a wealthy client of the firm. I recently met him at the tennis court. Then Anya told us that he had a long visit with Matilda just before we arrived to deliver the flowers. I think I would like to speak with him. Learn a little more about the family."

"Aunt Jess, I know that look. Everyone who loves you knows that look. Do you think this Julius guy killed Jason Courtland?"

I waved that thought away with both hands. "Not at all. Seriously, you would have to meet him to realize that he would be incapable of such a despicable act. But I am sure that Jason was murdered and I am relieved that now the police are sure as well. What I do think is that there are two people who know a lot about the Courtland family history: Anya Wiggins and Julius Machelli. I suspect that both are protective of Matilda, but they are less protective of the other family members. If there are skeletons to be found, Anya and Julius are the people most likely to know where they are buried."

Grady sat, lost in thought, and then stood. "If you met Machelli at the tennis court, he must live around here somewhere. Let's go find him."

I stood as well. "Actually, I know exactly where he lives. We'd better leave Donna a note."

Grady scribbled *Gone for a walk* on a piece of paper and left it under the saltshaker while I put our glasses in the sink. When we entered the lobby of Julius Machelli's apartment building, the concierge asked how he could assist us. From the look on his face, I could tell that Julius didn't receive much company.

"Just a moment, please." He walked to a telephone behind the reception counter, spoke briefly, and then returned to us. "Please come this way. Mr. Machelli lives in the penthouse. Elevator three will take you straight up."

When the elevator doors opened, Julius Machelli was waiting for us. "Mrs. Fletcher, what a pleasant surprise. And this is . . . ?"

"This is my nephew Grady Fletcher. But 'Mrs. Fletcher' sounds so formal. Please call me Jessica." I wanted our conversation to sound friendly and informal right from the start.

The two men shook hands, and Julius led us into a spacious living room. The drapes were wide open, affording us the vision of a panorama featuring a luxurious patio garden beyond which we could see what seemed to be a ribbon of sand leading to miles of ocean and sky.

I stood completely still, mesmerized by the view.

"Ah, Jessica, the way you look at the ocean, I think that you are a lover of every type of nature's magnificent waterways," Julius said.

"I must confess you are spot-on. I live in a small town in Maine named Cabot Cove, and our cove leads directly to the Atlantic Ocean. Here there is no cove, just ocean as far as the eye can see. You used the perfect word—'magnificent.'"

"Please, have a seat." Julius indicated a pale blue brocade couch and matching chairs grouped around an oval mahogany coffee table. "May I offer you some tea or coffee? Although it is a bit early for my taste, I happen to have a nice cabernet available, if that would be your preference."

As soon as Grady and I sat on the couch, I noticed we three were being watched by a man slightly stooped by age who stood near a doorway that I supposed led to the interior of the apartment. I wasn't sure if he was a servant or a bodyguard.

As soon as he mentioned the wine, I realized Julius had given me a nice opening for a friendly conversation. "If the wine is from your North Fork vineyard, I would dearly enjoy a taste."

Although I knew that wine was rarely his usual choice of drink, Grady followed my lead. Julius raised his hand in a signal and the other man set out wineglasses on the coffee table, left the room, and quickly returned with a bottle of wine in a standing silver ice bucket.

"Diego is a certified sommelier. He started working in my vineyard when he and I were both young men. He treats my wine as though it is more precious than rubies or diamonds or gold. Watch now how carefully he opens the bottle, how gently he pours."

After Diego poured a small taste and Julius swirled his glass and sipped, Julius nodded, indicating Diego could fill my glass and Grady's. I made a production of admiring the full-bodied taste and asked about the grapes. Knowing that he was speaking to novices, Julius kept his response short but informative.

"I am quite astonished. Have you always owned a vineyard?" I asked.

"Yes, it is a family business. In fact, that's how I know Matilda. We both grew up on the North Fork. My family owned a vineyard and her family owned a ferry service and boatyard."

Once he brought up Matilda's name, I told him I had tried to visit her earlier in the day but she was resting and could not be disturbed.

Then I said, "Anya mentioned that you had spent some time with Matilda earlier today. May I ask how she is feeling?"

"It breaks my heart to see her so devastated by the tragic loss of her son." Julius turned his head and stared out over the ocean; then his voice softened. "I loved her once, you know. Many years ago Matilda and I hoped to marry, but her family did not approve. They made a match for Matilda with Everett Courtland, who was from Southampton. Everett's family had been in banking for several generations and Matilda's father wanted that security for his daughter. Matilda entered a loveless marriage because she did not want to disobey her father or disappoint her family. Marriage to Everett would move Matilda many rungs up the social ladder and that would reflect well on her family."

Julius closed his eyes and sat, apparently lost in thought. Grady and I exchanged a glance but said nothing, waiting to see if he had anything more he wanted to tell us.

After a while he began speaking with more enthusiasm. "I was fortunate that Matilda broke my heart, because it was less than a year later that I met my true love, Irena, and we were happily married for forty-eight years until she passed away. Irena was the joy of my life. I am sorry to say that Matilda and Everett were not so fortunate. They had difficulties, and then a time came when they hit a particularly rough patch that lasted for quite a while. After it was resolved, Everett sold all his land in the Hamptons, bought a large plot of beachfront property here in Queens, and as far as I know, none of the Courtlands ever so much as visited out east again." Julius shook his head and seemed to age right before our eyes.

"It sounds as though there was a great misfortune," I said, wondering out loud.

"I guess you could call it that. I know for certain there was a death involved. Now, if you will excuse me, I am an old man and it is time for my afternoon nap. Diego will show you the way out."

Grady and I rode the elevator in total silence and said good-bye to the concierge, and once we were out of the building, both of us heaved deep sighs of relief.

"Boy, Aunt Jess, sitting there listening to Mr. Machelli was like watching an episode of a soap opera on a fifty-five-inch television screen. Love, money, death—all rolled into one story," Grady said. "I think we should walk home along the beach. 'Toes in the sand' sort of thing. It will help us escape the gloom. Here, I'll carry your sandals."

Within my first few steps of sand squishing between my toes, I was feeling better, sliding back into vacation mode.

Grady further cheered me when he said, "I almost forgot. I am going into the city tomorrow to see Mr. Hargreaves about the audit. I shouldn't be in Manhattan too long. I am planning on leaving here on the 12:15 ferry, which gets to Wall Street about one o'clock. If the timing works, we can come home on either the ferry that leaves around four or the one that leaves around five in the afternoon. Do you think you can work in a meeting with, er . . . I'm sorry. I forgot who you wanted to visit."

"My new publicist, Nancy Pollard. I've been with Ellen, my former publicist, for years, but she is retiring and highly recommended Nancy as her replacement. We have spoken on the phone and e-mailed but it has been strictly about work. I'd like to get a sense of her as a person. I thought a nice lunch in an elegant spot with a pleasant atmosphere would do the trick."

"How about Fraunces Tavern? You can't beat it for atmosphere," Grady suggested. "And it is only a few blocks from the ferry."

"If it's good enough for George Washington, it will definitely be good enough for Nancy and me," I said.

We were both laughing when someone called out, "Mrs. Fletcher, I hope you enjoyed your art lessons this morning."

Reggie Masterson was slow jogging in the sand and coming directly toward us.

"Oh, yes, very much indeed. I am fairly certain I have conquered the color green. Have you met my nephew Grady? He's Frank's father," I said.

"Oh, yes. Both Mr. and Mrs. Fletcher have come to class

with Frank. It is nice to see a family so interested in the art program. Many parents see it mainly as a way to keep the children occupied and out of their hair for a few hours. And I can tell you exactly which children are attending because they are made to and which children attend for the pure enjoyment. I guess I don't have to tell you that Frank is an eager learner. He's one of the students who makes me look forward to going to work each morning."

Grady flushed with pleasure and thanked Reggie for the compliment.

Reggie said, "This is my first year teaching here, so I wasn't quite sure what to expect."

"Well, you certainly seem to have it all well in hand." I sincerely meant the compliment. "Would you mind if I asked how you got this job?"

"I wouldn't mind at all. It is no secret. Carissa brought me on board. She has been working at the community center in the art program for a number of summers, but her main pottery studio is in Greenport, not far from my parents' home. That's how I know her. I actually spent a few months taking sculpture lessons from her to help me perfect my approach to the form of people and objects in my paintings."

"So you two are friends. How nice. And now you are working together," I said.

Reggie said, "Not exactly friends. More like colleagues. For the past few years, Jonas Littlefield was the painting instructor for the art project. But he had to withdraw this season, so Mr. Courtland asked Carissa to find a replacement. When she invited me to take over the watercolor class, I was happy to oblige. For one thing, the timing worked. I'd just closed what turned out to be a less-than-successful show in a gallery on the Bowery in Manhattan. So I was looking for a way to earn some money and still have time to paint. Speaking of painting, I am on my exercise break, so I'd better finish my run and get back to my canvas. Nice to see you both." Reggie waved and went on his way.

When we got to the bungalow, Donna and Frank were sitting on the porch playing an intense round of the colorful card game Uno. Grady stopped to watch but I went inside to call Nancy Pollard and set up a lunch date. She sounded as excited as I was that we would finally meet. She offered to call Fraunces Tavern to reserve a table, and I was happy to have one more chore off my to-do list.

I checked the time. Barring an emergency, Seth was sure to be available for a chat and probably somewhat irritated that I hadn't called sooner.

He answered in full doctor mode. "I thought perhaps you were in New York–Presbyterian Hospital with third-degree burns. I've been watching the weather. Mighty sunny in New York City these days. I hope you are using sunscreen and wearing a hat."

"You know full well that I am always extremely careful in the sun," I said.

"Ayuh, that's what all my patients say and then I have to take precancerous cells off their noses or their shoulders." Seth harrumphed.

"And how is my house?"

"Doing just fine without you. I am taking care of it as I always do. I have to say that your roses need a bit of work. A few nips with the pruning shears might come in handy. Living so close to Maeve O'Bannon, you can't afford to let your garden get all ragtag."

I changed the subject. "I texted Mort. Thanks to him, the detectives here have removed me from the suspect list."

"And I suppose by now you have a suspect list of your own." There was that harrumph again and I could almost see Seth raising his eyebrows.

I sighed. "I wish I did. However, I know so little about the people involved. Everyone here is new to me and you know I hate to jump to conclusions." I gently changed the subject. "So tell me, what am I missing in Cabot Cove?"

By the time Seth and I hung up, the Uno game was apparently over. Frank was sitting on the couch with a pile of books on his lap.

"How did the Uno game go?" I asked.

"I won. I was going to give Mom a chance to play again and maybe beat me, but a man stopped by to talk to her about work." Frank shrugged. "So I came in here to pick which library book I wanted to read next. Do you want to help me?"

"I'd love to."

As I walked to the couch, I glanced out the window and there was Lawrence Torsney standing on the porch, talking to Donna. He definitely was a man who popped up at the oddest times. I had to wonder what his real interest in the Courtlands could be.

Chapter Eleven

Donna dropped Grady and me off at the ferry dock in plenty of time for us to board the ferry scheduled to leave promptly at a quarter past noon. The sleek white vessel had outdoor seating on an upper deck and comfortable, thickly padded blue seats inside a clean and spacious cabin.

We walked up the ramp behind three passengers who stowed their bicycles along the main deck's railing. Then we followed them into the cabin, which had a gloriously high, wide window on each side that promised an entrancing view of everything we passed.

Grady must have been considering our surroundings as well, because he led me along the aisle until we were midcabin and then indicated a seat beside a window.

"Sit on this side of the ferry, Aunt Jess. I guarantee you will have the best view, especially when we sail past the Statue of Liberty."

The captain made a few brief announcements and then the engines revved up. They were quieter than I expected for a ship this size.

Once we were underway, Grady asked if I'd like coffee or tea from the food concession. "Unless you think that might give you a queasy stomach out here on the water."

"Seriously, Grady?" I laughed. "No Cabot Cove resident would ever admit to seasickness, and I'm grateful that is a problem I've never had. I would definitely love a cup of tea," I said.

When Grady returned with his coffee and my tea, I took it gratefully and said, "You know, I never had a chance to ask Donna. Did she happen to mention to you why Lawrence Torsney stopped by to speak with her yesterday?"

Grady said, "He's supposedly a client of Donna's company but Donna said she never met him before yesterday. He claimed that he was walking by and noticed her on our porch. He said he recognized her as being one of the ladies who was at Mrs. Courtland's house when he stopped by. Donna said he referred to Matilda as 'Jason's mom' and asked if Donna had any update on how she was doing."

"He's an odd duck," I said. "He turned up at Matilda's house and acted as though he was an old friend. He was, I guess I would say, almost put out when we didn't welcome him and bring him right in to see Matilda. But he covered it with a casual attitude."

"Knowing how your mind works, I guess you think he roamed around the complex until he spotted Donna as one of the people who might give him a way in, but why? Who would want to push their way into the family during this time of crisis? I don't get it." Grady shook his head.

"I don't either," I agreed. "But there is something curious about a man who shows up shortly after a murder and acts as though he has been part of the group all along. I can't put my finger on it. What is he up to?"

"Maybe he is a reporter looking for a scoop?" Grady ventured.

"That's possible, I suppose, but I would think the press would be more likely to be interested in the effect of Jason's death on the company. You know, money, chain of command, that sort of thing. Matilda would hardly be the one to ask. The one thing I am sure about is that a company as large as Courtland Finance has a whole slew of people who do nothing but deal with the media."

I watched through the window as the ferry glided effortlessly onto the dock ramp in Brooklyn to take on more passengers, and then we were on our way to the Financial District in Lower Manhattan.

"Grady, traveling on this ferry is so exhilarating. I'm an old hand at New York, and I've traveled all over the city on buses and trains, not to mention riding in more taxis than I can count. Did I ever mention that when I attended an event at the main library on Forty-second Street, I took a short ride in one of those bicycle rickshaws? I think they're technically called pedicabs. It was great fun, but I have to say a trip on the NYC Ferry tops them all."

Grady beamed, pleased that he was able to introduce me

to something that I was enjoying so much. I was still talking about how wonderful the ferry was when Grady pointed out the window. There she was in the distance: the ever-beautiful Lady Liberty. The closer we got, the more regal the Statue of Liberty appeared against the clear blue sky. Before I could get over the elation of sailing so close to her, directly in front of us the New York skyline came into view. It was glorious, with sunlight reflecting off the walls and windows of buildings of assorted ages, shapes, and sizes.

"Grady, do you remember when you were a youngster and Uncle Frank and I brought you to New York on vacation?" I asked.

"You mean the vacation when we visited Liberty Island and climbed right to the statue's crown? I certainly do. I felt like I was on top of the world, but I remember how tired my legs got. That circular staircase that winds its way through the statue's body was a tough hike for a little boy with short legs. Although looking back, I guess that staircase is difficult for everyone. Hey, Aunt Jess, 'The Circular Staircase,' wouldn't that be a great title for your next novel?"

"It is a great title for a mystery, but I'm afraid that an awe-inspiring mystery writer named Mary Roberts Rinehart beat me to it and wrote the definitive novel with that title long before I was born. Ask any librarian. It's still a classic today."

The ferry began to slow down and the other passengers started to close their laptops and gather their bags and briefcases. Grady looked at his phone. "Right on time. I guess it helps that there are no traffic jams on the water."

We followed the crowd off the ferry, along the dock, and out to the street. Grady took my arm at the corner of Water

Street while we waited for the light to change. Having lived in New York myself, I was not at all surprised by the brave, or perhaps foolhardy, New Yorkers who attempted to dodge between the cars when the light was not in their favor.

An extremely thin man with a shaved head and a graying handlebar mustache, and dressed in tan slacks and a pink golf shirt, came along the side street toward us and said, "Grady Fletcher, is that you? I can't believe it."

Grady looked befuddled for a few seconds and then said, "Anthony, what on earth?" He stuck out his hand and they shook vigorously. "You are the last person I expected to see here. You're retired. Off living the good life."

"I may have retired but I still live in the neighborhood. You did know I bought an apartment in the Cocoa Exchange, didn't you? Of course you did, but more important, who is this charming lady by your side?" He smiled pleasantly as he waited for an introduction.

At this point the traffic light changed to green and people were pushing past us to cross the street. We were clearly in the way but neither Grady nor his new friend seemed to care.

"This is my aunt Jessica Fletcher—"

Anthony whoever-he-was said, "Of course." Then he startled me when he took my hand and raised it to his lips. "According to office gossip, you are the mystery writer extraordinaire. I am Anthony Barlowe. I used to work at Courtland Finance."

Then it clicked. Anthony Barlowe, the man Donna had replaced in the global division of Courtland Finance and Investments. Donna had mentioned she was surprised when he retired, since he had recently moved into the Financial District so he could walk to work each day.

"Why, thank you," I said. "Did I hear you say you live in a cocoa exchange?"

"Well, the building was once the headquarters for the cocoa market here in New York, but really, in my opinion, headquarters for the entire world's cocoa market. But times do change and so does the use of buildings, so now it is home to me and to other New Yorkers who enjoy living in a distinctive building in the heart of the Financial District. I am sure you've seen the famous Flatiron Building on Fifth Avenue. The Cocoa Exchange is very similar. It was constructed where Pearl Street and Beaver Street converge at Wall Street."

Grady checked the time on his phone and said, "Well, it has been nice to see you, Anthony. I will certainly bring your regards to Donna, but unfortunately, I have to get to work. Audits, you know."

Anthony gave Grady a look of mock horror. "Surely you are not going to subjugate your aunt to sitting in the waiting room while you juggle numbers. How terribly boring."

"Actually, I won't be accompanying Grady to work. I have plans to meet a business associate for lunch at Fraunces Tavern," I interjected.

"Well, there is our solution. We can send Grady off to the coal mines as it were, and I shall escort you to Fraunces—a lovely place to eat, I might add."

Grady looked at me wide-eyed. "Er, Aunt Jess . . ."

"Now you run along. I'll be fine with Mr. Barlowe as my guide." I patted Grady's cheek in a gesture of dismissal that I knew he didn't care for, but I hoped he would take it as a signal that I really did want him to leave. I had questions that perhaps Mr. Barlowe could answer. "Oh, and, Grady, be sure to text me to let me know what time I should meet you at the ferry dock for our ride back to Rockaway Beach."

Grady gave me a thumbs-up, turned, and headed down the block.

Anthony said, "We can cross Water Street here, then walk up to Pearl and make a left turn. And in short order, we shall find Fraunces Tavern on the corner of Pearl and Broad streets."

"This is so kind of you. I am quite familiar with Midtown Manhattan, but this lower tip of the island is not a place I generally visit," I said.

"Well, now that you're here, I hope you'll enjoy yourself so that you will come visit us more often." Anthony skipped a beat and said, "Did I understand you to say that you took the ferry here from Rockaway Beach?"

"Oh, yes, Donna and Grady invited me to join them for a brief vacation. They are staying for a month." I tried to look totally innocent while I was luring him in.

"By any chance, are you staying in the Courtland bungalows?" Anthony's tone was nonchalant but he swiveled his head and peered at me carefully.

"Yes. Oh, but of course, since you were a colleague of Donna's, I'm sure you have spent time there. It's lovely, isn't it?" I smiled.

Anthony shifted his jaw and wrinkled his brow. "Actually, with one thing and another, I never had the pleasure of visiting the cottages, although I have heard it is a perfect vacation spot. Then you must have been there when Jason had his tragic accident."

I replied without correcting his assumption as to the cause

of Jason's death. "Yes, I was. Believe me, it was horrible. Poor Donna was the one who found him buried under a mound of tennis balls. I am sure he was battered beyond belief. Such an ordeal."

"How terrible for Donna. I hope she doesn't have nightmares. And the Courtland family? How are they coping?" he asked.

"Matilda Courtland is shattered, losing her son like that. Jason's wife, Linda, seemed inconsolable during the brief time I saw her after . . . the accident."

"And the rest of the family?" Anthony seemed genuinely concerned.

I took a chance. "Well, actually, Edwina and Dennis didn't seem broken up, but of course I suppose they are being stoic to provide support for their mother and sister-in-law. And I have not yet met Tyler Young, so I can't say how he reacted."

Anthony grimaced. "Tyler. Now, there is a shrewdie if ever I met one. Don't be surprised if you discover him singing and dancing because he isn't able to contain his joy that Jason is finally out of his way."

I pretended to be shocked. "Surely he wouldn't wish harm on his wife's brother?"

"I can't say that he would, but I can say with absolute certainty that should misfortune fall like a boulder on Jason Courtland, Tyler Young wouldn't be the least put out by it. In fact, he would probably find it cause for celebration."

Before I could ask why he thought so, Anthony waved his hand toward a nearby door bordered by high white columns. "Here you are, Jessica. Fraunces Tavern, where I am sure you and your colleague will have a delightful lunch. I sincerely hope we meet again."

With that, he turned on his heel and walked back in the direction from whence we'd come.

Nancy Pollard was as delightful in person as she had been in our e-mail exchanges and telephone conversations. It instantly felt as though we were old friends. She told me that she had two ancestors who had fought in the Revolution, including one who was an eleven-year-old drummer boy.

"I guess that is why my family has such an affinity for Fraunces Tavern as well as the dozens of other places along the Revolutionary War Heritage Trail. I have been visiting them all since I was a tiny girl." Her smile deepened her dimples and made her blue eyes twinkle. "I hope after lunch you have time for a visit to the museum upstairs. It is so interesting."

"I wouldn't miss it," I said as we both picked up our menus.

After we ate a leisurely lunch consisting of a Jefferson's Cobb Salad, mine with salmon and Nancy's with shrimp, we went to explore the museum. On the way I told Nancy that Cabot Cove has a long history of patriotism stemming from the Revolution and that the town holds a very popular reenactment every year. She was so enthusiastic, I promised to invite her to next year's Joshua Peabody Day.

"As much as I enjoy the reenactment every year, being here is truly exhilarating," I said. "We are standing in the very building where George Washington acknowledged to his officers that he had done his job and it was time, finally, to go home to Martha and Mount Vernon."

Nancy beamed. "Yes, the speech he made here was definite proof that Washington never intended to be a king or a dictator or anything of that sort. After what has been recorded as a very emotional farewell in December 1783, Washington left New York, rode to Maryland to resign his commission, and went home to Mount Vernon, envisioning a future as a gentleman farmer."

The story she described gave me chills, as did the artifacts in the museum: furniture and tableware, lithographs and engravings, that had all survived from the eighteenth century.

"Over here, Jessica, this is one of my favorites."

And she pointed to a small metal box poked with holes that sat on the floor in front of an antique hoop-backed Windsor chair.

"What on earth?" I said, and then I thought of what it must be. "Is that a foot warmer? I've heard that people not only used them in their homes but also carried them to meeting places and then lit the coals inside from the available hearth."

"Exactly." Nancy laughed. "Since women's shoes were not as protective as men's boots, the women often lugged their foot warmers to sewing circles and other gatherings. Arduous, to say the least."

I laughed along with her and then a bust on a shelf caught my eye. It was identified as a plaster cast of Marie-Joseph Paul Yves Roch Gilbert du Motier, Marquis de Lafayette. I pulled out my phone and snapped several pictures, positive that Frank would be thrilled to see them.

I was enjoying myself so much that I didn't hear my text notification. Fortunately, I checked my messages and learned that Grady had finished his audit and would meet me at the ferry dock shortly. Nancy walked back to Water Street with me, where we said good-bye and promised to get together the next time I was in the city.

Once I got to the dock I had to walk only a few yards before I saw Grady waving. As excited as I was to tell him about my adventures in Fraunces Tavern, I was more interested in getting his take on Anthony Barlowe and his relationship to the Courtland family, particularly Tyler Young. We'd have plenty to talk about on the ride home.

Chapter Twelve

I was happy to hear that Grady's audit had gone off without a hitch.

"I couldn't believe it. We were finished in record time. Mr. Hargreaves actually gave me an attaboy."

Relief was so evident on Grady's face that I leaned in to give him a brief congratulatory hug.

We got in line to board the ferry, and once we settled into our seats, I noticed that there were a lot more passengers heading to Rockaway than had accompanied us on the way to Manhattan.

"That's because it's the end of the workday. At this hour we're riding with the regular commuters who use the ferry as their daily route to work. Speaking of work, how did your meeting go?"

I told him how much I had enjoyed finally having the opportunity to spend time with Nancy and that I was sure we would be a terrific team going forward. I admitted to being awed by Fraunces Tavern and then segued.

"How well do you know Anthony Barlowe?"

"Not well at all." Grady shrugged. "I met him a number of times when Donna brought me to events like the Courtland annual picnic, holiday parties, awards dinners, and the like, but since Donna didn't work with him closely, we were not friendly. In fact, I was kind of surprised that he recognized me on the street this morning."

I lowered my voice. "Well, I consider it fortunate that he did, because he made a not-so-subtle suggestion to me that Tyler Young would be more likely to celebrate than to mourn the death of his brother-in-law."

"Really? Why would Anthony say something like that?" Grady sounded puzzled. "He's been gone from Courtland's for nearly a year. Oh, wait. I suppose he could have a gossip source who still works at the company. If that's the case, we should warn Donna. Every single person who is on her staff now once worked for Anthony. I hope they're not blabbering about her."

"I don't think you need to worry. Donna is a sweet person and by every account a competent employee. Remember the kind words Jason had for her when we were at Matilda's house? I would imagine that the most detrimental thing anyone could say about her is that she is far too nice to be in such a cutthroat business."

With that, Grady's phone rang. He broke into a grin. "It's the lady herself. Hi, honey. Nope, don't worry. Not a problem at all. Aunt Jess and I will see you at home."

Grady tapped his phone to end the call and turned to me.

"Donna and Frank spent the afternoon at the beach, and he was sitting on the couch reading one of his new library books and fell asleep. I told her not to wake him. She needn't pick us up. We can get back to the bungalow on our own."

"We certainly can," I said. "I have both Lyft and Uber apps on my phone. Don't you?"

Grady nodded. "Of course I do, but we may not need them. I wouldn't be surprised if there will be cabs or cars from a private service at the dock waiting for ferry passengers. I noticed a couple when we left. I expect they meet every ferry and they would be sure to show up at this time of day."

And he was right. When we got off the ferry, people were piling into private cars, black cars from car services, and green taxicabs—all of which were waiting outside the gate on Beach Channel Drive. We were back at the Courtland property in less than fifteen minutes.

After the cab dropped us off, Grady turned around to watch it leave the parking lot. "Aunt Jess, Anya Wiggins looks like she is struggling with those packages. Let's give her a hand."

He pointed and I saw Anya walking into the lot from the main road, carrying more grocery sacks than she could easily handle. We hurried to help her.

As Grady took the packages out of her arms, Anya said, "Thank you so much for rescuing me. Tilly has needed me around her every minute since . . . since Jason. About an hour ago, she finally admitted to being worn out and needing time to herself. She went to her room to rest. When I was sure she had fallen into a deep sleep, which I can tell you she desperately needed, I decided to run out and pick up a few things from the grocery. Unfortunately, I bought more than I could manage to carry. I felt like my arms were about to fall off."

Grady, balancing the grocery sacks as best he could, hurried ahead of us toward Matilda's house. I asked Anya if she wanted to stop for a moment's rest, but she declined.

"The thing I know for sure is that it is best for everyone if I am there when Matilda wakes up. In all these years, this is the worst I've ever seen her, even worse than the awful time . . . Never mind."

I sensed there was something Anya wanted to say, so I persisted. "Do you mean the loss of her son has affected her more than the loss of her husband?"

Anya shook her head. "That was bad, but to be totally honest about it, most of Matilda's feelings were wrapped in sadness for her children and grandchildren. And she had to carry her own guilt for not loving him the way a wife should love a husband. No, her heart was broken decades ago. But in this, in losing her firstborn, Jason, her suffering is so much worse."

We took a few silent steps until I said, "I never had children of my own, but my nephew Grady came to live with my husband and me when he was quite young, after his parents were tragically killed in a terrible car accident. If anything were to happen to Grady or Donna or Frank . . ." I stopped.

Anya nodded. "Then you do understand."

I said, "Yes, loss of a child must be a different kind of loss. Unfathomable. I suppose that Matilda suffered a great deal of unhappiness when her parents wouldn't let her marry Julius Machelli but I imagine the pain she endured then was nothing compared to how she feels today."

Anya came to an abrupt stop and studied me closely,

clearly taken aback that I was party to a family secret. Her chin bobbled but no words came out until she said, "You mentioned that you had met Julius, but now I can see you know far more about the Courtland family than I realized."

She resumed walking and I stayed by her side. After a while she said, "I suppose there is no harm in telling you the rest. There was a man. He came along many years after Julius. Tilly was married, a mother of three, and a society matron. She had no business falling in love, but she did, and heaven help me, I was the go-between who delivered constant messages between them. He was married as well and also had children. We all knew their liaison was dangerous. I couldn't see happiness in their future, so I kept hoping that eventually it would end somehow. But their love grew more intense; their desire to be together overshadowed every waking hour and I guess even their dreams. The time came when their love reached a point where they were determined to rip both families apart and build a new life together."

Anya went completely silent again. I waited patiently for the end of the story. When she began to speak once more, there were tears in her voice if not in her eyes. "At the last minute, Tilly decided she could not bring herself to cause such a heartbreaking disturbance in the lives of her children. She ordered me to call her lover and tell him of her decision.

"I will never forget how joyful he sounded when he heard my voice. I'm sure he expected me to say that Tilly was ready; her plans had been finalized. Of course they *had* been finalized, but not the way he'd hoped. Listening to him cry on the phone was the most pitiful sound I'd ever heard. The last thing he said to me was 'I will come and talk to her.' He disconnected the line before I could tell him how foolish that would be. I warned Tilly, and for the rest of the day and long into the night, we were both frantic. But our panic was for nothing. He never arrived. At midnight, while we sat in the kitchen, Tilly told me she was relieved that he'd come to his senses and accepted her decision.

"Everything changed the next morning when I saw the front page of the *Hampton News*. The headline read JAMES-PORT LAWYER KILLED IN CAR CRASH. I did not have to see the victim's name. I knew. Only death would have kept him from Tilly. She took responsibility for his death as if she had driven a stake through his heart. Believe me when I say, she has never recovered. Now with Jason gone, I'm afraid she will sink deeper into the pit. She is very fragile. I am so worried."

Grady was waiting for us on the screened-in porch. "The rear door was open, so I brought the groceries inside and left them on the kitchen counter."

Anya was able to muster a wan smile. "You are a kind young man. Thank you for your much-needed help. When things return to normal, I promise to bake you a pie."

When she turned to me, she took both of my hands in hers and looked directly into my eyes. "I am so sorry to have burdened you with my grief and Tilly's pain. Please fling it all away. Now I must go."

I watched her walk, shoulders slumped, into the house and push the door closed behind her. Anya had let the difficult emotions caused by Jason's death allow her to be indiscreet. And I was sure she already regretted it. I would have to find a way to reassure her that Matilda's secret would always be safe with me.

When Grady and I got to the bungalow, Detective Tieri was sitting on the porch.

Grady muttered, "What now?" but I was glad to see him. I hoped he had news about the murder.

Tieri put his finger to his lips and semiwhispered, "The boy is asleep in the living room, Mrs. Fletcher said." He raised his palms apologetically. "That is, the other Mrs. Fletcher said I could wait here for you. I have a few questions. Maybe we could take a walk so we don't have to worry about waking the boy."

In truth I wanted nothing more than to lounge on the porch with a glass of iced tea but I realized that he was right. The porch would be the worst possible place for the conversation I hoped we were going to have—one sharing information about the progress of the investigation into Jason Courtland's murder. We walked around the bungalows and over to the tennis court and sat on what was rapidly becoming, in my mind, my usual bench.

Tieri started with a direct question. "So tell me, Mrs. Fletcher, what do you know about Dennis Courtland?"

"Well, I know he is the chief financial officer of Courtland Finance and Investments and the youngest child of the company's founder. And while I can't confirm this, I have a strong notion that he is a lecherous man."

The detective laughed. "Mrs. Fletcher! Did that sly buzzard hit on you?"

"Dear me, no. But I observed both his behavior around my niece Donna and her machinations to stay out of his grasp. That led me to believe he has, shall we say, an ongoing problem when he is around pretty young women or perhaps any women at all."

Tieri nodded. "I am beginning to see what Mort Metzger meant when he said that you analyze things that most other folks don't even notice."

I am sure I blushed when I said, "Mort is a dear friend and has always been very kind, even when I, you might say, interfere in his investigations."

"Speaking of Mort, I was blown away when I asked how Adele was doing and he said they've been divorced for years. I never saw that coming."

I thought about how to respond about a close friend's private life and then said, "While Mort has loved living in Cabot Cove from the moment he arrived, Adele was never truly happy there. I think over time her discontent with her surroundings grew. A number of years ago, she returned to New York City, and from all reports, or at least from the handwritten notes on the Christmas and birthday cards she sends to me, I can honestly say that she is settled into a life that pleases her."

"What about Mort? How did he handle it? That had to be tough."

I was impressed that Detective Tieri seemed genuinely concerned.

"Oh, he was at loose ends for a while, as anyone would be. However, after a couple of years, he began dating. Fortunately, he met Maureen, a lively redhead who both adores and energizes him. And he was smart enough to marry her. They seem quite happy together," I said. "Personally, I think they are a perfect match."

"Well, that's good to hear. Mort is a great guy and deserves to be happy," Tieri said. Then he switched back to the topic at hand. "Now, about Dennis Courtland, you got anything else you think I should know?"

"Well, I am curious why you are focused on Dennis specifically. I have become much more interested in Tyler Young."

"Ah, the brother-in-law." Tieri scrunched his eyebrows until they met. "Hmm, possible, I guess, but Dennis is the next in line to run the company and that puts him at the top of my suspect list. What has you looking at Tyler Young?"

"Conversations I had with two different people who worked for him," I said. "Jason ran the company and I surmise that Tyler, who is in charge of the global division, reported directly to Jason. My niece Donna supervises a unit within Tyler's domain, but she was chosen for the job specifically by Jason over Tyler's objections."

"Bosses do stuff like that all the time, don't they? At least in my job they do." Tieri grinned.

"Of course they do. It is their right to make what they consider to be the best decisions for the organization. But time has passed, Donna has proved herself to be valuable in her new role, and yet Tyler has been consistently adamant that Donna never speak to Jason about any business matters in the global division. Why is that, do you think?"

Before he could answer, I continued. "In fact, Tyler was apoplectic when Jason announced that Donna would be the employee awarded this month at the Courtland property here in Rockaway. Tyler told her in no uncertain terms that she was to . . . I believe the phrase he used was 'keep her business off the beach.' What is he hiding? What was he afraid Jason would find out? And after the events that happened on this very tennis court, he doesn't have that problem anymore, does he?"

"Point taken. We'll have a look, but personally I think Tyler doesn't trust Donna because she was Jason's pick, not because he has anything to hide," Detective Tieri said.

He started to rise from his seat but I placed my hand on his arm, indicating I had more to say. "I might agree with you except that I had occasion to speak to the person whose retirement led to the job opening that Donna filled."

He dropped back onto the bench. "Okay, spill. I'm listening."

When I told him Anthony Barlowe's assessment that Tyler would not necessarily wish misfortune on Jason but was certain to be dancing in the streets if such an event happened, Detective Tieri said, "You win. I'm convinced. We'll take a closer look, maybe even get around to talking to this guy Barlowe. Anyone else on your mind?"

I almost mentioned Lawrence Torsney but decided to ask Donna about her conversation with him first. He might actually be what he claimed: a concerned client wishing to express his condolences. If so, I'd be wasting the NYPD's time if I passed his name along to Detective Tieri. I decided that I would look further into Mr. Torsney myself.

Chapter Thirteen

I was both hungry and tired as I walked back to the bungalow, but my mind was in complete turmoil. Although I was due to go home in a few days, I was reluctant to leave Grady, Donna, and Frank here at the beach while there was a killer on the loose. I was sure that the murderer had a very strong connection to the Courtlands, and through the auspices of Donna's job, not to mention their vacation in the bungalow, so did my beloved family.

As I walked past one of the larger houses, I saw Edwina Courtland-Young sitting by herself on the porch.

"Jessica! Come and join me for a while. I just finished my tour of duty with Linda and I could use some cheery company. Can I bribe you with a glass of iced tea?" She held up a pitcher that was nearly full.

It was too good an opportunity to pass up.

"You certainly can. I was just thinking how nice a glass of something cold would feel right about now, and here you pop up like a genie about to fulfill my wish," I said.

Edwina uprighted a clean glass from the midtable lazy Susan and opened the ice bucket that sat dead center. By the time I was settling into a chair opposite hers, she was handing me the glass filled with tea and ice cubes. At least that is what I assumed.

As soon as I brought the glass to my lips, I detected a strange odor. Spices perhaps? I started to take a sip and realized there was more than a spice or two added to the tea. I pretended to take a small sip.

Edwina smiled, quite pleased with herself. "You really needed that, didn't you? I always think a splotch of bourbon helps the iced tea pack the punch it should have."

I nodded and set my glass back on the table. I wouldn't be gulping the rest of the contents anytime soon, that was for sure.

"I have had a terribly long day. Grady and I took the ferry to Wall Street so I could meet my publicist for lunch at Fraunces Tavern. It's the first time I've ever been there, but I'll definitely dine there again in the future. I was enthralled."

"It's quite charming and so authentic." Edwina nodded. "I have enjoyed it many times. At the company we've often had small private award events there as well as celebratory dinners for the directors. You know—for birthdays and the like."

We went on talking about the social niceties of the Financial District until, for no apparent reason, Edwina burst into tears. She held a napkin to her face and sobbed. Should she need it, I placed my napkin in front of her and waited. It took some time but she eventually regained her composure and apologized to me.

"I don't know what is wrong. I'm not usually like this but for some reason I can't seem to keep my emotions in check."

I did wonder how much bourbon laced the iced tea she had drunk, but I merely said, "Please. No apology is necessary. I can only imagine how overwhelmed you must be by your brother's death. And I suppose the medical examiner's office hasn't released his body as yet, so there is so much emotional turmoil still to come."

"I *wish* I was overwhelmed. At least that would be normal. The problem is that I am, in a twisted way, almost happy he's gone." Edwina stared at her glass of bourbon tea. "For most of my life I have been extremely angry with him." Then she picked up the glass and took an extra-long gulp.

"Let me tell you exactly what happened. See what you think. When we were both teenagers, we went to one of those 'parents won't be home so anything goes' parties at a beach house owned by the family of one of Jason's buddies. Even though we were underage, we both drank a lot of beer, and long story short, we were driving home with Jason at the wheel and he crashed into a tree. He received only a few minor bruises, but I wound up with a crushed pelvis and shredded fallopian tubes."

I patted her hand, murmured words of sympathy, and waited for her to continue.

"So there you have it," Edwina said. "My entire adult life I have been surrounded by nieces and nephews, and as years flew by, my precious grandnieces and grandnephews, but to my sorrow, I have never been able to conceive a child of my own. Every day, every single day over all these long years, I have blamed Jason. I have hated him for depriving me of the joy of having my own children. But now Jason is dead and, I am ashamed to admit, I don't know where to direct my anger anymore."

Edwina was filled with such anguish, I knew I had to tread carefully. "My husband, Frank, and I never had children of our own, but we were fortunate to have our nephew Grady, and today I am here with you because of the loving relationship I have not only with Grady but with Donna and their wonderful son. Sometimes it is best to focus on how lucky you are to have all those nieces and nephews, not to mention the adorable grandnieces and grandnephews. You are fortunate to be surrounded by a loving family. There are many people who are completely alone."

"Family, yes, there's my family." Edwina sniffled. "I dread that we all have to go through all the formalities associated with Jason's funeral, followed by his burial. My husband didn't get along well with Jason, and now I'm sure he and Dennis will be at each other's throats. And I am terribly worried about my mother. I'm also worried about Anya. I can tell you there were long periods of time over the years when Anya was more of a mother to us than Lady Matilda would even pretend to be."

From what Anya had told me, I certainly understood how that could have happened. "But regardless of his feelings for your brother, you do have your husband. I am sure Tyler has been a great comfort to you during this terrible time," I said.

"Oh, I'm glad you're sure. I have *never* been sure that he married me because he loved me. It always seemed far more likely that we got married because he wanted to secure a spot as part of the top management team of Courtland Finance and Investments. He has always had delusions of grandeur, and now with Jason out of the way, he and Dennis can do pistols at fifty paces for the top prize: chief executive officer. Stick around, Jessica. It could get quite entertaining here on the Courtland estate, as Dennis likes to call our beach houses."

Edwina stood, lurched to one side, and steadied herself by leaning on the back of her chair. "If you'll excuse me, I do believe it is time for me to have a lie down."

She opened the door, entered the house, and slammed the door behind her, leaving me sitting on the porch with so much to think about. Tyler versus Dennis, could that be the fight of the century? Or had such a fight already happened and Jason Courtland turned out to be the loser? There was a lot about the Courtland men to sort out.

I decided to circle each of the cottages to see who else might be taking a walk or sitting on their porch. Perhaps I could glean more information and begin to tie pieces together.

The sun was no longer high in the sky. Dusk was moving in slowly. There was a light, gentle wind that smelled of the ocean and reminded me of my morning bike rides in Cabot Cove. I didn't see a soul anywhere on the Courtland property and was about to give up when I heard voices that seemed to be coming from the house on the far side of Matilda's. I turned the corner and Dennis Courtland was sitting on the porch of what I supposed was his house with, of all people, Lawrence Torsney. From what I could hear, Torsney was asking Dennis about his plans for the future of the firm.

I slowed my pace and proceeded to walk casually by just

as Dennis began to respond. When he saw me, he stopped talking business and spoke to me instead.

"Out for an evening stroll, I see, Mrs. Fletcher."

"Yes, I am, Mr. Courtland. There is such a lovely breeze. And how are you this evening, Mr. Torsney?"

As soon as I mentioned Torsney by name, it startled them both.

Lawrence Torsney stumbled over his answer. "I'm sorry . . . I don't recall . . . Have we had the pleasure?"

"Why, yes, of course we have. I was one of the women you approached yesterday when you attempted to pay a condolence call on Matilda Courtland. You also visited my niece Donna Fletcher. Although we didn't actually meet that time, I am staying at her bungalow and happened to see you speaking to her."

The entire time I was talking I had my eye on Dennis and noticed that he became rattled as soon as I mentioned Donna. "And now here you are. You seem to be all over the place."

"Lawrence is an old family friend," Dennis said. "Now, if you will excuse us, we were about to have dinner."

And for the second time in the past few minutes, a member of the Courtland family entered their home and closed the door practically in my face.

I was more puzzled by Lawrence Torsney than by anyone else I'd met since I arrived at the beach. I didn't understand where he fit into either the Courtland family or their financial company. I decided that I'd better ask Donna about her conversation with him, and then I would definitely pass his name along to Detective Tieri.

Even before I reached Donna's bungalow, I could smell

beef on the grill. As I got closer, I saw Grady tending the barbecue while Donna was setting a table on the porch.

"Those sizzling steaks smell delicious," I said. "And I am starving."

"You have a couple of minutes to wash up," Donna said. "It's such a gorgeous evening, we've decided to eat out here. I should warn you: Frank is awake and has been super energized by his nap, so he will probably be chattering like a magpie."

"After the bizarre conversations I've had with adults today, believe me, Frank's chatter will be a welcome respite." I could definitely use some grandnephew time.

Aware that I had left some time ago with Detective Tieri, Donna gave me a questioning look but I waved her off.

"Nothing important. Perhaps you and I can talk after dinner. I did hear some trifling things that I would like you to confirm."

Frank was hopping around the living room to music that was unfamiliar to me. He held up his wrist. "It's my watch, Aunt Jessica, playing the theme from *Inspector Gadget*. I have been watching the old shows and they are really funny. Now I can play the theme and remember something I saw that was funny anytime I want to."

I was pleased that the watch brought Frank so much enjoyment and told him so. "Now I am going to wash up for dinner, and from the look of the steaks on your father's grill, I suggest you do the same."

Dinner was relaxing and fun, not to mention delicious. Donna had prepared a spinach salad with tomatoes and mushrooms along with sweet potato fries. Both complemented Grady's steaks, which he had barbecued perfectly to my taste, medium to medium well.

While we talked and laughed, describing how each of our days had gone, my mind drifted back to Edwina. She'd allowed herself to stay mired in grief and to hold on to her anger at her brother, instead of looking for the joy her extended family could provide. I had to wonder if she'd hated him enough to kill him.

Donna was clearing the table when I remembered I had something I wanted to share with Frank. I went inside and brought back my phone. I tapped my picture gallery and brought up the plaster bust of Lafayette.

I handed the phone to Frank and said, "Guess who."

Frank stared. "Well, with that kind of hair and those curls, he was certainly alive during the time around the Revolutionary War. I'm sure it's not George Washington or Thomas Jefferson. I've seen their pictures lots of times."

His stare became a squint.

After a few more seconds, I decided to give him a hint. "Have you read any good books lately?"

Frank's eyes grew wide. "Is that him? Is that Lafayette?"

I told him to scroll down to the next picture, a different view of the bust. "Yes, sir. It is indeed the heroic Frenchman Marie-Joseph Paul Yves Roch Gilbert du Motier, Marquis de Lafayette."

Frank bounced out of his chair. "Where is this? Did you actually see it?"

I told him about my lunch in Fraunces Tavern and all the Revolutionary War items I had seen in the tavern's museum.

Frank turned to Grady, and before he could get the question out, Grady answered, "Of course. Once we're home, we can go to lunch at Fraunces, I promise."

"And visit the museum?" Frank asked.

Grady's answer of "Absolutely" was met with a loud war whoop.

Donna and I clapped with delight at Frank's excitement. Then Donna said, "This calls for a celebration. Ice cream, anyone?"

After we finished dessert, Grady and Frank went to the beachfront to play a game of catch while Donna and I cleaned the aftermath of dinner.

Once she and I were alone in the kitchen, I said, "Earlier I saw Dennis Courtland and Lawrence Torsney talking on Dennis's porch. I did wonder what that conversation was about. Torsney asked a question about the business, but Dennis went absolutely silent when he saw me and changed the subject."

Donna looked surprised and then shrugged. "Torsney seems to know everyone and turn up everywhere."

"My thought exactly, and I have to wonder why. You don't know of any long-term financial relationship he has with the firm, yet he claims to be a client. And of course he is walking around here as though he is part of the Courtland family." I shook my head. "There is something off about him. I'm not sure exactly what but something is definitely off. For example, you don't know him, but when he stopped by yesterday, he said he recognized you from when he approached us on Matilda's porch. I was standing right next to you on the porch, and yet when I met him just now he had no idea that he'd ever seen me before today."

"Nothing's been right since Jason—" Donna's eyes welled with tears.

"There, there." I gave her a gentle hug. "We are all together and enjoying the beach as much as we can, given the sad situation compounded by a police investigation. Still, I think there are a few things we can do to help Detective Tieri without putting ourselves in danger. In fact, Donna, you can do one thing right now that would be of immeasurable help to the investigation."

"Aunt Jess, really? I don't think I have your aptitude for identifying criminals and solving crimes. I'm an accountant, not a mystery writer." Even as she objected, she stopped crying and looked encouraged. "But if you think I can help."

I told her exactly what I wanted her to do.

Chapter Fourteen

Donna put her hand over the phone's mouthpiece and said, "It's ringing. Now I'm nervous."

"Act natural and do it the way we practiced. You'll be fine," I whispered in case the line engaged.

We were sitting in the kitchen and I could see that Donna was edgy. I, on the other hand, was excited to see if my strategy would bring any new information to light.

Donna wiggled her fingers at me, which I took as a signal the conversation was about to begin.

"Anthony? Hi, it's Donna Fletcher."

Anthony Barlowe must have given her a lengthy greeting, because Donna began tapping her fingers on the kitchen table and rolling her eyes at me.

At long last he stopped talking and she was able to respond, "Yes, yes, I know. That's why I am calling. It was extremely thoughtful of you to escort Aunt Jessica to Fraunces

Tavern. You know, she lives in a small town in Maine, and well, New York City can be overwhelming for out-of-towners. I do worry when she goes off by herself."

I raised my eyes to heaven. "Aunt Jessica who can't take care of herself" was definitely not part of the script I'd provided. Still, I had to admit Donna sounded casual, just two old colleagues having a chat.

While laughing at something Anthony said, Donna signaled me with a thumb raised high in the air.

"Yes," she said into the phone. "It was tragic. Everyone here is . . . traumatized. Totally devastated is probably the description I am looking for. When I see how submerged in distress the entire family is, well, I don't know how the business will survive."

Anthony spent what seemed to my writer's mind like several paragraphs reassuring her. Finally Donna smiled at me and switched topics.

"Anthony, you are such a comfort. Can I bother you with one more thing? A man named Lawrence Torsney suddenly appeared immediately after Jason died, and he has been sort of stalking anyone associated with Courtland Finance. He's asking an awful lot of questions about the company. He told me he is a client, but I've never heard of him. Wheelchair? Good heavens, no."

Donna picked up the pen and began scribbling on the pad sitting at her elbow. "About forty, tall, blond, stocky build. No, no, he's White. Really? Thank you. I will look him up in the computer base. Of course I will warn the others." Donna shook her head at me as she said that last part.

After some rather lengthy good-byes, Donna pressed the

off button and then glimpsed at her phone to make sure it disconnected.

"Aunt Jess, we did it," Donna crowed.

"No, my dear. *You* did it. I must say your performance was superb." I wanted to quiz Donna while her conversation was fresh in her mind. "Now tell me what we learned."

"Lawrence Torsney has been a client of Courtland Finance forever. He was originally brought into the firm decades ago by Everett Courtland when he was still actively growing the business. When Mr. Torsney became interested in foreign investments, Everett appointed Anthony to work as his adviser."

"So Anthony can actually confirm that Lawrence Torsney is a legitimate client," I mused.

"Far from it. The Lawrence Torsney who Anthony described stopped actively investing a long time ago. His account is inactive except for the funds he withdraws each month. He lives quite comfortably in a town called Jupiter in Palm Beach County, Florida."

The look on Donna's face told me she had more surprises to come.

I played along. "Well, I suppose Torsney could be vacationing in New York for the summer. Florida gets quite warm this time of year. But you look as though you have more to say."

Donna nodded. "Oh, I certainly do. You are going to love this, Aunt Jess. Anthony told me that he once visited Florida to have Mr. Torsney sign some papers. That is not a service we generally provide, but Anthony made the accommodation because—get this—Mr. Torsney uses a wheelchair at all times now. And according to Anthony's description, he is an elderly Black man."

I leaned back in my seat and clasped my hands in front of me. "So then whoever the man is who is snooping around the Courtlands—"

"He is not Lawrence Torsney!" Donna finished my sentence.

"Donna, don't you ever again tell me you are not cut out for investigative work." I gave her a kiss on the cheek. "Now, you go see what the boys are up to. I am going to my bedroom to call Detective Tieri. At long last I have some information that he may find useful."

After the sixth ring with no answer on Tieri's cell phone, I was expecting voice mail to pick up, but then I heard, "Good evening, Mrs. Fletcher. I was surprised to see your name pop up on my phone this late. Are you in trouble?" He sounded concerned.

"No, not at all," I said, sorry that I had alarmed him.

"Well, that's terrific news, because I really don't want to rush back to work. I am pushed back in my recliner with my feet up, watching the Mets trounce the Dodgers six to three in the bottom of the seventh inning. Looking good for the home team."

He was completely relaxed. I felt as though I was talking to Mort's friend Vinny, not the NYPD detective.

"I'm glad to hear it," I said. "Would you rather we talk tomorrow?"

"No, we're good. I actually DVR every game. Then I start watching about ten or fifteen minutes after the ump yells,

'Play ball.' If I get interrupted by, say, a phone call, I can hit pause, so I never miss all the best plays. I do it with football, too. Jets fan in case you were wondering. Now, what's up?"

Friendly Vinny was gone and Detective Tieri was all business.

"Has the name Lawrence Torsney come up in the course of your investigation?" I asked.

"Can't say that it has. Matter of fact, right before Aisha and I signed out this evening, we spent half an hour going over the list of interviewees, the list of witnesses, and the list of possible suspects. His name wasn't on any of 'em. Who is this guy?" He sounded eager.

I gave a brief description about how Torsney began showing up immediately following Jason Courtland's murder. "I thought it could be a coincidence. After all, the entire Rockaway peninsula is a beach community and it's the height of summer. Lots of people coming and going."

"But then?" He sounded anxious to hear the rest.

"Well, this is almost impossible to believe, but the man who is glad-handing everyone as Lawrence Torsney is an impostor." I emphasized that final word.

"Are you sure?" Tieri squawked. "What kind of evidence have you got?"

I told him about Donna's conversation with Anthony.

"That does seem to nail it," he confirmed. "Listen, stay close to home. Aisha and I will stop by to speak with you and the other Mrs. Fletcher sometime around noon if you think that will work. We'll be in court on another case in the morning. You can leave a message on my cell if the time doesn't work for either of you. Now, if it's okay with you, I'm going to get back to the Mets."

"I'm sure tomorrow will be fine and I thank you, Detective, for taking my call," I said.

He laughed. "The way this investigation is going, I got a feeling you should probably call me Vinny." And he clicked off his phone.

Grady and Frank were watching television while Donna sat tapping on her iPad. When I walked into the living room, she looked up and answered my expansive smile with one of her own.

Grady noticed and asked, "What have you two got going on?"

Our simultaneous one-word response, "Nothing," made him only more suspicious.

He cocked one eyebrow and in his best tough-guy voice said, "I'll get it out of youse if it takes all night."

Donna and I howled with laughter, and although Frank might not have understood what was so funny about Grady's performance, he joined in. As I looked around, I once again felt sorry for Edwina, who had never allowed herself to appreciate the family she had.

At breakfast the next morning, Grady asked about everyone's plans for the day. When I said that I was going to art school, Frank clapped his hands.

"I was hoping you would come every day and so far you have. You are the coolest aunt."

Donna said, "Aunt Jess, perhaps later in the day, you and I could go for a ride. You haven't really had a chance to discover the great places to see and the fun things to do here in the Rockaways. I'd love to be your travel guide."

Frank jumped off his chair. "And I will be your assistant travel guide."

As he started to turn out of the kitchen and into the hall, Grady said, "Wait a minute, Sport. What did you forget to say?"

Frank looked perplexed for a moment and then the light bulb lit. "Sorry, Dad. May I be excused?" With one hand on his waist and the other on his back, he took a formal bow.

Donna bowed her head in response. "Yes, you may."

Frank spun out of the room.

Grady said, "I wish I had his energy."

"Don't we all." I chuckled. "Donna, before I forget, the detectives are going to be here around noon to speak with us about Lawrence Torsney." I turned to Grady. "He's—"

"The impostor. I know, Donna told me. Aunt Jessica, I really would prefer if the two of you stayed as far away from him as possible." Grady tried not to make it sound like an order but it clearly was.

"Don't worry. We have no intention of confronting him. Last night I called Detective Tieri, who, by the way, has asked me to call him Vinny," I said with a grin, "and he'll stop by around noon to talk to Donna. And then, unless Torsney comes knocking on the front door again, we are finished. We've done our part."

Of course, just like in a scene in a bad horror movie, at that precise moment there was a knock on the front door.

Grady said, "I'll get that," and hurried to the door as if we were going to try to rush to get there before he did.

We heard a mumbled voice. Grady said, "Thank you," and then the door shut. He came back to the kitchen with what smelled like a freshly baked pie.

"If you can believe it, that was Anya at the door. She baked a cherry pie to thank me for carrying her packages yesterday. With all she has going on, I am amazed that she could think of me, much less take the time to do this." He set the pie on the kitchen counter.

"Sometimes people must keep busy in a crisis or they will fall apart," I said. "Look at the time. Frank and I have to leave for art school soon."

And I headed to my room to get ready for the day.

Frank and I got to the community center early and signed in with Mrs. Ingram. Since I was wondering if Carissa Potter was still as upset as she'd been the last time we had a chance to speak, I was delighted that we had sculpture class first. When we went into the room, Carissa was arranging the materials for the day's lesson on a long table. She gave us a warm welcome.

"Mrs. Fletcher, it is so nice to see you again. You are becoming a regular participant."

"Well, I did promise Frank that we'd spend as much time together as we possibly can, and art is so much fun. By the way, please, call me Jessica."

"Jessica it is," she said. "Frank, could you do me a favor? I'm trying a new project today. We're going to make soap dishes and I want to take notes as to how everyone manages to make thick rectangular plates with raised drain ridges in the center. I brought my notebook but I forgot my pen. Would you please ask Mrs. Ingram if she has a spare pen I could borrow?"

"Yes, Miss Carissa, I'd be happy to." And Frank bounded out of the room.

I took advantage of the fact that we were alone and asked Carissa how she was feeling.

She looked puzzled, then realized what I meant. "Why, I'm fine, Jessica. Absolutely fine. I did have nightmares that first night but I'm much better now."

"And the police? Have you spent much time talking to them?"

"Why, as a matter of fact, Detective Kelly came by my apartment yesterday, but it was the strangest interview. She asked me the same questions that she and her partner asked us when you and I met with them at the tennis court. So repetitive. And when I asked her how Jason's mother was coping, she didn't seem to know." Carissa shrugged and shook her head as if mystified. "I mean, how could she not?"

"Carissa, I do think detectives are more used to asking questions than answering them," I said gently.

"True, but it was Jason's mother I was asking about. How could that detective ignore the sorrow of the victim's mother?" Carissa seemed unduly upset, close to agitated.

Frank came back and handed Carissa two pens. "Mrs. Ingram said to tell you that you can keep those. She has plenty. See, Aunt Jess? I told you that Mrs. Ingram can solve any problem."

"You certainly did," I said.

"Like right now. She's telling Mr. Courtland that Madeline

and Juliet are welcome back to class, but if they become upset, she will call him right away, take the girls out of class, and keep them with her by the snack table until he comes back to take them home. I think it would be easier if he just stayed."

Frank shrugged and made a face that clearly showed he was confounded by the ways of grown-ups. Then he immediately offered to help Carissa, who put him right to work.

I stepped into the doorway and saw Jamie Ingram ushering Madeline and Juliet into the watercolor room. Dennis Courtland had turned and was heading out the door.

I called, "Mr. Courtland."

"Oh, Mrs. Fletcher. For a second I was afraid my granddaughters hadn't even made it to their seats and Mrs. Ingram was calling me to take them home," he said. "This has been more difficult for them than I would have imagined."

"I'm sure. My grandnephew, Frank, is only ten but he has expressed real concern for all the children in your family, and he has been extra clingy when we are together. Not that I mind that part, of course." I smiled.

"I have to be honest, Mrs. Fletcher. With the shock of Jason's death, we are all worried about Mother, Anya, and Linda. Naturally the business is front and center." He smoothed his gray hair by running a hand over his head. "Everyone's future depends on its continued success. But having to deal with children's fears and nightmares, well, that was totally unexpected. At least by me."

I gave him a look as filled with admiration as I could muster. "Speaking of the business, I suppose you would be the board's natural choice to replace your brother as the chief executive officer."

Dennis stood a smidge taller and puffed out his chest. "I am sure that until the shock wears off, none of us is thinking that far ahead, but I suppose as the chief financial officer, I would be the logical choice."

"And when you and Mr. Torsney dined together last night, did he happen to express an opinion one way or another regarding the firm's future? Since he's a client, I would think he'd have an interest," I said.

Dennis looked somewhat taken aback, as if the wishes of the company's client base had never occurred to him. He pursed his lips and then he said, "Well, we have been a family-owned and -operated business since the firm opened, and our clients have trusted us to take care of them and their financial interests. I must assume that trust has not dissipated with the loss of my brother at the helm. Good day, Mrs. Fletcher."

I was chiding myself for not getting any real information from Dennis Courtland when Frank came out to let me know class was about to begin. I would have to put my sleuthing on hold until after school was out.

Chapter Fifteen

From Carissa's earlier verbal description, I was expecting us to make a rectangle, slightly larger than a bar of soap, that had ridges to keep the soap high and allow excess water to drain into the dish. Her vision was more modern. Carissa showed us a drawing of a soap dish that had walls on three sides. Instead of us building high ridges in the dish, they were actually formed by deep cuts in the dish that ran straight to the fourth side, allowing the water to run out. Hopefully we'd all put that edge on the side of the sink basin or the edge of the tub.

At the end of class, the children ran out of the room directly to the snack table.

Frank looked at me. "Can I get you anything, Aunt Jess?"

"I'd love a bottle of water."

And he left with the other children, laughing and talking with his friends.

Mrs. Ingram came into the room, nodded a hello at me, and said to Carissa, "The two Courtland girls are here today. They did quite well in watercolor. If the day becomes too long for them and they get fidgety or start to act out or cry, let me know immediately and I will call the family."

Carissa nodded and began setting up for her next group. Reggie Masterson came into the room. He gave me a friendly wave and then said to Carissa, "I heard Jamie Ingram give you the heads-up and I wanted to let you know that Madeline and Juliet did well in my watercolor class. They were attentive and seemed to be having fun."

Carissa merely nodded, so I interjected, "I think it's better to keep the children busy. Luckily we are in a beach community like this where there is so much fun going on around them."

Reggie said, "You make a good point, Mrs. Fletcher. The families are here on vacation, and all of a sudden, there's a great tragedy. Ruins everything. So if we can distract the children, that's good for the entire family. Well, I'd better get myself a bottle of water and a snack before classes start up again. I'll see you in a few."

As soon as he left, I said to Carissa, "He's such a nice young man, and he really seems to enjoy working with the children. He mentioned that you were instrumental in helping him get the job."

"Reggie is a talented artist," Carissa said. "He studied form with me, and he had such a cool demeanor that when this opportunity came about, I thought of him as a person who would not be rattled by anything the children do or say. Of course, who could have predicted a murder? That could upset anyone."

"He also told me that you have a studio on Long Island. I sometimes visit friends in the Hamptons. The next time I am out that way, perhaps I could visit the studio to see some of your work," I said.

"Oh, I'm nowhere near the Hamptons. Too posh by half. I like the cozy North Fork of the island's tip. That's home to me. Look at the time. You'd better find Frank and get to Reggie's session. We'll both begin our classes in about five minutes."

After seeing my pictures of the bust of Lafayette last night, Frank and Grady had managed to transfer them to Frank's smart watch, and that was enough to make him decide to read the book by Nathan Hale one more time. As soon as we got home from art school, he curled up on the porch with a banana and buried his nose in the book.

In the kitchen, Donna had taken a tin of apple-cinnamon muffins out of the oven and was transferring them to a serving plate.

"Oh, my, that smells delicious," I said.

"I am glad you think so. We were becoming overrun with apples, so I thought this was the best way to have them eaten quickly. Since the detectives are coming over, perhaps we can soften them up with muffins and iced tea," Donna said.

"I hope we don't need to. I think after our conversation last night, Detective Tieri—or, as he has told me to call him, 'my friend Vinny' . . ." A thought popped into my mind. "Wait.

Wasn't that a movie? Oh, no, that was *My Cousin Vinny*. Anyway, I think that he and Detective Kelly realize we are all on the same team now."

Frank burst through the front door and swung into the kitchen. "Mom, those detectives are here. They want to see the two Mrs. Fletchers. Something sure smells good in here." He looked at the muffins.

Donna said, "Please ask the detectives to come in. By the time you show them the way to the kitchen, I'll have a muffin and a glass of milk waiting for you to take back out to the porch."

"Will do."

I had to smile when I heard Frank say, "Right this way, please."

He led the detectives to the kitchen and traded them for milk and a muffin. He tossed me a quick wave and went back to the porch and *Lafayette!*

Vinny Tieri looked as though he'd already put in a long day. I guessed his session in court had been grueling. Donna offered them seats and I asked how the Mets had fared last night, which earned me a beaming grin.

"They sent the Dodgers home with three losses in a row. Made my week, I can tell you."

Detective Kelly looked as fresh and unflappable as she always seemed to, in a light blue linen suit, which I assumed was her standard court attire. Both detectives accepted a glass of iced tea, and Donna encouraged them to try a muffin, which they happily did.

I waited until Vinny took a healthy bite of his muffin and then said, "And please, there will be no more referring to us as the two Mrs. Fletchers. I am Jessica and my niece is Donna. Please feel free to use our first names. Is that okay with you, Vinny?"

For a split second, I feared he would choke on his muffin, but he managed to swallow and then sputtered, "Sure. Didn't I tell you on the phone you could call me Vinny? Mort says you call him Mort and he calls you Mrs. F., but with an aunt and a niece with the same last name, I figured that wouldn't work. But I can manage Jessica and Donna."

Detective Kelly added, "And I wouldn't mind being called Aisha in our informal conversations."

I admired that she was cautious enough to realize that, cozy as we all were at the moment, there was always the possibility that Donna and I could be cold-blooded killers pulling a scam and that she might have to arrest us in the near future.

Vinny wiped his mouth with a napkin and instantly turned into a detective definitely on the case.

He asked Donna to repeat to him as accurately as she could her conversation last night with Anthony Barlowe. She repeated the conversation and answered the detectives' questions succinctly.

Both detectives were taking copious notes and finally Vinny said, "We are going to need Mr. Barlowe's contact information so that we can, at some point, interview him. And we would appreciate it if you did not tell him that we may be in touch. For the time being, we are keeping the Torsney part of this investigation close to the vest."

Donna immediately looked troubled. Vinny barely glanced at her, but it was enough for him to ask, "Okay, now, exactly who did you tell?"

Close to tears, Donna said, "Grady. I told my husband, Grady."

Vinny relaxed. "Not a problem. No reason why you shouldn't have, but let's keep this information within your immediate family, okay? No close friends, no distant cousins, just you three."

Donna nodded and leaned back in her chair. I could see that she was much relieved.

"Now, Jessica, can you tell us where and when this Torsney guy showed up?"

"Donna and I both saw him when we were with Anya on Matilda Courtland's porch. That was . . . the day after the murder. And a few hours later, he showed up here to talk to Donna."

In effect, I tossed the ball to Donna. She explained that Torsney's visit was part condolence call and part questioning who in the firm she thought might take over as CEO. And that was a question Donna certainly wasn't prepared to answer for someone she'd just met.

Aisha interrupted. "You didn't think that was strange? A man you didn't know came around asking about the hierarchy of the company you work for so soon after the death of the CEO?"

Donna said, "He claimed to be a client and I had seen him at Matilda Courtland's house a few hours earlier. And this is the first time I am here at the beach with the Courtland family, so I really don't know who fits in and who doesn't."

In reply to the obvious next question from Vinny, Donna explained how we all came to be together in this bungalow at this particular time.

Vinny nodded as though he was satisfied for now, but I had more information to share, so I hastily said, "If you wanted to find out how and when this fake Mr. Torsney came to the Rockaways, I understand that he lives in a place called the Tides in a community called Arverne by the Sea. At least, that is where he said he resides."

"The Tides, huh? Now, that is a nice place. Not flashy enough to be called swanky, but the apartments are undeniably upscale. And it's all rental units, so he could sublease for a while. No one would notice who comes and goes except the doorman or concierge," Vinny said. "Of course, if he does live there, we can't be sure what name he used to get the rental, since we don't know who he actually is."

He closed his notebook, a sure sign he thought we were done, but I still had a question or two.

"May I ask if you have had any luck finding the remote control that operates the TeachTennis machine?"

Vinny shook his head. "You remember we used divers but they couldn't find it. We also had a team search around the perimeter of the tennis court. They filtered through the seagrass, checked flowerpots, trash cans, bike sheds, and gardens for a half-mile radius. They even crawled under every porch, but no luck, I'm sorry to say."

"I guess even if you found it, any fingerprints would be long gone," I said.

"Well, that's true, but never let it be said that our techs lack ingenuity," Vinny said with pride. "They called the company that makes the machine and found out they could get a remote that could sync to this particular machine from a store over on Flatbush Avenue in Brooklyn. Someone ran over and picked up a remote, brought it to the lab, and tried to operate the machine. They assured us the TeachTennis was not broken. That machine responded to every button on the remote—on, off, alter speed, change direction, whatever. Now we are positive that whatever happened to Jason Courtland, it happened on purpose."

The fact that I had been sure Jason was murdered the moment I knelt by his body and couldn't find a pulse didn't make Vinny's pronouncement sound any less dire.

After the detectives left, Grady took Frank to the beach while Donna and I opted to do some shopping.

As she pulled the car out of the parking space, Donna asked if I wanted to accompany her only to the supermarket or if I wanted to do a little sightseeing as we had discussed.

"Donna, I'd love that. Of course Frank will be disappointed he won't be your assistant travel guide today. Until Grady and I took the ferry to Manhattan, I had no idea how much there is to see here. I got a brief glimpse of all those tiny shops, as well as fishermen and crabbers finding their catch along the edge of Jamaica Bay. I would love to have a chance to take a leisurely ride and really get to know the community," I said.

"Great. We'll start at Fort Tilden." And Donna swung a left out of the parking lot.

"Is that a military facility? Right here on the beach?"

"Oh, yes. Of course, it is decommissioned now and technically named the Fort Tilden Historic District. The site is administered by the National Park Service, but yes, in its day Fort Tilden played an important role in guarding New York Harbor. From time to time since—oh, I'm not sure—possibly the founding of our nation but certainly since the early eighteen hundreds, the fort was used off and on as a military installation to guard the entrance to New York Harbor. In World War One, it was well fortified with heavy weapons. When World War Two came along, the army built huge casements to protect the large guns and ammunition. One of the casements, called Battery Harris East, has a lovely open-air observatory on top of it. From there you can see the ocean, the wetlands, and even the Manhattan skyline. Edwina told me it is especially lovely around dusk."

"Well, perhaps one evening, Frank and I can roast marshmallows on the grill and tell each other ghost stories while you and Grady visit the observatory," I said.

"Oh, Aunt Jess, you are such a romantic." Donna laughed. Then she turned onto a road with lush greenery on both sides. "Now, this is one of the few roads we can take into Fort Tilden. I'll drive along a little more so you get a sense of the place and then we'll hit the stores."

The fort had a long beachfront exactly like the one in front of our bungalow, but there were no lifeguards and swimming was forbidden. I did wonder how many swimmers and surfers violated the rules.

After we left Fort Tilden, we drove along the main streets of Rockaway. There were so many storefronts. Naturally there were a number of surf shops, and eateries were in high demand, along with plenty of retail stores of every description.

I said I was surprised that there was so much variety in a vacation spot, but Donna corrected me.

"A huge number of the residents of the peninsula live here

full-time. Perhaps this was once primarily a vacation community, but not anymore. Would you like to do a little browsing?"

We stopped at an L-shaped mall with colorfully decorated storefronts and a burger stand in case the shoppers got hungry. We window-shopped to get the lay of the land and then Donna went into the Suit Up Shop to look for a new bathing suit, while I decided to browse in the thrift shop next door.

Within a few minutes I came across a chess set, and amazingly, the pieces were American Revolutionary War soldiers and British redcoats. I thought it would be perfect for Frank. I couldn't wait to hear whether he was going to make Lafayette a bishop or a rook. I thought it was a steal for ten dollars.

An older woman—wearing a name tag frame that read I'M A VOLUNTEER, with the name *Sally* written in with blue Magic Marker—saw me holding the chess set and asked if she could help me.

"I was wondering, do you have any gift bags or boxes?"

She pointed behind me. "Next aisle. Go all the way to the back. Look on your left-hand side. Want me to show you?"

"Thank you, no," I said. "I'll be fine."

I was partway down the aisle when the idea hit. I laughed to myself. I could almost hear Seth Hazlitt say, *That's foolish, woman, plain foolish.* But I shook him off. I spotted a blue-and-green-striped gift bag that was sized perfectly for the chess set. Nearby, I found an open pack of white tissue paper with a few sheets left that was selling for a dime. On the next shelf I saw a small silver gift box marked twenty-five cents. Perfect.

I wandered down the next aisle, and among the bottles of

cologne and perfume, I managed to find one that fit inside the gift box. I was good to go.

I purchased my treasures and walked to the bathing suit shop. Donna was coming through the door. I was delighted that she had a package in hand.

"Got something, did you? Let me see."

"Actually I got two suits." Donna was excited but then her voice turned to slightly apologetic. "They were on sale."

"Donna," I scoffed, "sale or no sale, you are staying at the beach, a place where you surely need bathing suits."

We both laughed. Then I told her I'd found the perfect chess set for Frank.

As soon as I described it, Donna said, "Aunt Jess, you are so good to him. He will absolutely love it."

"Now," I said as we linked arms and walked to the car, "I have an idea. Since we're out to explore, is it far to Beach Sixty-ninth Street?"

"Not far at all. Would you like to take a ride?" Donna gave me a look that I usually get from Grady. It's the look that says, *What are you up to?*

So I told her.

A few minutes later, she was pulling the car into a spot in the visitors' parking lot of a pristine terraced building called the Tides in a beach community called Arverne by the Sea.

Chapter Sixteen

The doorman gave us a welcoming smile and opened the door wide. The lobby was spacious and designed in sleek modern decor. Three well-dressed women of a certain age were sitting on chairs that circled a glass-topped coffee table a few feet to the left of the concierge desk. The lady who sat facing in our direction looked at her watch and said, "Where is Elaine? If she doesn't hurry, we'll miss our reservation."

I heard an elevator door open and the clatter of heels on the tile floor. A statuesque blond raised her hand and waved, her keys rattling as she did so. "Here I am. I know it's my turn to drive but I couldn't find my car keys. But we're all set. I have them now." She jangled the keys again.

Her impatient friend scoffed. "Really, Elaine! You lose your keys so often. I keep telling you to have a spare set made for George to keep behind the desk in case you need them. Isn't that right, George? Haven't I said that a million times?"

The concierge, nattily dressed in a crisp white short-sleeved shirt and a royal blue bow tie, said, "Now, now, Mrs. Lopez, don't get me in trouble. I've told you before, management doesn't want the front desk to take responsibility for car keys. Suppose I lose the keys? Suppose someone steals the car? Sorry, no."

Mrs. Lopez dismissed management with a wave of her hand, and she and her friends brushed by Donna and me as they went out the door, chattering and laughing.

Good, I thought, *the staff is used to batty older ladies. That's a role I can play well.*

George looked at us and said, "Good day, ladies. How can I help you?"

"Well, if you could find Mr. Torsney for us, that would be a huge help." I tried to look as confused as possible.

He thought for a minute and then asked, "Are you ladies supposed to meet the gentleman here in the lobby?"

"Oh, good gracious, no. We don't even know him." I widened my eyes and shook my head.

Following my lead, Donna did the same. I would have to remember to congratulate her. Her acting skills were on-target.

"Mr. Torsney, Lawrence Torsney. He lives here. Right in this building."

George took a breath. "No, ma'am, I am sorry but he does not."

"Well, that can't be right. It just can't be right." I opened my purse and took out the silver gift box I'd bought in the thrift shop. "You see, this is his and I have to give it to him."

I shook the box slightly so George could hear the bottle of cologne rattle from side to side.

George started to apologize again but I cut him off. "Can't you look in the register or on the list or in there." I pointed to the computer screen next to him. "Check for his name. He won this prize during the two-dollar raffle at the church supper last night but he went home without it. Momma said he left it right there on the table by his napkin."

I turned to Donna. "Isn't that what Grandma said?"

Donna said, "Yes, that is exactly what she said. Right by his *used* napkin." And she wrinkled her nose as if the thought of something so unsanitary was revolting to her.

I almost laughed out loud.

George, who was clearly a man with the patience of a saint, agreed to pull up the alphabetical list of tenants and search. I was sure he hoped that would enable him to get rid of us for good.

"What was the name?"

"Torsney, Lawrence Torsney." I was starting to feel a wee bit guilty for sending George on this wild-goose chase.

"No, ma'am. He definitely is not a resident here at the Tides." George looked genuinely sorry with just a touch of relief that we would finally go away.

No such luck.

"Well, you know, Momma is no spring chicken. She might have gotten the name partly wrong. Perhaps you might know who we mean if we describe him?"

I could practically hear George grit his teeth, but he nodded politely.

I turned to Donna, who had spent more time with the Torsney impostor than I had, and said, "Darlin', you were at Grandma's table during the church supper. Do you happen to remember what Mr. Torsney looked like?"

Donna gave a detailed description, but once she got past general height, weight, and hair color, no matter what she added, George looked down, rubbed his hand on the countertop, and said, "I'm sorry, ladies. You have the wrong address."

At long last we apologized profusely and thanked him.

Neither Donna nor I said a word until we were in the car with the doors and windows closed. Then we burst into peals of laughter.

Donna said, "Oh, Aunt Jess, I can't remember when I have had so much fun. That poor man! I'm sure he thinks we are crazy."

I said, "I'm sure he's glad we're gone."

And we started laughing again.

"I do have to say, Donna, that you are a natural. I always say that I enjoy these little skits when I need them to try to find out some information, because it reminds me of the days I worked in a summer stock company. I did so want to be on the stage, but no, I wound up behind the stage, painting scenery and helping with split-second wardrobe changes. Did you ever have an interest in the theater?"

"Not really, Aunt Jess." She started the car. "This was fast and easy, but real acting would involve studying lines and lots of rehearsals. I don't think I'd have the patience, and I know I don't have the time."

We zipped through the market, gathering everything on Donna's list in record time. At the last second, Donna left me in the checkout line while she ran across to the dairy department for a wedge of Parmesan cheese.

As she put it in the cart, she said, "Much as I love this opportunity for living at the beach, I miss my own kitchen. I am forever reaching for ingredients that aren't there. And now that I have the cheese, I am hoping there is a cheese grater in the utility drawer."

"May I recommend a solution?" I said as we began placing groceries on the conveyor belt.

We both laughed and said, "Takeout!"

Donna texted Grady, so he and Frank were waiting for us in the parking lot when we got back to the beach. Frank was eager to show us how strong he was by reaching into the trunk and trying to snatch up as many packages as possible. I leaned into the trunk, and blocking his view with my shoulder, I reached past him and pushed the gift bag from the thrift shop far to the back. At the same time, I slid two supermarket bags toward him. I picked up the bag with Donna's bathing suits and announced we had everything, and I quickly closed the trunk.

There was much laughter and bumping into one another in the kitchen as all four of us emptied the packages and attempted to put the purchases away. The problem was that neither Frank nor I had the vaguest idea where anything actually went. Finally Donna politely dismissed us, saying, "There is half an hour until dinner. Why don't you two play a game or go for a walk?"

Or, I thought, *we could go for a walk and find a game.*

I had been planning to wait until after dinner to give Frank his chess set, but since we seemed to be under Donna's feet in the kitchen, I asked Grady for his car keys, explaining that I'd left something in the car. As soon as I said it, Donna's eyes lit up, so I knew she thought getting the chess set now was a good idea.

I took the sparkly gift bag out of the trunk, and since it looked so much like a present, I was surprised that Frank didn't ask me what was in it.

"Good evening, Mrs. Fletcher. Are you two on your way out or just coming home?"

Dennis Courtland was standing a few feet away. Red embers glowed through the ash of the cigar he was holding.

I already knew I didn't like the man, but he was technically one of our hosts, not to mention a top executive in Donna's firm, so I smiled politely and said, "Actually, Mr. Courtland, we are just picking up a package that I inadvertently left in the trunk earlier today. The truth is that I don't drive, so without Grady or Donna, Frank and I aren't able to go to or come from anywhere."

"Ah, I see. And how is your lovely niece? I must stop by and check to make sure she is recovered from the shock of the other morning. After all, with Jason gone, I have to be sure that all our employees know how much they are cared for by the new executive team."

He puffed on his cigar and then tapped it lightly until the ash began to fall toward the ground, but an ocean breeze came along, lifted it up, and twirled it around until it landed on the sleeve of my blouse.

Apologizing profusely, Dennis jumped forward but, oddly

enough, rather than hastily brushing the ashes away, he slid his hand along my arm in a way that felt very close to being a caress. Instantly I stepped back, put my arm around Frank's shoulder, and bade Dennis a good evening.

"One more thing before you go, Mrs. Fletcher. Anya mentioned that my mother has some of your books and she would enjoy having them signed. I hope that you will remain here long enough to be able to accommodate her once this unpleasantness is over, or even more to my liking, perhaps you and I could meet the next time you are in the city. I could bring the books—"

"Anya and I have already spoken about my signing the books. You can rest assured she and I will manage to make the book signing happen before I leave. Now, I do have to get Frank home for dinner."

Dennis Courtland had gone too far, and my smile was getting more forced by the minute.

His smile, however, was beginning to have what I read as more than a touch of a leer to it. "Well, I certainly hope to see you again before you leave. Good night, Mrs. Fletcher, or may I call you Jessica? And I insist you call me Dennis."

And it took every ounce of social grace in my being for me to say, "Of course, Dennis. Have a good evening."

As we walked toward the bungalow, Frank took my hand and said, "Oh, Aunt Jess, you aren't leaving yet, are you? That would make me sad. We still have a lot of things to do together."

"We certainly do." I held the gift bag in front of him. "And once we get to the porch, you can take a look in this bag to see if it brings anything to mind. You just might find something that we can enjoy doing together."

"A present?" Frank squealed. "Is that a present for me?"

"You'll find out," I teased as I began to skip ahead of him.

He immediately began to run, and we had a mock race to the porch steps. I stopped on the bottom step to ensure that Frank won the race to the top. I motioned him to the table, and he sat down and folded his hands as though we were playing school and he was the most well-mannered student in the class.

"Should I close my eyes?" His voice was tinged with anticipation.

"Great idea," I said.

With his eyes closed tightly, Frank said, "You know, Aunt Jess, my smart watch was such a super present that I can't believe you got me something else. You really do spoil me."

He was so serious that I could have kissed him. Instead I took the chess set out of the bag and I lifted the lid so that he could see the pieces laid out in the box exactly as I had seen them when I came across the set in the thrift shop.

"One, two, three, and open," I said.

Frank was so quiet that at first I thought he didn't recognize the American Revolutionary Army in their uniforms and the British redcoats in theirs. Then he said, "Aunt Jess, this is amazing. Where did you find . . . Never mind. I can't thank you enough."

He pushed his chair back and gave me a hug. "I'm so lucky you're my aunt, not for the presents, which I do like, but mostly I like that we have so much fun together."

I admit to getting misty-eyed but I managed to ward off flowing tears. Frank was such a decent, gentle boy, so much like Grady. This was one of those moments I wished my husband, Frank, had lived long enough to meet his namesake.

I shook off any melancholy before it took hold and said, "Now let's go show your parents."

As soon as dinner ended, Frank and I settled in the living room to play a game of chess. I had no doubt I would be the redcoats.

Donna and Grady decided to go for a walk. I hoped they'd enjoy the serenity of the evening. Frank beat me handily in our first game and was ahead by a pawn and a bishop in the second when they came home.

I could see that Donna was distressed, but before I could ask, Grady pointed to Frank and shook his head. Message received.

It took Frank a bit longer to defeat me in the second game, but defeat me he did. The Americans were clearly unstoppable.

I said, "No wonder they won the war. George Washington must have been a tactical genius like you."

"I belong to a chess club that meets after school on Fridays," Frank said. "Playing there regularly has really improved my game."

Grady, who'd been watching us play, said, "I'll take a turn at being the Brits. Perhaps I can change their luck. Aunt Jess, why don't you go find Donna? I think she is in our bedroom."

I tapped gently on the door in case Donna was resting, but she opened it immediately, ushered me inside, and offered me the smallish oval-shaped club chair under the window. Donna sat on the edge of the bed.

"Aunt Jess, I don't know how much longer we can stay here. I mean, I know the detectives don't want us to leave, but there is so much anger here." She raised her hands in despair.

Since I was sure leaving was not yet an option, I asked what had happened when she and Grady went for their walk.

"It's such a pretty night. We strolled along the seagrass, but the flies were out in force this evening, so we decided to walk over to the bay and back. As we got closer to Matilda's house, we heard Anya yelling. We were afraid that something had happened to Matilda and that Anya needed help."

"That would be my first thought as well," I said to let her know I understood.

"We were hurrying to the porch when the front door opened and Tyler Young came rushing out. Anya stood in the doorway yelling after him, 'Don't you come round here with any more of your nonsense. Tilly doesn't care about the business. She only cares that her son is dead, which doesn't seem to bother you at all.' And Anya slammed the door shut."

"Oh, my, that was a terrible scene for you to witness, especially since Tyler is your boss," I said.

Donna said, "The only saving grace was that Tyler was in such a fury that he stormed down the porch steps and around the corner of the house. I doubt he even saw us. At least I hope he didn't. How awkward would that be?"

I comforted Donna as best I could. Then I said good night to the boys, who were intently wrapped in the American Revolution via chess.

I went to bed, hoping for a good night's sleep. Instead I was restless with conflicting ideas about Jason Courtland's murder floating in and out of my brain, often waking me, which led to my tossing and turning. All in all, not a great night.

In the morning the sun shone brightly, and since there was no art school, Donna, Grady, and Frank decided to enjoy themselves down by the water's edge. I pleaded "work to catch up on" since I would have the bungalow entirely to myself. In reality, it was the perfect time for me to focus on Jason Courtland's murder and to put the people who'd spent the night scrambling around in my head together in a list that had some semblance of order. If I could review the events and conversations of the past few days, I hoped to figure out the order of suspects I should consider, from most likely to least likely or, if I had perfect clarity, from most likely to not a chance.

I sat at the kitchen table and wrote down the names of everyone I had met since I arrived at Rockaway Beach. Then I added the adult children of both Jason and Dennis Courtland even though they arrived at the bungalow colony after the fact. But I had heard that each of them lived in Manhattan, and my jaunt to meet Nancy for lunch had taught me that it was a reasonably short trip from Manhattan to Rockaway Beach by ferry. I was sure that, like most of New York City, the community was also easily accessible by train or by car.

With the exception of the ever-elusive Lawrence Torsney, I was sure everyone on my list was connected in some way to the east end of Long Island, either to the North Fork, as I heard it referred to time and time again, or to the Hamptons–

Montauk Point area, which Carissa referred to as the South Fork, but for some reason is most often known under the collective title the Hamptons.

I crossed Torsney's name off my group list and put it at the top of a pristine new page. Once Vinny and Aisha's investigation discovered who he really was and they shared the information with me, I expected his story would fill a page, perhaps even two.

At first I went down the list slowly, saying each name aloud. After I had the order solidly in my head, I moved back to the first names I'd written and looked with an eye toward whether they could have, or would have, killed Jason Courtland.

Chapter Seventeen

I shook my head at the first two names. Matilda and Anya were nonstarters. I wasn't even sure why I had written their names on the list at all, other than the fact that the teacher inside me always insisted that lists be neat and complete. It was impossible for me to imagine Matilda killing her own son and I was sure Anya would never do anything that would cause Matilda such pain.

Next, of course, was Linda Courtland. I didn't know anything about her relationship with her husband. Did they get along or fight in public? Was one or the other of them guilty of infidelity? Those answers would be hard to come by.

I did realize that Dennis Courtland was someone worth considering. For one thing, I already knew he was an ambitious man. When I came upon him sitting on his porch with the Torsney impostor, the little bit I overheard let me know that I'd interrupted a conversation that was clearly about how the business would be run going forward. It was not out of the realm of possibility that they were conspirators of some sort. The sooner Vinny Tieri outed "Lawrence Torsney" and brought him in for a thorough interview, the more likely it would be that we could find out what kind of plan he and Dennis Courtland were hatching.

I stared at the next name for a long time, knowing I really had to think long and hard about Dennis's sister. Although Edwina Courtland-Young had held on to a burgeoning animosity toward Jason for her entire adult life, I had difficulty believing that she would suddenly pick this time and this place to kill him. She would have had strong motivation if, when she had first realized the damage caused to her body by his drunk driving, she had lashed out in a fit of rage. It was even more likely in my mind that a few years later, when she was married and her friends and siblings were starting to have their families, the bitterness could have burst forth with a vengeance, but now, at this stage of her life? No, I couldn't make sense of it. What possible motive could she have?

Next up was her husband, Tyler. Now, his was a different story entirely. I definitely considered him to be a man with motive aplenty. And his most obvious motive, similar to that of his brother-in-law, Dennis, was a desire to take control of Courtland Finance. In addition, he had a penchant for keeping the activities of the global division shrouded in secrecy from everyone else in the firm, including Jason during the time he was alive and functioning as CEO. What was Tyler hiding? Illegal international transactions? Fraudulent trades? Stealing from clients' accounts? In the world of finance, the list of possibilities was endless.

I revisited the names and the scant information I had gleaned about the next generation of Courtlands. Two of Jason's children were employed at the family firm: a son who was an attorney and another son who was a supervising investment analyst. The third and final son was a dentist. I knew that all three had immediately come to the beach community to comfort their mother, and I suppose each other, but I hadn't so much as seen them sitting on the porch, nor had Frank reported that Jason's grandchildren were present on the beach or in the community center.

Dennis Courtland's daughter worked for a high-powered finance magazine, while his son was a certified public accountant at Courtland Finance. I had no idea which one of them was a parent to Madeline and Juliet. I'd have to check with Donna. She probably knew Dennis's son from the office and might know if he had children. Not that it mattered. I put my pen down and sighed. I had all the information about the Courtlands that was available to me at the moment. It was time to move on.

I got up and put the kettle on to make tea. I'd been drinking so much iced tea that I'd begun longing for a nice hot cuppa. Once I had a steaming cup of Irish breakfast tea at my elbow, I continued the list that I hoped would keep my thoughts organized.

I knew that, through Matilda and her late husband, all of the Courtlands had an early connection to the Hamptons, and yet here they were, summering in a beach community a hundred miles to the west.

Like Matilda and Anya, I was fairly certain Reggie Masterson shouldn't even be on my list. Although his parents lived on the North Fork of Long Island, he was at the community center this summer strictly by chance. If the original water-color teacher had not resigned, Reggie wouldn't have been here at all. Still, there could have been some unusual, not widely known connection between Reggie and Jason. I suppose Jason's company could have given terrible investment advice to someone in Reggie's family who wound up bankrupt. When the job was offered, Reggie took it, realizing he would have the opportunity for revenge . . .

I rested my chin in the palm of my hand. *Slow down, Jessica. This isn't an imaginary murder you are creating out of whole cloth for one of your books. You need facts, not fiction.*

I took a sip of tea, counted to ten, and began analyzing again. Jason Courtland was the sponsor of the art program and paid everyone's salaries, so there was that, but the truth was, Reggie Masterson's original connection to the Courtland family was through Carissa Potter. I reminded myself that Carissa had taught at the community center for a number of summers and probably had a friendlier relationship with Jason than Reggie did. And Jason had certainly grown to trust her, because when he needed a watercolor teacher, he hired Reggie on Carissa's recommendation.

I thought that was a key indicator, because Jason would have wanted to be certain that any teachers he hired would always keep the children's safety at the top of their minds. After all, Jason's own grandchildren and their cousins all took classes at the community center at various times over the summer.

I opened my iPad and searched for Reggie Masterson. I was surprised that he, as an established artist, had such a short list of links until I reminded myself that he was still a very young man. I could see instantly by the paintings that came up in my search that he had an extraordinary way with color and shading. One particular work, being displayed by a gallery in Cleveland, Ohio, was called *Grapevine* and showed Reggie's gift to perfection. Shades of browns and grays competed to dominate the knotted trunks and wooden posts that kept the vines from drooping to the ground. Heavy bunches of grapes ranging in color from pale blue to dark purple hung from branches laden with broad green leaves, some spotted by the sun while others were quite dusky. His website indicated that he had attended a number of prestigious art schools and his work had been shown in Boston, Southampton, Manhattan, and Philadelphia. He also had a section listing his experience as a teacher. I was both surprised and impressed to see that he was licensed by the New York City Department of Education. That might have been more of an edge to help him land the job at the community center than Carissa's recommendation. Again I was reminded to be careful not to mix realities with assumptions.

Carissa had a much longer list of web links that went on for page after page. I started by viewing her website. The opening page was a large picture of the front window of her pottery-and-sculpture studio and included some remarkable pieces. One large purple vase with a small branch of pink flowers painted on the front caught my eye. The flowers reminded me of the swamp milkweed bouquet young Frank had presented to me at the airport; that bouquet was still bright and lively in a vase on the dresser in my room.

Right below the picture was the address of Carissa's studio in Mattituck, New York. I clicked over to Google Maps and found that Mattituck was on the North Fork of Long Island. When Reggie mentioned that he had taken lessons from Carissa, he also said her studio was near his parents. I wondered if they were in Mattituck or in a nearby town. Not that it mattered at the moment. There were dozens of links to articles and announcements that heralded Carissa's rising success in the world of sculpture. I did enjoy looking at pictures of her work, but there was nothing in any of the links that helped me discover how she came to be spending her summers at Rockaway Beach.

I decided I would skip the next few pages of links and then see what turned up in some of the less prominent articles. The first thing I noticed was a picture of a much younger Carissa Potter. Her pottery was smaller and the colors less vivid. I opened a few links and was about to quit when I came across several early biographies. I was surprised to learn that in college Carissa Potter had been known as Carrie Stockly, an art major who volunteered at a food bank and played soccer, tennis, and golf. She had also done an art internship at the Accademia di Belle Arti di Firenze in Italy. I understood why she would give up being called Carrie, which was probably her nickname when she was a young girl. Carissa sounded much more professional. As to Potter and Stockly, I did wonder if she'd been married at one point. She certainly didn't seem to be married now. Or had she adopted the name Potter in order to promote her work? Perhaps she wanted to sound more artsy. *Hi, I'm Carissa Potter and I sell pottery.* That sounded to me like a version of the old "A, my name is Alice" game my friends and I played while bouncing a pink rubber ball we called a spaldeen.

I heard the front door open and Frank yelled, "Aunt Jess, we're home."

I turned off my iPad and gathered up my papers. "I'm in the kitchen. Does anyone want a cup of tea?"

We sat around the table munching on the remains of Donna's apple-cinnamon muffins while Frank showed me pictures on his smart watch of the latest sand tunnel he'd built.

"Dad, show Aunt Jessica the picture you took of me with my tunnel," Frank said.

Grady tapped his phone and passed it to me, and there was Frank with a triumphant smile on his face, lying in the sand beside his newest tunnel.

"Aunt Jess, look at the huge tunnel I was able to build. It's nearly as long as I am tall." Frank beamed with pride.

"It certainly is," I replied. "You are the most amazing sand designer I have ever met. Tunnels and bridges. Why, I believe you could build an entire highway system."

Grady laughed. "You must have been eavesdropping. Frank told us as we were walking back to the bungalow that he would like to do just that."

"Last night before bed, I actually drew a few pictures of the kinds of highways I want to build. Wait. I'll show you." And Frank ran to his room to get his drawings.

Donna and Grady exchanged a look that I recognized because I'd seen it many times before. It told me they had something they wanted to discuss with me. It was far too early to talk about our plans for the winter holidays, so I thought perhaps they were thinking about getting away by themselves for a while and wanted to see when my schedule would allow me to stay in Manhattan and care for Frank for a few days.

"Donna and I both think that, with all this chaos caused by Jason's, er"—Grady looked down the hall in the direction of Frank's bedroom—"his accident, well, we were wondering if you could stay a few extra days to make up for all the disruptions we've had? I mean, it's bound to calm down and—"

"Stop right there." I held up my hand.

Grady looked crestfallen. "I know how busy you are but—"

"But nothing," I said. "To tell you the truth, I have been thinking the same thing myself. A few extra days at the beach with you all would do me a world of good."

Of course, that wasn't exactly the truth. As the day of my planned departure came ever closer, I was growing more reluctant to leave my family living a few houses away from the murder scene while Jason Courtland's murderer was still at large.

Frank charged into the room. "Yay, did I hear right? Aunt Jess, are you really going to stay with us for extra days?"

When I nodded, he let out a double *whoop, whoop* and asked, "How many?"

I hadn't gotten that far in my thoughts, and I certainly didn't want to tell a ten-year-old that I wasn't planning on leaving until a murderer was caught, so I left my answer purposely vague.

"I'm not quite sure but I'm going to talk to my friend Susan, who makes my travel arrangements, and see what kind of flight changes she can manage."

For the next little while, we admired Frank's half dozen drawings of roads peppered with bridges and tunnels.

"I just have to decide which one I want to try first. Maybe you all could vote," Frank said.

Grady said, "I think you and I should go over each of these and rate them in order of easiest to hardest to build. Then we could—"

"Start with the easy ones and work our way up," Frank shouted as he raised his hands and danced around the room like a boxer in the ring who'd scored a knockout.

Donna said, "Why don't you two take the drawings out to the porch and rate your highways? I am going to need you out of my kitchen. I have to cook dinner."

I offered to help but Donna shooed me away.

Now that we were all agreed I would extend my visit, I decided to call Susan Shevlin and ask her to cancel my trip home.

After I finished assuring her that my vacation was peaceful and relaxing, she laughed.

"Don't give me that, Jessica. I had my hair done yesterday and Loretta told me that Sheriff Metzger received a phone call from a New York City detective who told him you were involved in a murder."

It was no surprise to see that the gossip mill in Cabot Cove was as current as ever.

"'Involved' isn't the word I would use. But I am here in a tight-knit family community and the police would rather we all stay put until they say we can leave."

"You mean, you're under house arrest?" Susan sounded appalled.

"No, nothing like that. We are all potential witnesses. That is why I'd like you to cancel my return trip but leave the replacement date open-ended. I'll call you again as soon as I am sure when I'll be coming home."

There was a knock on my door and Grady, sounding as perplexed as I'd ever heard him, said, "Aunt Jess, please. You have company. You'd better come."

I said good-bye to Susan and opened the door. "Company? Who on earth would be looking for me here?"

I walked into the living room and couldn't understand why Vinny Tieri was grinning like the Cheshire cat from *Alice's Adventures in Wonderland* until I saw the person standing next to him. Lawrence Torsney.

Chapter Eighteen

Grady stood by my side with his hand holding my elbow as I eyed them both warily and asked, "What can I do for you, Detective?"

I must have sounded strained, because those few words were enough to bring Donna out of the kitchen, drying her hands on a dish towel.

If Vinny noticed that I had reverted from first names to his official title, he certainly didn't seem to care. His grin only widened, which, quite frankly, I wouldn't have thought was possible.

"Mrs. Fletcher," he began, clearly deciding two could play the formality game, "I'd like you to meet—"

"I assure you, Mr. Torsney and I are already acquainted," I said, fully aware that it was not news to Vinny.

"I know you think you are," he said, "but have you met

Special Agent Josh Keppler of the Federal Bureau of Investigation?"

My jaw dropped. Whatever I had been expecting, that wasn't it.

"Vinny, what on earth is going on here?" I demanded. "Do you mean to tell me—"

Vinny laughed uproariously as though he had pulled off the most spectacular practical joke, and I suppose in a way he had.

"The look on your face when you walked into the room was priceless. Absolutely priceless." He took a handkerchief out of his pocket and wiped his face.

Torsney/Keppler put a hand on Vinny's arm. "Detective, if I could . . ."

"Be my guest."

Vinny was still chuckling. Personally I thought the detective was enjoying himself far too much.

Torsney/Keppler began, "I am glad that the three of you are all here, because—"

The front door banged open, startling us all.

"Dad, are you coming back to finish our game?" Frank started talking before he came around the door. When he saw all five of us frozen like statues in the living room, he looked stricken.

"Excuse me. I'll wait on the porch," he said in his best "talking to grown-ups" voice, and he closed the door behind him.

When Vinny remarked, "Well-mannered kid you got there," both Donna and Grady automatically thanked him.

I was having none of it. "Mr. . . . Agent Keppler, if that is your true name, please tell us what is going on. What are you doing here? And why all the subterfuge?"

Vinny said, "I guarantee this is going to take a while. Maybe we could all sit down?"

And he waved Donna, Grady, and me toward the couch.

Grady and I made eye contact. He shot me a nearly invisible nod and I shrugged. *Why not?* At least for the moment, we could politely listen. When the three of us were settled on the sofa, the detective and the special agent each sat in the armchairs across the room.

I think Grady surprised everyone when he opened the conversation. "Just to be clear, you've both come into my home without an appointment or an invitation. I'd like you to explain why you are here. Then we'll decide if there is a need for further conversation."

Keppler looked at Vinny. "Maybe the cloak-and-dagger wasn't our best approach. We apologize."

Vinny was smart enough to nod in agreement.

Keppler went on. "Mr. Fletcher, I know you were busy with your son when we turned up on your porch, and again, I apologize for interrupting, but Detective Tieri and I didn't arrive together. We planned, strategically, to arrive at the exact same moment so no one other than the people in this room would see us together. Vinny walked to your cottage from the west and I stood at the end of that large patch of seagrass between here and the beachfront. When he came into view, I followed him onto your porch."

Vinny added, "We chose dinnertime because we thought we'd be less likely to be seen by any of the occupants of the surrounding bungalows. My choice would have been to invite you all to, ah, my office at the station house, but remembering your aversion to that idea the last time I suggested it, we came up with this plan."

I was about to erupt at both of them but Donna beat me to it for an entirely different reason.

"Dinner! You'll have to excuse me. I have something in the oven." And she hurried to the kitchen.

Vinny turned to Keppler and said, "I don't suppose there is room for all of us in the kitchen."

Agent Keppler burst out laughing, and as if he'd stuck a pin in a giant balloon, the tension in the room evaporated.

Donna came back, smiling. "Caught it in time. Everything in the kitchen is under control. What did I miss?"

Keppler said, "We would never start without you. You are a key person in my inquiry into the Courtland Finance and Investments firm, and my inquiry is now inextricably tied to Detective Tieri's investigation of what we now know to be Jason Courtland's murder."

"You wait a minute," Grady said. "My wife is a . . . a saint. She would never harm a fly, much less kill a person. And she is honest. The most honest person I've ever known."

Keppler and Vinny exchanged a glance and then the agent said, "That is nearly word for word how Jason Courtland described her when he and I spoke."

I was flabbergasted. "Do you mean to tell us that Jason Courtland knew you were investigating his company?"

"Jason Courtland was the interested party who requested the investigation," Keppler said.

I thought we were finally getting somewhere.

Grady apparently thought that Donna was not under any

cloud, because he said, "If you can assure me that my wife is not a suspect in anything that either of you is investigating, I am going to join my son on the porch." He turned to Donna. "I don't like leaving him alone on the porch this long; either I go out or we bring him in."

Donna didn't hesitate. "Go outside and keep him busy. Aunt Jessica and I will be fine."

"If you need me, holler," Grady said to Donna and me, and then, without asking permission to leave from either of the two law enforcement officers, Grady walked out to the porch.

Before Grady had fully closed the front door behind him, I said, "Excuse me, Agent Keppler, but may I ask exactly when you had the opportunity to speak to Jason Courtland?"

"It is a long story. Some time ago, Jason Courtland went to the Securities and Exchange Commission to report that he'd detected some . . . I guess you could call them problems in the company. He'd brought outside auditors into the firm for a thorough examination but they failed to discover anything other than a few easily made and easily corrected errors."

Keppler stopped to give Donna and me a moment to adjust to this incontrovertible evidence of the fact that Jason Courtland had requested an investigation into his own company.

I asked for clarification. "Nonetheless, they were financial errors, I assume."

"Exactly right, Mrs. Fletcher, and Jason wasn't convinced that the auditors had been comprehensive enough. While he was pondering his next step, a gentleman named Anthony Barlowe retired rather unexpectedly. Since Mr. Barlowe had worked in the division of the firm that was of concern to Mr. Courtland, Barlowe's replacement was of paramount importance. Although she lacked experience in that particular area of global investments, Jason Courtland chose Donna Fletcher because, as he put it, besides being smart, she is flawlessly honest. The promotion would also put her in the direct line of command under the person Jason suspected of somehow making large amounts of money disappear from the company coffers."

Donna's right hand flew to cover her mouth as she gasped. "Tyler? Jason suspected Tyler of . . . of what? Bad management? Stealing? Misusing information? What?"

"I suppose I could say all of the above. And more. As CEO, Jason thought he should be privy to every file, every e-mail, the minutes from every meeting, and, most important, have the full confidence of every employee, particularly the senior staff. You know the drill. He was the top dog. And yet for a number of years, he often felt like the global division was stonewalling him."

"Are you saying Jason put Donna in her current position so she could be his spy?" My indignation was beginning to show.

"I certainly didn't mean to imply that at all. No. He put Donna there because, in addition to her innate honesty, Jason believed that while she was learning about a new-to-her element of the company's work, her staff would generally be supportive due to her reputation as a collegial person and a caring supervisor. He was betting that Tyler would be tiptoeing around his own division because he could never be sure that while showing Donna everything they thought she should know, a staffer wouldn't accidentally trip over something that looked out of place in some odd way. Jason was trying to buy time for the SEC to finish their work. He also expected that Tyler would be more cautious because Donna was an unknown. While Tyler wouldn't try to recruit her as an accomplice, he absolutely wouldn't want her getting in his way."

Donna nodded. "And now it makes sense . . ."

"What does?" Keppler asked.

"Well, as I told Aunt Jess, Tyler had a penchant for privacy. We were all constantly instructed not to speak about our work to anyone outside the global division. He would say, 'And if anyone—and I mean anyone, even Jason Courtland—asks you the simplest question, you are to refer that person to me.' It was a running joke. I am not sure if you are familiar with the movie, but the staff laughed about it a lot. We called ourselves the Fight Club of Courtland Finance."

I'd read the book by Chuck Palahniuk, and the others had either read the book or seen the movie, because we all laughed at the commonplace office humor.

"If you are here, Agent Keppler," I said, bringing us back to the topic at hand, "that would lead us to believe that the Securities and Exchange Commission's investigation led them to find criminal activity."

Keppler nodded. "Not conclusively. However, there were enough warning signs that a boss in the SEC Division of Enforcement sent my boss a criminal referral."

Vinny leaned forward in his chair, rested his elbows on his knees, and said, "Now we're getting to the good part."

I couldn't help but flash him my sternest teacher look. What part of the topic under discussion could be considered good?

I hoped he got my message. In any event, he leaned back in his chair and Keppler continued.

"I reviewed the documents we received from the SEC. Then I met with Jason several times. We went over and over every suspicion he had, and it was clear to me he was targeting his brother-in-law, Tyler Young."

"And did you agree that Tyler Young was guilty of misdeeds?" I asked.

"I agreed that he *could be* guilty, but based on the scant evidence we'd uncovered, there were a couple of other people on my radar screen, including Jason's brother, Dennis. Plus, if there was fraud or theft at Courtland's, I couldn't automatically eliminate Jason just because he was the one who brought us the complaint. During my career several devious criminals have done just that. Knowing they couldn't hide the company's problems forever, they'd come forward and point the finger at someone else. If that was the case here, Jason Courtland wouldn't have been the first criminal to have tried it."

Although I said nothing, I had to agree. Courtland Finance had been tightly controlled by family since its inception. My instinct was that anyone who worked in the company would have been considered an outsider by the family, and if that person tried to pull off a scam, one or more members of the family were bound to have noticed.

Keppler continued. "It was Jason who came up with the idea of my assuming the identity of an actual client with a long-dormant account and showing up here at the beach and using my 'client status' to gain entry to the family. If anyone checked the records, Lawrence Torsney has an account with a very attractive balance. The firm's records would show that he—er, I—no longer actively participate in account management."

"Because at this point he's taking only distributions, the real Lawrence Torsney would likely be unknown to any member of the firm," I said.

Keppler nodded. "When Jason died, I hoped it was an accident and spent a few days trying to talk to the family. I even lightly interviewed Mrs. Fletcher here." He indicated Donna. "But once I realized murder was a strong possibility, I went right to the local precinct."

"By the time Josh came in to talk to us"—Vinny waggled a finger from me to Donna and back again—"I had the pleasure of telling him that you two Mrs. Fletchers had already discovered that he was nosing around here under a false identity."

"I have to hand it to you, ladies. I thought that if anyone was going to realize I was . . . What did you say they called me, Vinny, an impostor?"

Vinny nodded.

Keppler started again. "I thought if anyone was going to figure out that I was an impostor, it would be one of the Courtland family members. I am going to have to brush up on my clandestine-operation skills." He chuckled. "All my hard work only to find out that two women I'd barely spoken to had nailed me as a fake. How did you do it? Where did I go wrong?"

Donna turned to me as if to say, *You tell him.*

"I guess it was a lot of little things. Not one was a glaring error, but taken together, they nagged at the back of my mind. For example, when you approached us on Matilda's porch, you tried to project the image of a longtime client and friend of the family. If that were so, it was likely that you, or at the very least the name Lawrence Torsney, should have seemed familiar to Anya, yet she drew a complete blank."

Vinny said, "I get your point, but didn't you take into account that, at her age, her memory might not be what it once was?"

Keppler gave Vinny a "thanks, pal" wave and then asked, "What else? Believe me, I want to know so I don't make the same mistakes the next time I do some undercover work."

"Well, when you saw Donna on the porch the other day, you stopped to talk to her. You claimed you recognized her because she had been on Matilda's porch when you visited to make a condolence call. But when I saw you on Dennis Courtland's porch and called you by your Torsney name, you had no idea that we'd ever met. There were only three of us on Matilda's porch, so it wasn't like I expected you to remember me from a large crowd, but from a group of three, well, if you remembered Donna, you should have remembered me. I began to suspect that you recognized Donna because you had reviewed pictures of Courtland personnel. Now I realize it was because Jason mentioned her particularly as a potential ally."

"I will say you are a very astute woman," Keppler said as he looked at his watch.

"Thank you. That's the way my mind has always worked. It doesn't like discrepancies. Oh, and as it happens, Donna and I stopped by the Tides to visit Mr. Torsney and he doesn't live there," I said.

"Astute and thorough. A killer combination."

Even as he spoke, the FBI agent's attention was already

moving elsewhere. He signaled Vinny. "I think we're done here. I'd better leave first. I'll be in touch."

He got up, and when he had his hand on the doorknob, he turned and said, "Thank you, ladies, for an enlightening interview."

No sooner had the door closed than it opened again and Grady came in. "Well?"

Vinny said, "With these two ladies on your side, you are one lucky man."

Grady walked over, put one arm around Donna and the other arm around me, and said, "Don't I know it."

After dinner the family sat around the table on the porch and played two games of Clue. There was great merriment because the mystery writer couldn't manage to figure out the "who with what and where" before the ten-year-old solved the murder. Twice.

Later, in my room, I picked up the papers of my suspect lists, written earlier in the day. I took the blank page that had Lawrence Torsney's name across the top in big bold letters. Now that was definitely headed for the recycling bin. I ripped it in half. Then I looked at the list of my remaining suspects and drew a very large asterisk next to one name—Tyler Young.

Chapter Nineteen

While Frank and I were having lunch after art class the next day, I said to Donna, "I have been thinking the boardwalk would be a great place to ride a bicycle. Do you know of any bike rental shops around here?"

"You don't need one. There are several bicycles available out in the storage shack behind the garden shed. When we first arrived, Mrs. Courtland told us that although they are rarely used, they are in great condition and we were welcome to use them anytime we wanted to. I'm glad you brought up the idea. With everything going on, well, I'm sorry, but a bike ride never even occurred to me. I should have thought of it, though, because I do know how much you enjoy riding. After lunch Frank can show you where they are," Donna said.

"Bike riding on the boardwalk. That's a great idea," Frank said. "I'd love to go along."

He looked at Donna with pleading eyes.

Donna sighed. "Well, if Aunt Jessica doesn't mind having you along, that would be fine, but only if Dad or I am around to drive you to the boardwalk. Aunt Jess can ride on the streets from here to the top of the boardwalk, but you absolutely cannot."

I could see the word "but" on Frank's face, so I quickly changed the subject. "Speaking of Grady, where is he?"

"His office called. So he's on lockdown in our bedroom doing a small favor for Mr. Hargreaves." Donna held up her hands and put finger quotes around the words "small favor." "I'm not sure how long he'll be."

"Look at these bikes!" Frank was awed at first sight of the four bicycles leaning one against the other along the shed's rear wall. "Trek makes the best road bikes. I never thought I'd get to ride one. Oh, I hope there is one that fits me."

I knew Trek had a stellar reputation for both durability and safety. I picked up the bicycle closest to me. It was dark blue and sized for an adult. I put my hand on the seat and bounced it. The tires definitely needed air. Not surprising, since I had no idea how long the bike had been sitting unused. The next bike was a twin to the first, but the third was dark green and slightly smaller. I hoped it was sized appropriately for Frank.

He looked at it and looked at me. "What do you think, Aunt Jessica?"

I pointed behind him. "I think you should get the red tire

pump off that shelf. Then we can pump up the tires and see if you and this bicycle are a match," I said.

Once the tires were pumped, I made sure that Frank could straddle the seat while keeping his feet flat on the floor. I deemed it adequate. Then Frank insisted on pumping the tires of the bike I'd chosen, so I busied myself by dusting down his new "ride" with the paper towels I pulled from the holder nailed to the wall.

In no time at all, we finished pumping tires and dusting seats, handlebars, fenders, and crossbars. We were sure we had the two bicycles at the ready when we heard a knock. Grady was standing in the doorway with a blue-and-yellow can in his hand. He looked at the tire pump sitting on the floor in the midst of a pile of used paper towels.

"Wow, you two have been busy. Did you check the chain and the brakes yet?" he asked.

I had to confess that it had never occurred to me. But within a few minutes, Grady did a quick lube job on both bicycles.

Then he said, "We'll let that sit overnight and tomorrow you two will be ready to roll."

"Tomorrow?" Frank was disappointed.

"I'm afraid so, Sport," Grady said. "We have no idea how long it's been since these bicycles were used, much less oiled. Safety maintenance is a dad's main job."

Frank perked up. "You always say that."

Grady ruffled the boy's hair. "I say it 'cause it's true. Now, let's clean up this mess and I promise I will drive you to the boardwalk tomorrow for a good long bicycle ride."

"Deal," Frank said, and began picking up the paper towels while I reshelved the pump.

As we were walking back to the bungalow, Edwina Courtland was coming toward us with the two little girls I remembered as Madeline and Juliet.

The girls ran up to us, or I should say to Frank, and one said, "Aunt Edwina is taking us to the playground. Do you want to come?"

I guess with bike riding out of the question for the afternoon, Frank decided it was a good option, because he quickly agreed.

"These two are such a handful, perhaps he'll keep them busy while I rest on a bench." Edwina's smile was halfhearted and I was sure I detected bourbon on her breath.

That set off alarms in my head, and I guess in Grady's as well, because he said immediately, "If you wouldn't mind, Mrs. Courtland-Young, I haven't actually seen the playground yet. I'd just as soon come along. Aunt Jess?"

"Oh, my, yes. I love playgrounds. It is always entertaining to watch the children play on the equipment."

I thought I heard Edwina murmur something that sounded like "Not for me."

We walked two short blocks to the playground. I noticed that Edwina was flushed and somewhat winded by the time we got there. She seemed to be in poor physical shape, considering that she summered in such a health-inspiring place.

The little girls ran straight for a large red, tan, and yellow geo dome climber.

Frank looked at Grady, who waved him ahead, then said,

"Aunt Jessica, why don't you and Mrs. Courtland-Young have a seat on that bench?" Then he followed the children.

I took Edwina by the arm and guided her to the bench, which was fully in the shade of a leafy old tree. It was a comfortable spot with a full view of the playground.

We sat down and Edwina immediately opened her oversized purse and pulled out a thermos.

"I don't suppose you want any of my special iced tea," she said with a crooked smile.

"Not right now, thank you," I said.

"It's been a rough couple of days—I can tell you that," Edwina said before taking a long drink of the "tea" she'd poured into the thermos cup.

"I'm sure it has been."

I hesitated to mention Jason's death for fear she'd begin talking about their personal history again. Besides, I was far more interested in her thoughts on the company's future.

"I guess in your role as a member of the board of directors, you will have to join the others in making quite a few decisions in the very near future," I said.

Edwina slumped toward me. "You don't know the half of it. Where do you think my husband is right at this very minute? Where is he? Well, I'll tell you. He rounded up Jason's sons—well, not the dentist, but the other two—and he dragged them into the office."

She looked appropriately outraged. "I mean, shouldn't they be with their mother and . . . and . . . my mother? Noooo. Tyler had other plans."

"Plans? What sort of plans?" I was seriously curious.

"This morning when Dennis asked me, I never should have agreed to watch the girls. That's how all the trouble started."

I have to admit that confused me. I pointed to the geo dome, where Juliet was hanging by her knees from a midlevel bar and Madeline was balanced victoriously on the very top.

I asked, "Those sweet little girls?"

Edwina nodded, although she looked more like a bobblehead that someone had accidentally touched. "Well, Tyler was having his coffee in the kitchen while the girls were watching television, some PBS kiddie show, in the living room. One of them went into the kitchen and asked if she and her sister could have some juice. While Tyler was pouring the juice, he asked—and I am sure he meant it in a nice way, not a snide way—he asked, 'How am I so lucky to have two pretty little girls spend the morning with me?' And she answered, 'Grandpa was supposed to stay with us but he had to go to work. Everyone else had to talk to the man and the lady.'"

"The man and the lady?" I couldn't decipher that.

"That's how we refer to the detectives in front of the children. They had scheduled family interviews today. My mother's doctor finally said the police could speak to her for a few minutes, and I guess it made sense for them to talk to my niece and nephews since everyone is hunkered down here. They'd already spoken to Dennis, Tyler, and me more times than I can count."

"Believe me, I know the feeling." I tried to sound sympathetic, but I wanted her to get back to my main area of interest. Why was her husband in his office at Courtland Finance? "So then what happened after the little girl told your husband that her grandfather went to work?"

"What happened?" Edwina shrieked loud enough that Grady turned to look at me, but I warned him off with a slight wave of my hand.

"What do you think happened? Tyler went ballistic. He wouldn't yell and scream in front of the children, but he spent the better part of ten minutes seething at me through clenched teeth about how my older brother was always trying to sandbag his career and he wasn't going to let my younger brother do the same thing."

She opened the thermos and this time didn't bother with the cup. "He was cruel and vitriolic, lambasting my brothers over and over again. Then he called Jason's sons to tell them that Dennis was about to betray the entire family. He has the local car service on speed dial, and within five minutes, off he went with our nephews in tow. That was a really bad sign."

"What was? Do you mean the nephews or the car service?" I was confused.

"The car service. Calling them meant he was so upset, he didn't trust himself to drive. A few years ago, Tyler got really upset at work. He and Jason nearly came to blows. It was summer and we were staying here. Tyler jumped in his car and was driving home on the Belt Parkway when he felt disoriented. Fortunately, he pulled off to the side of the road to rest. Within a few minutes, he lost his vision. He got out of the car and fell to the ground. A passing firefighter stopped to give emergency aid and I'm sure nine-one-one got a hundred calls. Anyway, the ambulance came and he went to the hospital, where he was diagnosed with a TIA. Do you know what that is?"

I nodded. "A transient ischemic attack, more commonly called a ministroke."

"Yes, he is convinced he was close to dying right there on the side of the highway and that the firefighter saved his life, which he probably did. After that, Tyler swore he would never again drive when he was upset. And he never has."

She leaned against the back of the bench and pointed to the children, who were now playing on a colorful open spiral slide.

"Such sweet, innocent little girls, and yet they managed to set him off. Go figure."

"Oh, it really wasn't the girls." I tried to strike a compassionate tone. "I would suppose that as an in-law rather than a blood relative, your husband may have hidden the fact that he always felt insecure about his place in the company. Now with the CEO position vacant, well, that insecurity has magnified. It's possible he sees your brother Dennis as a threat."

"Oh, no, it's more than that. Tyler sees Dennis exactly how he always viewed Jason: as a sworn enemy to his own ambition. Tyler will never be satisfied until Courtland Finance is his and his alone. Even though that can never be. He is not a Courtland."

Her blond curls bouncing, Juliet ran over to us and climbed onto the bench. "I'm thirsty. Can we go back to the house now?"

When we got home, Donna was sitting on the porch with her laptop open. "How were the bicycles? Any good?"

Frank shouted that Trek bikes are the best, and the green bike was his size. He went through the steps we had taken to get the bikes ready to ride and ended with "Dad is going to drive Aunt Jess and me to the boardwalk tomorrow morning."

Grady said, "Okay, Frank, I know you're excited, but quiet down. We don't want the whole boardwalk filled with folks curious to see you and Aunt Jess riding."

"How long is the boardwalk, Dad?"

Before Grady could answer, Donna pushed her laptop in Frank's direction. "Why don't you look it up? I'm sure Dad and Aunt Jess would like some iced tea." And she signaled us to follow her inside.

I burst out laughing. Since I'd met Edwina, I would never quite think of iced tea the same way.

As soon as we sat around the kitchen table, Donna poured a glass of tea for herself and Grady. I opted for water. She sat down and told us what was on her mind.

"I got the strangest text from Carole, my assistant at the office. It said that tonight I should be sure to count noses when everyone comes home from work. I didn't think anyone here was going to work, what with the family being in mourning and the police investigation. I was about to call her when Frank ran up the porch steps and there you all were."

"I think I can explain at least some of what Carole is referring to," I said, and proceeded to give Donna and Grady a brief explanation of everything Edwina had told me while we sat in the playground.

Donna looked more and more distressed. And when I finished, she said, "Yesterday Carole texted me to see if I could confirm that Courtland Finance and Investments is slated to go out of business because there was no one capable of stepping up to replace Jason. I assured her that within a few weeks the ship would be righted, so to speak. Now, with the entire staff already on edge, Dennis and Tyler choose today to go into work and do what? Wrangle for control of the executive suite? In front of everyone?"

Grady leaned in to put a comforting arm around her. "I admit it doesn't look good, but, hon, there was not a thing you could have done to prevent it."

I said, "Grady's right. Perhaps later on you could call Carole and see how today played out. Having a firsthand account of today's events in the office will give you a better idea of how to cope with . . . with whatever is going on between Tyler and Dennis."

In the back of my mind, I had to wonder: If Tyler Young, who was at the top of my suspect list, had murdered Jason Courtland, why would he risk calling attention to himself by going after Dennis Courtland so publicly?

The front door slammed and Frank rushed in from the porch. "That man from the other day is here. The one who came with the detective. And he wants to talk to you, Mom."

Lawrence Torsney, aka Special Agent Josh Keppler. What now?

Chapter Twenty

When he found us all sitting around the kitchen table, looking for all the world like a family enjoying a tea break and some light conversation, Agent Keppler seemed genuinely apologetic.

"I'm sorry to barge in like this—"

Donna cut him off. "It's no bother. Please join us." She waved toward an empty chair. "Can I offer you some iced tea or a cold glass of water?"

"Water would be great. Listen, Vinny Tieri called me with sort of a heads-up. He and Aisha arranged to interview the entire Courtland family today now that Matilda Courtland's doctor has given the okay. But when the detective arrived, Dennis Courtland, Tyler Young, and two of Jason Courtland's sons were nowhere to be found. Someone told him they'd all gone into the office, so Vinny called me to see if I had them. I think he was actually hoping we'd brought them into the office on some ruse so we could question them, but I had no idea they weren't right here at the beach. In fact, Mrs. Fletcher, er, Donna Fletcher, I thought it was possible that the board of directors had ordered all staff in for a kind of 'we're all in this together' meeting, but since you are here, that is clearly not the case."

I made a quick decision and said, "Actually, I believe I can explain, Agent Keppler. As you know, Edwina Courtland-Young is a director of the company, and I happened to speak to her this afternoon."

As I told him everything about Dennis and Tyler that I'd learned from Edwina, I watched him shake his head once and raise his eyes heavenward twice. When I finished speaking, he sat mutely. I thought for a moment that he was going to stand up and leave without a word.

Then he said softly, "Have they no consideration for their staff? Fighting for control before the CEO is even buried is tasteless enough, but to do so in the office in front of the very people whose livelihoods depend on the company's continued existence is downright cruel."

Grady said, "If you'd been around Matilda Courtland's house two nights ago, you'd have learned that at least one of the executive staff has no consideration for anyone."

He went on to explain what he and Donna had witnessed between Anya and Tyler.

I turned to Donna, and without mentioning Carole by name, I said, "Perhaps you could recount your recent texts with your office friend. That will give Agent Keppler an idea of how the staff is responding to all this chaos."

While Donna confirmed Keppler's thoughts on the staff's

response to the rift between Dennis Courtland and Tyler Young, I was wondering if internal strife would help or hurt Keppler's ability to construct a case. If there *was* a case at all. Suppose the war between Dennis and Tyler was no more than an extension of what Donna liked to call the sibling rivalry that bubbled among the Courtlands?

Eventually Agent Keppler thanked Donna for her information and apologized for keeping us from our dinner. As he was leaving, I said, "For such a small family, there seems to be a lot of turmoil."

He smiled and said, "I need to remind myself that it is best to keep in mind how astute you are. Good evening."

Donna's chicken casserole was delicious in spite of the fact that it had sat in the oven set on "warm" for far longer than it should have.

The next morning Grady put the two Trek bicycles in the trunk of his SUV and drove Frank and me to the nearest corner where we could enter the Rockaway Beach boardwalk.

After he unloaded the bikes, he said, "I'll keep my phone near me at all times. I will pick you up here ten minutes after you text me that you are ready to come home. Got it?"

Frank and I both assured him that we did.

We walked our bikes up the ramp, and when we turned onto the boardwalk, I remarked that it seemed to go on forever.

"It's five and a half miles long," Frank said. "Remember Mom told me to look it up on her laptop? Should we ride to the end and back again?"

In spite of Frank's enthusiasm, I thought the eleven-mile round-trip might be too much for our first go, especially on unfamiliar bikes.

"I'll tell you what," I said. "Why don't we ride for a while and then turn around. There is no need to measure miles. If you don't think we've gone far enough today, we can add more distance to our next ride."

"You mean, we can ride again?" Frank squealed.

"As long as the bikes work well and the sun shines, why not?" His enthusiasm was contagious.

Even at this early hour, there were plenty of walkers, joggers, skateboarders, and other bike riders going in both directions, but since the boardwalk was probably a good thirty feet wide, there was room for us all to stay out of one another's way.

After a mile or so, we stopped to watch a group of birds strutting around on the sand. One of the larger birds, with a long red beak, poked in the sand, brought out something, and fed it to a smaller bird. I pointed it out to Frank.

"Look at the beak on that bird. It is extremely long and bright red. I wonder what kind of species that is."

"I saw a few like that at the wildlife refuge. Tariq called them American oystercatchers. I guess he needs a really long beak to dig deep enough to find oysters," Frank observed.

Farther along, we saw a group of surfers and stopped to watch. Frank told me he had asked his parents if he could learn to surf, but they thought he was too young. "But look out there. Some of those surfers look like they are my size."

A familiar voice said, "Don't let the distance fool you. Everyone out there is much older than you are."

We turned and I barely recognized Jamie Ingram from the

community center. She was wearing a wide-brimmed hat, oversized sunglasses, and a navy blue backpack. She had an attractive wooden walking stick in each hand. The tips of the sticks reached as high as her chin.

"Good morning. I see you practice Nordic walking." I gestured to the sticks.

"I do. Some years ago I broke my leg. As part of my recovery, I used a walker and then a cane. A friend suggested I try using walking sticks and do some serious walking to rebuild my muscles and my confidence."

"Well, it seems to have worked for you," I said.

"Sure did, and the bonus was that by using the sticks, my walking routine works both my upper- and lower-body muscles." Jamie flexed a biceps to show us what she meant.

"Mrs. Ingram, do you mean those sticks help you build muscles? That is awesome," Frank said.

"They do. Would you like to try walking with them? I can teach you in a hot minute," she said.

Frank glanced at me, and as soon as I nodded, he hopped off his bike, dropped the kickstand, and stood ready to try the sticks.

Mrs. Ingram gave him a brief lesson and then he took a few steps while she cautioned, "Remember, these particular sticks are too big for you, so you have to be extra careful to hold them straight up. Can't have them leaning back and hitting you in the head. Good lifting."

As we watched Frank walk back and forth, Jamie asked me how the Courtlands were doing. I replied that it was hard for everyone, and I was surprised by her response.

"Well, I can tell you there was one person who got lucky

when Jason Courtland died, and that's Reggie Masterson." She cocked her head in an "ask me more" kind of position.

I immediately obliged. "But I understood that Reggie was the newest addition to the community center and barely knew Jason."

"Be that as it may, I can assure you Reggie did know that Jason was on the verge of firing him. They had a fairly loud conversation about it the day before Jason's accident. Personally, I think the kid is doing a great job. But Jason paid the bills and he didn't like Reggie's focus on teaching color rather than actual painting. Not that it would have mattered for Jason's grandchildren. Believe me, I have seen their paintings. Rembrandt himself couldn't make artists out of the likes of them."

After we said good-bye to Mrs. Ingram, Frank was extremely enthusiastic about walking sticks. As he chattered on, I reminded myself how quickly I had dismissed Reggie Masterson from my list of likely suspects. I'd have to look at him again.

I sent Grady a text when we were ready to leave, and he was waiting at the boardwalk ramp just as he promised. Before we had even gotten the bicycles into the car, Frank was singing the glories of walking sticks, which allowed me to remain lost in thought while he and Grady talked on the brief ride home about the pros and cons of that form of exercise.

When we got to the bungalow, Donna had snacks waiting on the porch.

"Grapes and cheddar cheese. My favorites," Frank said.

Donna offered me an iced-coffee shake, which was unfamiliar to me but turned out to be quite delicious. When I asked what the secret ingredient was, she told me she added two tablespoons of ice cream—sometimes coffee, sometimes vanilla, depending on what she had in the freezer. I had a hunch that chocolate ice cream would work as well and decided to buy some the next time I went to the market.

While Grady, Donna, and Frank planned their activities for the day, I decided not to join them on the beach.

"Since I've changed my plans and opted to stay here for a while longer, I have some personal matters that need to be taken care of," I said.

Grady raised an inquiring eyebrow and I quickly answered, "Believe me, there is nothing urgent. I have a couple of bills to pay in case I don't get home before they are due. I also realized that I'd better call Seth Hazlitt to be sure he knows I have changed my plans, so he'll continue to check on my house. And I am thinking of taking a bit of a rest this afternoon. Frank is quite a speedy bike rider. It took a lot of energy for me to keep up."

Frank preened, his parents laughed, and I was pleased to get a block of time to myself.

Seth picked up on the second ring. "Ayuh, Jessica, Mort Metzger says you've managed to ruin still another vacation. Turns out that body you found was definitely a murder victim. Amazing how that seems to happen so often." He chuckled.

"Seth, really. How can you laugh? As a doctor, you of all people should know that death is no joking matter. And I didn't discover the body. My poor niece Donna did. And to make matters worse, the deceased is her CEO."

Every word I spoke increased my worry for Donna. Her life was in total upheaval.

"Now, that is a serious matter. I'm sorry I was so flippant. I hate to see a sweet person like your niece go through that kind of severe trauma. Tell me, does she still have her job or did the business die with the boss?"

Seth was more on-target than he knew.

"So far the company seems stable," I said. "But as a family-owned business, it has an awful lot of complications."

"And all those complications come in the form of other family members messing about, I expect," Seth said.

"You couldn't be more correct. Anyway, given the circumstances, I've extended my stay indefinitely, and I was wondering—"

"No need to wonder. I'll keep an eye on your house. However, I will expect payment in the form of a lobster dinner followed by your famous cranberry muffins once you get back into your own kitchen."

"Done," I said.

"Before you hang up, let me share the latest gossip with you. Eve Simpson is crowing all over town that she has finally unloaded—actually she uses the word 'sold,' but 'unloaded' seems more accurate to me—the old Crenshaw place. It seems that Dan Andrews is about to become a homeowner."

"Now, that is news. I thought he'd wait longer to pick a permanent home, but I must say, the Crenshaw house does come with a beautiful yard and garden, and the location is so near the *Gazette* office, he can walk to work."

"Jessica Fletcher, eternal optimist," Seth said. "Neither the house nor the land has had anyone look after it for more than fifteen years, probably closer to twenty. I don't know how Dan will possibly be able to renovate the house, clear and replant the property, and run the town newspaper. Last I heard he isn't Superman."

"Oh, Seth, for goodness' sake, don't discourage him. He doesn't need to accomplish it all in one weekend," I said.

I hung up after Seth elicited a promise from me to take care of Donna and to call him as soon as I knew when I would be on my way home to Cabot Cove. In return, Seth promised not to tease Eve Simpson or Dan Andrews mercilessly about the Crenshaw property.

My most pressing chore now behind me, I opened my iPad and searched Reggie Masterson once again. I couldn't find anything more than my previous search had revealed. He had absolutely nothing in his background that screamed "criminal," much less "murderer."

It was possible that there were shadows in his past that a simple Internet search would not reveal.

Then something occurred to me. In her offhand, casual-conversation sort of way, Jamie Ingram had been quick to point a finger at Reggie without seeming to do so. I tended to think of Carissa and Reggie as employees of the art program, but never thought of Jamie Ingram that way. Yet she took attendance; purchased, stored, and distributed refreshments; and probably had other duties that I was not aware of. Just as Donna was Jason's employee at Courtland Finance, Jamie Ingram was his employee in the art program, and based on our conversations, she had been so for some time. I had to wonder if she had pointed to Reggie in the hope that I would go back to the Courtlands and spread the word that Reggie had had an ax to grind with Jason. And how had I found this out? Ah, the ever-loyal Mrs. Ingram told me. Or was she simply trying to steer anyone who might be curious about her off into another direction? Now, that sounded bizarre, even to my fertile imagination, as Jamie Ingram's name had never come up in any conversations I'd had. And as far as I knew, Detectives Tieri and Kelly were more focused on the family and, with Agent Keppler's encouragement, on the company. No one paid any attention to the activities at the community center but me.

I went back to my trusty iPad and started a computer search for Jamie Ingram. The first link was to her Facebook page, which had a few pictures of the beach and some terrific pictures of flowers growing in what I presumed to be her garden. The only thing I learned there was that Jamie's given name was actually Jamilla.

The next link was to an article about church ladies organizing a fundraiser for missionaries working in countries around the world. In one blurry group picture, Jamie was identified as being second from the left. On the same page was a picture of a globe with the continents clearly defined. In front of the globe was a small collection box. The caption credited Jamie Ingram as the creator of the papier-mâché globe. Well, that did explain her interest in the art program. There were a few other links, all to events at the same church.

I gave up. I was looking for clues that weren't there. Although I told Grady and Donna that I was going to rest, I really had no intention of taking a nap. I decided to sit on the porch for some quality reading time. I had a copy of the latest Inspector Ian Rutledge book by the wonderfully talented mother-and-son team of Caroline and Charles Todd, who used Charles Todd as their author name.

I had the book in my hand and was nearly at the front door when someone knocked with such force that I hesitated to answer.

I looked out the window and Tyler Young was pacing back and forth with his head down and his hands in his pockets. He stopped, turned toward the door, and began banging again.

Chapter Twenty-One

Keeping the fact that Tyler was Donna's immediate supervisor uppermost in my mind, I opened the door, intending to politely tell him that Donna was not at home while I resisted the urge to chide him for banging so rudely.

However, he didn't give me the opportunity to say a word. I had barely opened the door halfway when he pushed against it with his left hand and started jabbing the index finger of his right hand directly at my face.

"You! Mystery writer! I understand you have been nosing around, trying to get information about my brother-in-law's death for one of those silly books you write. Well, let me tell you, there is no mystery here. And no murder. A machine malfunctioned and poor Jason is dead. Period. It has nothing to do with Courtland Finance and Investments. So stop asking so many questions."

To say I was shocked at his behavior was putting it mildly. I gathered my resolve and said quite firmly, "Mr. Young, I have no idea what you are talking about. I most certainly am not writing a book about Jason Courtland's death. Where would you get such an idea?"

When he saw how indignant I was, he stammered, "Well, well, that is, I was told you write about murders and that you thought Jason's death could easily be a murder. Then one of the detectives asked about the financial assets of our company. They wanted to know where the money comes from and where it goes."

I was beginning to consider that he had a drinking problem similar to his wife's, when all of a sudden, he did a complete reversal. "I am sorry, Mrs. Fletcher. Obviously, I've been misled by . . . Let's just say by someone who doesn't always think straight. Please forgive my intrusion. Enjoy the rest of your day."

I watched him pull out his cell phone as he walked away, but I couldn't hear whom he called. I had to wonder if someone was trying to rattle him and had used me to do so, or if my asking a few questions here and there was beginning to cause serious concern among the Courtland family. For the moment I decided to let the present slip away while I joined Inspector Rutledge in long-ago England. Maybe reading about his crime fighting would nudge the puzzle pieces that I was sure were floating around in my brain and refusing to fit together.

As usual, Ian Rutledge kept me so captivated that I was startled when someone spoke my name and brought me back to present-day Rockaway Beach.

I looked up and was surprised to see Carissa Potter and Reggie Masterson standing at the bottom of the porch steps.

"Hello, you two. Are you enjoying your day off?" I asked.

Carissa shrugged her shoulders until they nearly reached her ears. "It's hardly a day off for us. More like a command performance. A man called me on my cell and said he was speaking on behalf of Mrs. Matilda Courtland and basically ordered me to come to her house. I couldn't believe that with her son dead, the poor woman wanted to see me. So I checked with Reggie, and surprise, surprise, he got the same call."

Reggie said, "I thought perhaps the family was going to cancel the program for the rest of the summer. I wouldn't blame them if they had, but Carissa pointed out that a woman who just lost her oldest child would be so lost in grief that the art program should be furthest from her mind."

"I can't even imagine the pain, the devastation that the mother is going through. Even more so than his wife or even his children." Carissa shuddered and wiped an invisible tear from her eye.

"Well, what happened? Did you both go to the house?" My curiosity was on high alert.

"We did, and it was really, really strange," Reggie said, and then he turned to Carissa. "You've been here longer. You know who these people are. Perhaps you should tell the story."

Carissa nodded. "We decided that we would walk over to the house together because whatever Mrs. Courtland wanted to discuss, she wanted to speak to us both. When we got to the house, a tall woman with a long apron opened the door and asked us what we wanted. When I told her who we were and that Mrs. Matilda Courtland had sent for us, she said that was impossible."

Reggie picked up the story. "We told her we each had re-

224

ceived a phone call within the past hour, and that made her hesitate, especially when I mentioned that a man had called."

"But then," Carissa continued, "she said she was sorry but Mrs. Courtland is not up to visitors. We tried to explain that we weren't visitors and that we had been summoned to a meeting, but it was no use. She politely but firmly closed the door."

"My goodness, what on earth did you do?" I asked.

"What *could* we do? We started down the porch steps when Mr. Dennis Courtland came hurrying across the garden. He said, 'There you are. Sorry I'm late.' Neither of us thought it wise to tell him we believed we had an appointment with his mother, so we waited to see what he had to say, which was that the family, particularly his mother, had decided to fund the art program for the rest of the summer in honor of Jason," Carissa finished.

"As if he couldn't tell us that on the telephone. For that matter, why bring it up at all if nothing is going to change?" Reggie said. "It felt like he needed to speak to us at his mother's house, as though he had some authority issues to work through. After all, he'd just seen us at the community center a day or so ago."

"Well, that's certainly true," I said mildly. "And what about Mrs. Ingram? Did Dennis Courtland contact her? I wonder."

Reggie and Carissa turned questioning eyes to each other.

"I don't know. I didn't hear from her, did you?" Reggie asked.

Carissa shook her head. "I didn't think of her. To be honest, I don't think anyone does. She's just the juice lady. But you're right. She is as much an employee of the program as we are. Why didn't the Courtlands send for her as well?"

"I suppose it's because she is easily replaceable, while if one or the other of you decided to look for another job because you were afraid the program would be cut short, well, it would be difficult to find a person with your skill set to complete the summer program," I suggested.

"That's very kind of you," Reggie said. "And perhaps you are right. I just don't get why Mr. Courtland pretended Mrs. Courtland wanted to see us."

I was confident I knew the answer. "During the brief time I was here before Jason died, I did have reason to learn that he used his mother as a shield to protect his decisions from being criticized by the rest of the family. I suspect that Dennis is trying to set himself up to follow that pattern."

"That does make sense, at least in the short term," Carissa said. "I was beginning to fear that the senior Mrs. Courtland was getting, well, a bit dotty while she struggled with the loss of her son. You know, I thought she'd told Dennis to call us and then forgotten why. That sort of thing."

Reggie said, "Well, you've certainly helped to put our minds at ease. We'll return the favor by letting you get back to your book."

Carissa followed his lead, adding, "I hope you will be able to come back to class again before you go home. Frank so enjoys your company."

Between first Tyler Young and then his brother-in-law Dennis Courtland causing disruptions, I had a little difficulty getting my head back into the crime Ian Rutledge was trying to resolve. I kept wondering who would tell Tyler that I was writing a book about Jason's murder. I also didn't understand why Dennis was using the art school as a place to flaunt the authority he hoped to have. A test run perhaps?

Fortunately it took reading only a few pages for the writing of the wonderfully gifted Todds to draw me into a cleverly woven story.

"Aunt Jess, Aunt Jess." Frank waved as he ran up the path, pulling his sand sled behind him. "We missed you at the beach, but Dad said I should tell you that I hope you had a good rest."

I almost giggled at Frank's innocent way of making his point of missing me while still obeying his father.

"I did enjoy spending time with an old friend." I held up my book. "But now that you are back, perhaps we can play a game of chess, unless your parents have other plans?"

"Great idea!" Frank pulled his sled to its resting place on the side of the house and then called, "After I get the sand off in the outside shower and change my clothes, I will be ready to beat those redcoats."

Grady and Donna were right behind him and they didn't seem to have half his energy. I asked how they had enjoyed their afternoon.

"Wonderful. The ocean was so calm that even I could swim without fear. You know upstate in Fishkill, we swam in pools and lakes. We didn't get bounced around by ocean waves," Donna said. "With all that swimming and building sand bridges, I am in need of a rest. Aunt Jessica, would you mind terribly if I just toss together a salad while Grady picks up a pizza for dinner tonight?"

"That sounds extremely appealing. My only suggestion is

that you allow me to make the salad while you lie down for half an hour or so."

Donna was usually so insistent on treating me like company, never letting me do a thing, that I knew she had to be exhausted when she agreed. Frank was perfectly content to postpone our chess game until after dinner. He was happy enough to ride along with his father to bring home the pizza.

I found a head of romaine lettuce and some mushrooms, cucumber, and tomatoes in the refrigerator and washed and dried them all. There was a nice-sized bowl in the cabinet that I thought would do nicely to hold a large salad. I shredded the lettuce and was slicing the cucumbers when Donna came into the kitchen wearing a sunny yellow shift. Her hair, still wet from the shower, was tied in a bun on top of her head. She looked like a teenager and I told her so.

"Oh, Aunt Jess, you are always so kind. I have to confess I don't feel like a teenager. Staying here was supposed to be the vacation of a lifetime for all of us. But it has just been one stressful event after another. And now with this investigation by the FBI, I would give anything to go home, but that's not a serious option."

Donna sat, dropped her elbows to the table, and rested her chin in her hands.

"No, it isn't," I said. "Besides the fact that the police have asked us all to remain here until their investigation is complete, you, my dear, are here because of your job, and that definitely prevents you from leaving the beach even when the police say we can leave."

Donna heaved a long, drawn-out sigh. "You're right about that, but every time Agent Keppler comes around with his questions, I wonder if I'll even have a job by the time this vacation ends. Will Courtland Finance and Investments remain in existence for any length of time?"

I put down my knife, pulled out a chair, and sat beside her. "No matter what happens at Courtland, you are a talented, highly qualified accountant, and any company would be happy to have you on their staff. Didn't you hear how Jason Courtland praised you to Josh Keppler when the investigation first began?"

Donna held up her hands in mock surrender. "Yes, I did. But Jason isn't here to give me a glowing reference, is he? If Courtland goes bye-bye under a cloud of scandal, I'll have no future whatsoever in accounting."

Rather than let her wallow in anxiety, I said, perhaps a little too brusquely, "Well, there is no point in worrying about that now. Not when we have two hungry men coming through the door at any minute."

I handed Donna a sharp knife along with two large ripe tomatoes and asked her to wedge them.

She gave me a tiny smile. "You always do manage to point out the important things in life. Time to get the men fed."

We had the salad ready and the table set when Grady carried in a large pizza box. Right behind him Frank carried two white bags.

He stood in the center of the room and said, "Mom, guess what! Tell me your favorite food from the pizza place and I will make it appear."

Donna furrowed her brow as if she was thinking long and hard. Then she said, "Spinach calzone."

Frank raised the bag in his right hand as high as he could.

"Ding, ding, ding, ding, ding. You win the prize." He thrust the bag at his mother.

Donna peeked inside the bag and gave Frank a big hug and kiss. Frank gallantly stepped aside and said, "It was Dad's idea."

Donna said, "Well, since I gave you the hug and kiss I should have given to Dad, you can keep it. I have another one for him."

As she gave Grady a big loud kiss on the cheek, we all laughed, and as I looked on, I thought that no matter what happened with Courtland Finance or Donna's job, my family would be fine.

Once we were all seated with salad and pizza on our plates, I asked Donna about the spinach calzone, which she had put in the middle of the table on a serving plate. She cut me a healthy wedge.

I thought it was tasty and told her so. Just then the doorbell rang. Grady jumped up and ran before it rang a second time. The doorbell reminded me that at some point I was going to have to tell Donna about my encounter with Tyler Young. And she probably should know about the episode Carissa and Reggie had had with Dennis Courtland at Matilda's house, but I was sure it could wait until tomorrow or even later.

Grady came back and said, "Aunt Jessica, it is Anya Wiggins at the door. She needs to speak with you for a minute."

Donna and I both looked at him wide-eyed, but he merely shrugged and whispered, "She looks like she's been crying."

Chapter Twenty-Two

Anya's eyes were red and she was carrying a shredded wad of tissues. She clearly had been crying, but I made no mention of it. I said good evening and then patiently waited for her to tell me why she was looking for me and if it had anything to do with the fact that she was so distraught. I led her to a couple of Adirondack chairs at the far end of the porch. For a while we sat looking at the waves shimmering on the ocean and at the few puffy cumulus clouds that seemed to float above it.

When I began to think she would never speak, I said, "Anya, you seem so upset. If you need to just sit for a while, I am happy to sit here quietly, but if you've come to me for help, tell me what I can do. Please tell me how I can be of assistance to you or to Matilda."

She started to speak, but her voice was so raspy, I offered her a cup of tea. She nodded and I went inside.

Grady followed me to the kitchen. "Aunt Jess, what is going on?"

I put the kettle on and took a teapot and two mugs out of the cabinet. "I'm not sure, but Anya needs a friend, or at least a momentary confidante, and I am more than willing to be that person. We may be on the porch for a while."

As soon as the kettle whistled, I filled the teapot and set it on a tray with the mugs, a sugar bowl, and a small creamer filled with milk. Grady walked ahead of me and opened the door. I set the tray on the porch table and filled the mugs. Anya declined milk and sugar. We both sat sipping hot tea as I waited for her to speak.

"Tilly is not leaving her bed. This morning I couldn't even talk her into taking a shower. When I offered her a sponge bath, she threw me out of the room. What's worse is that Edwina, Dennis, and even Tyler keep barging in the front door, demanding to see her, and when she won't see them, they blame me like I'm holding her hostage or something." Anya took another sip of tea.

"Why, that is awful," I said. "How can they blame you?"

"Easily, I'm afraid. Dennis was the worst. He told me if I didn't lighten up, that my job as 'gatekeeper'—that's what he called me—would be gone and I'd have nothing. The man forgets who changed his diapers more times than his mother ever did. So, anyway, it has been a long, hard day. I'm sorry that all poured out when I opened my mouth. That really isn't why I am here." Anya straightened up and looked directly into my eyes.

"Tilly asked for you specifically. She needs a favor."

"Of course, anything at all I can do."

I patted Anya's hand to comfort her. I assumed she was going to ask me to sign Tilly's books.

"With her children showing up at the house whenever they choose, Tilly has no privacy," Anya said. "So we hatched a scheme. She has asked me to tell them that Father Donovan will be coming to hear her confession and to bring her Communion at ten o'clock tomorrow morning. She wants me to ask them to respect her privacy and not come to visit until the afternoon."

"Well, that does sound like a way for Tilly to get some quiet time, and I am sure that a visit from a clergyman will do her a world of good," I said.

"Oh, no, I'm sorry I wasn't clear. We haven't called Father Donovan. Tilly is pretending to have scheduled a peaceful time alone with Father because she wants you to come to see her in the morning, and she doesn't want her children to know. She'd like your conversation to be completely private."

Clearly, Tilly's request did not involve a book signing. Still, I was extremely curious what she wanted, and accepted the invitation readily.

I offered Anya more tea but she declined. "No, thank you. I've had tea and a small rest, and thanks to you, I have accomplished what Tilly asked me to do. It would be best if I go right home. I don't like to leave her alone too long."

I walked with Anya to the edge of the garden path and then I watched her walk home until she was out of sight. When I got back to the porch, Donna was clearing away the tea service.

She said, "Grady heard you both leave, so I thought I would tidy up. Is everything okay? Grady said that Anya looked awful. He actually described her as 'bereft,' and that's a word I've seldom heard him use."

I smiled to reassure her. "We'll talk inside."

When Donna and I came into the living room, Grady was sprawled out on the couch, reading a magazine. Donna asked where Frank had disappeared to, and Grady said he had gone to his room.

I said, "I'm going to have to disturb him because I want to let him know that I won't be able to go to art school with him tomorrow. Something has come up."

Grady said, "Now, that sounds serious. Will you fill me in later? Oh, and tell Frank I'll be glad to come along to art class if he wants some company."

I stopped outside Frank's door and searched my memory for the appropriate set of Morse code dots and dashes. I was fairly sure that dot, dot, dash, dot had worked the other day, so I gave it a try.

"If your first initial is dot, dash, dash, dash, please enter," Frank said in a regal tone worthy of the Marquis de Lafayette himself.

I stifled a giggle and opened the door. Frank was lying on the floor and had his chess pieces arranged as opposing armies. The British forces were camped on top of a bed pillow, while the pawns dressed in America uniforms were climbing on one of Frank's sandals to the top of the pillow behind the British. The rest of the Americans were hiding behind Frank's other sandal in front of the pillow, clearly waiting for the British to flee in their direction.

"That's quite a battle you have brewing," I said.

"The coolest thing about this chess set is that I can use it to play chess or use it to play army. It is always lots of fun whichever way I play," Frank said. "Did you come to find me because you want to play chess? I can end this game if you like."

"Oh, that is a very tempting offer, but you have put so much effort into setting up a strategic battle that I wouldn't dream of intruding," I said, and I was not surprised that he didn't seem all that disappointed that I wasn't looking for a playmate.

"I did want to let you know that I have an appointment tomorrow morning, so I won't be able to go to art class with you. Your dad said he'd be happy to tag along if you wanted company," I said.

"Oh, that's okay. I don't mind being on my own at all. Most of the other kids are fun. And Mrs. Ingram is really nice to us whether we have a grown-up with us or not. When we were digging tunnels a few days before you came, Billy and Shane told me that they were really worried when she started being the juice lady, because of the trouble, but she was always nice to them and to all the kids," Frank said as if stating a well-known fact.

"Trouble? I wasn't aware that Mrs. Ingram had any trouble."

"Well, Billy said that the trouble was about Mr. Ingram. He committed a crime and was sent to jail. Then Billy's grandfather gave Mrs. Ingram the job as juice lady so she would have some money for food and stuff like that. He told me Mrs. Ingram also watches over the bungalows during the winter when no one else is here. Then that nosy Madeline butted in and said that was the least Uncle Jason could do because he was the one who sent Mr. Ingram to jail. Then Billy told her she didn't know what she was talking about and to mind her own business and go build her stupid castle. I did tell you how she likes castles, right?"

My brain was so busy processing Frank's revelation about Mrs. Ingram and Jason Courtland, it took me a few seconds to answer. "Yes, that's right. You did mention that she and her sister preferred castles to tunnels and bridges."

I sat on the bed and watched the battle commence. Frank narrated minute by minute until the redcoats were soundly thumped. I pretended to be enthusiastic but my mind was elsewhere, so I was glad to say good night when Donna came to remind Frank that it was time for bed.

I pulled out my trusty iPad and discovered that New York State had a criminal-history record site available for an online search. However, I soon realized that without a first name and birth date for Jamie Ingram's husband, I wouldn't be able to find any information regarding whatever crime might have taken place.

I'd already searched Jamie Ingram but that had only led to my learning about her activities in a local church and her apparent talent for making objects out of papier-mâché. I assumed that a search of Jason Courtland's name would lead to recent articles covering his death, which would be followed by pages and pages of links to his activities as CEO of Courtland Finance and Investments. I would be hard-pressed to find how or why, at least according to some of the Courtland children, Jason had sent Mr. Ingram to jail. I almost decided to search for Jason anyway when I got a better idea.

I typed Courtland and Ingram into the search box. A number of links came up for a law firm in Nevada that included those names and three others as their masthead.

I scrolled past a number of links that, like the law firm, had nothing to do with what I was trying to find and moved from page to page. Then, near the top of the fourth page, I saw the words Edward Ingram Found Guilty in a link to a news article. That was certainly worth a chance.

I opened the article and learned that an Edward Ingram of Rockaway and two other men had been arrested for stealing pleasure boats in New York's boroughs of Queens and Brooklyn; altering the hull identification numbers, which I supposed was the same as a car's vehicle identification number; repainting the boats; and selling them to purchasers as far south as Myrtle Beach, South Carolina.

The two other men had opted for separate trials, which had been scheduled to begin shortly after the date of the article. The next couple of links added nothing to what I'd already learned. Now that I had a given name for Mr. Ingram, I decided to do a more specific search. I entered Edward Ingram and Jason Courtland in the search box, and hit the jackpot.

I skimmed through the article and then slowed down and read it more carefully. As the stories I'd read earlier indicated, Edward Ingram had gone on trial for stealing and reselling motorboats a little more than three years ago. At two thirty in the morning on the night in question, as lawyers and apparently reporters liked to say, Mr. Ingram entered the Moonbeam Gateway Marina and broke into a Marex 320 Aft Cabin Cruiser. He then started it up and glided it right out of its slip. Mr. Jason Courtland, who had two boats docked in nearby slips, happened to be visiting one of his boats, looking for a misplaced wallet. He explained that while preparing for bed, he discovered his wallet was missing. After scouring his house and his car with no luck, he decided to drive to the marina to see if he'd dropped it on the boat that he and a business associate had taken out earlier in the day.

While walking toward his own boat, he'd caught sight of someone moving around on the white-and-tan Marex. He took a few steps closer but relaxed when he saw it was Mr. Ingram, whom he recognized because he often did repairs on boats in the marina. Mr. Courtland assumed Mr. Ingram was working on some sort of emergency and continued on to his own boat, failed to find his wallet, and then went home. The next day, as word spread through the marina community that the Marex had been stolen, Mr. Courtland reported what he had seen the night before, and the police found the boat in a garage that Ingram used to store his tools and work equipment.

"Caught red-handed," I said to myself.

I clicked a few more links and read slightly different reports, then put my iPad down. Young Madeline was correct. Uncle Jason certainly had played a role in sending Edward Ingram to jail. And then, perhaps out of guilt for his role in her husband's incarceration, he offered Jamie Ingram a job at the community center and some sort of caretaker role at the cottages. I would have liked to think he'd offered her the jobs out of compassion, but unless she was financially desperate, I couldn't, for the life of me, understand why she'd accepted.

Chapter Twenty-Three

As I walked to Matilda Courtland's house, I was sorry I'd agreed to visit her. After the information that I had uncovered last night, I would much rather have gone to art school with Frank on the off chance of having a private word with Jamie Ingram. I didn't think Detectives Tieri and Kelly were making much progress in solving Jason Courtland's murder. Perhaps Jamie would know if either of her husband's associates from the boat-napping incident was a violent man, and, if so, whether they were out of prison or not. Or was it possible that Edward Ingram had been working for a nationwide ring of thieves? If that was the case, then Jason had absolutely hampered their operation. Those organizations could be dangerous and were often run by the type of people who demanded revenge. And with all the bustling businesses I'd seen in and around Rockaway Beach, why would Jamie

Ingram take a job that would keep her connected to Jason Courtland? That seemed, to me, to be the oddest point of all.

Anya had left the front door open but, prudently, had locked the screen door. I knocked on the frame. No one came to the door. I waited a few minutes, then called out, "Anya, it's Jessica."

I watched her walk toward me across the living room. The sad, nearly broken Anya of yesterday was gone, and Anya with the purposeful stride and cheery smile was back.

"Thank you so much for coming," she said. "Tilly had a fitful night but she is calmer this morning, although I couldn't talk her into getting out of bed to face the day. She did, however, take a shower, and then demanded her prettiest nightgown and bed jacket, since she was having company, so I took that as a good sign. So much better than her lying in bed, crying till her tears run dry."

"I am happy to help in any way I can. Do you know exactly why Mrs. Courtland sent for me?" I asked, and then hastily added, "I want to be prepared. I don't want to disappoint her by saying or doing the wrong thing. As you have mentioned the other day, she is fragile."

Anya shook her head. "Mrs. Fletcher, you know that I have known Tilly my entire adult life. Becoming Jason's nanny was my first real job, and over the many years, my job has gradually turned into my being nanny to his mother. I have kept her secrets and run her private errands, but there are times when she will not confide in me, and during those times, I do not pressure her. She did ask me to bring your books to her room and leave them on her dressing table, but I really don't think that they have anything to do with why she has invited you here."

"Really? I had assumed—"

"Well, let me bring you in to see her and we will find out."

Tilly led me down a hallway, its walls lined with paintings of beach scenes. The last door at the end was partially closed. Anya knocked before pushing it wide open.

"Tilly, your company is here."

The room was painted a pale yellow. Green-and-yellow tweed carpet covered the floor. Everything else—the furniture, the curtains, even Tilly's bed coverlet—was so white that the sun coming through the window made the room nearly blinding. Tilly sat up in bed, leaning against a mound of pillows. Her bed jacket was pale blue with a splash of pink rosebuds. Without it, she might have gone totally unseen surrounded by the coverlet and the pillows.

"Jessica, it was so nice of you to come. I have been longing for company."

Mrs. Courtland reached out with two hands to greet me.

I went to her bedside and took her hands in mine. I noticed they were cold despite the sunny day.

"Mrs. Courtland, Matilda, I am so very sorry for your loss."

"I appreciate your kind words and I am so grateful for the exquisite flowers you and your niece brought to me that first day. I am only sorry I was not able to receive you."

Tilly waved her hand to indicate a small white armchair near the bed. "Please sit. We can talk for a while. Anya, would you mind bringing us some coffee? Or, Jessica, would you prefer tea?"

What I didn't say was that I would have preferred to find out why I had been summoned. Instead, I agreed that coffee would be fine and said I took mine black.

When Anya left the room, Tilly said, "She is a gem. I often wonder how I would have survived my life, especially the difficult parts, without Anya."

"Perhaps you should be saying that directly to Anya instead of telling me," I said. My words were cloaked in candor rather than malice.

"After all we have been through together, I don't question that she knows how important she is to me, how much I depend on her. But you are right. Sometimes the words need to be said. That is something for me to think about. Perhaps when everything else is settled, I will take the time to tell her how much she is valued. Thank you for reminding me that gratitude should be expressed."

Tilly took a tissue from a white china holder that sat on her night table and carefully wiped her eyes. "I also wish I had been a better mother to Jason, expressed my love and appreciation to him before . . . before there was no time left."

She dabbed at her eyes again and I had a flash of intuition that I might be close to hearing the real reason for my visit.

Anya came in carrying a tray with our coffee. She set the tray on the dresser and put Matilda's cup on her night table. Then she brought over a small white wooden table that had been next to the dresser, and placed it beside my chair. Before she brought my coffee, Anya asked if I wanted a cookie or two, which I declined.

"Jessica, did you notice how she keeps the sweets out of my

reach?" Tilly said. "Anya watches my blood sugar level far more carefully than I do."

"If it was up to you, every meal would have sugary treats, and you'd be in the emergency room at the hospital more often than not. We did that once. Never again. If there is nothing else you need right now, I'll be in the kitchen," Anya said, and left the room.

I sipped my coffee, waiting for Matilda to speak, and when she did, it was heartrending.

"Jessica, did you ever notice that sometimes the sins of the past"—Tilly hesitated and then went on—"will come back to haunt us at the worst possible times?"

"Oh, yes, I do believe that is very true. Any tragic or sad occurrence can easily stir up the memories of earlier unhappy incidents, and the despair of those reminiscences, once aroused, can come flooding back, mixing with the desolation of the present situation."

I was beginning to believe that what Matilda Courtland needed most was a good cry with a person who didn't know her history and yet was someone she believed she could trust not to repeat whatever was said. In her limited surroundings, I might have fit the bill. I was a stranger, and yet she might have felt that I was familiar because she read my books. So I was surprised when the conversation took a turn.

"Jessica, when we met, I was impressed that you are quite humble—down to earth, as it were—for a person of your fame and stature," Tilly said.

I was always uncomfortable when anyone approached me as if I were a film star or a pop singer. I knew Matilda thought she was complimenting me, but to my ears, her words were awkward and unnerving. However, with all she was going through, plus the fact that she obviously wanted to speak to me about something that was of major importance to her, there was no need for me to respond. I simply smiled.

"I need a favor, an extremely special one," Tilly said, and looked so hopeful that I knew that I would be inclined to say yes, regardless of her request.

"I have read your mysteries for years and enjoyed them. So naturally whenever I come across your name in a newspaper or magazine, I will read the article."

Tilly seemed to be expecting a response, so I said, "That's very kind of you."

She nodded her acknowledgment of my thanks and went on. "I was surprised how many of those stories were about your involvement in true crime, actual murders. I was once in love with someone who died in a disastrous car accident." Tilly drew a deep breath and then exhaled slowly. "My children, who know nothing of the past, keep telling me that Jason's death was accidental, some sort of mechanical failure. I can tell you that the human heart knows the difference between an accidental loss of love and a loss that is planned and executed by someone with a villainous soul. My heart, broken as it was, recognized that long-ago death as an accident, just as it knows now that a monster whose heart is filled with evil killed my son. It was cold-blooded murder. Don't you agree?"

"Unfortunately, I do." I patted her hand. "And I cannot even imagine how painful this is for you. I wish there was something I could do—"

"Oh, but there is. That is why I asked Anya to invite you here this morning. I want you to solve Jason's murder."

I was flummoxed. It was one thing for me to snoop (as Seth Hazlitt liked to call it) to satisfy my own curiosity, and quite another to investigate on behalf of the mother of the victim.

"Really, Matilda, I don't think that I can help you. While it is true that on occasion I have been helpful to the authorities with some of *their* investigations, I would be hard-pressed to promise you that I could act as your private detective and solve Jason's murder." I tried to sound compassionate but firm.

"Oh, but, Jessica, I am sure that any effort on your part will lead to answering some of the questions I have," Tilly said. "For example, what was Jason doing at the tennis court so early in the morning? For that matter, what was he doing on the court at all? Unlike Linda, he was barely interested in the game and rarely played."

I had to admit that Matilda made a valid point. I'd assumed that tennis was an interest that Jason and Linda shared, particularly because when I saw Jason's body, he was dressed in tennis whites.

"Still, Matilda, I don't want you to rely on me to—"

"Your mother has company. This isn't a good time." Anya spoke so loudly that I was sure she wanted to be certain that Matilda and I were alerted to the fact that someone else was in the house.

A man answered, "Don't be silly. I just want a quick word and then I am on my way. Now, where is she? Her bedroom?"

Dennis Courtland.

We heard two sets of footsteps coming down the hall.

Anya was still arguing when Dennis came into the bedroom. Whoever he expected, by the look on his face, I could tell it wasn't me. He stopped short and confirmed it.

"Ah, Mrs. Fletcher, I didn't expect you to be here."

Matilda was so used to her children popping in at odd moments that she didn't miss an opportunity to answer sharply, "J. B. Fletcher is one of my favorite authors, and Jessica was kind enough to offer to sign my book collection. Now, if you would be so kind as to allow us to get on with it, I will have Anya call to let you know when I am free."

I caught a glint of suspicion in Dennis's eye. "Sign what books? I don't see any books."

"Oh, for heaven's sake." Matilda grew more exasperated with every passing moment. She gestured toward the dressing table. "Unlike some members of this family, I still have manners, so I offered Jessica a cup of coffee before she started writing her name over and over again, interrupting her holiday as a special favor to me."

Dennis walked to the dressing table and picked up the first book on the stack and read the title aloud. "*The Umbrella Murders* by J. B. Fletcher." He put it down and pulled a book from the middle. "*The Corpse at Vespers* by J. B. Fletcher. Apparently you are quite prolific, Jessica. I shall have to borrow some of Mother's books to enjoy your stories."

He looked squarely at his mother and nodded his head as if the pile of books had convinced him of the purpose of my visit.

Matilda, her patience clearly exhausted, said, "If you are done interfering, would you please leave so that Jessica and I can have our coffee in peace? I specifically directed that I did not wish to have any visitors this morning, and yet here you are."

"Mother, Anya called yesterday and told me that Father Donovan would be here, so you would prefer privacy this morning. When I noticed that his car wasn't in the parking lot, I assumed he'd been here and gone. Where is the good father, by the way?"

Dennis's sly smile was his not-so-subtle way of accusing his mother, or at least Anya, of lying, but Matilda was ready for the question.

"The rectory secretary called this morning to tell me that Father Donovan was called out on an emergency—the death of a longtime parishioner, I believe—and so he was forced to cancel. I took the opportunity to invite Jessica and was delighted when she made this time available. Now, if there is nothing else . . ."

Dennis slid past my chair and leaned down to kiss his mother on the forehead, and then he headed for the door. Once in the doorway, he turned back and asked, "Has my sister stopped by this morning by any chance?"

Matilda pursed her lips and raised her eyes to the ceiling. I hoped she was measuring her words carefully.

Apparently she wasn't. "When I see your sister is no business of yours, just as your sister needn't know that you barged in here today. Now, go about your business and leave me to mine."

We sat in silence and listened to his footsteps echo down the hallway, and from the sound of the way he slammed the front door, Dennis must have been thoroughly vexed by Matilda's comments.

Anya rushed into the room. "Are you okay, Tilly? I stood in the hallway and listened to his ranting. Dennis was in rare form as usual."

"Anya, I am fine," Matilda said. "Perhaps you could bring a few books over here and spread them on my bed so we can avoid unpleasantness if Edwina or Tyler bursts through the front door on a spying mission."

She sat up a little straighter and leaned toward me. "Now you see what I am up against. The competition among my children for my attention has always been strong, perhaps because there were times when I gave them too little. But once their father died, their rivalry grew bitter, spiteful, because from that point on my love could be measured in how I supported each of their positions regarding the company. Of course, Jason was the oldest . . . but now he is gone."

Anya set a couple of books on the bed and put the rest on the small table by my chair, careful to remove my coffee cup. She handed me several pens and said, as if to lighten the mood, "Now, Miss World-Famous Author, those autographs aren't going to write themselves."

As I signed each book, Anya showed the title page to Matilda and then put the books on the dresser. The time went by quickly and I could see that Matilda had been drained by the morning's events and needed a rest. Even if I hadn't been aware, Anya certainly was.

I hoped Matilda had forgotten her earlier request, but as I stood to leave, she said quietly, "Jessica, you won't forget what I asked of you?"

And I assured her I would not.

Once outside, I checked my watch and was pleased. I had just enough time to walk to the community center and meet Frank at the end of art class. Perhaps I'd be lucky enough to get a chance to speak to Jamie Ingram.

Chapter Twenty-Four

Class must have just ended as I got to the community center, but I didn't see Jamie Ingram. As the children came out, they were proudly showing paintings to the waiting adults, who were oohing and aahing their appreciation. Frank came out talking to two boys, one about his age and one who was probably a year or two older. I heard him mention Lafayette. When he saw me, he said good-bye to the boys and ran to show me his painting.

I admired the gray feathers shaded from medium to dark and the reddish orange chest of his bird. "You've really learned a lot about mixing colors and blending from light to dark. This robin redbreast is really well done."

Frank beamed. "I'm learning so much. Wait until you see the doorstop I am working on in pottery class."

"Mrs. Fletcher, Frank's work is really exceptional." Carissa

Potter came up to us. "Why don't you tell your aunt what to-day's homework assignment is?"

Frank laughed. "We have to go to the beach and collect enough sand to pour through the hole in the back of our doorstops before we seal them. Did you know that a lot of doorstops have sand inside to make them heavy enough to hold a door open?"

"No, I did not." I noticed Carissa was craning her neck, searching through the jumble of junior artists and their adult companions. "Carissa, are you looking for someone? As it happens, I was hoping to speak to Jamie Ingram. Is she around?"

"Jamie left early to take her mother to a doctor's appointment. No, I am looking for Billy and Shane Courtland." She continued to peer around the area in front of the community center. "Where could they have gone so quickly?"

"Aunt Jess, you saw them. We came out of class together, but then I saw you."

"Well, then, you are correct, Frank. I did see them. When you came over to me, I noticed they ran in the direction of the bungalows."

"Oh, I am sorry I missed them," Carissa said. "Today was their first day back in class since they lost their grandfather. I wanted to talk to them privately, see how they feel, and encourage them to come to class regularly. I could have even consoled them if it seemed necessary. I told you I lost my father in a disastrous car accident when I was even younger than they are, so I know how a family death can devastate a child."

"And I am so sorry that you had that experience." I slued my eyes toward Frank to remind her that he was listening to every word. "In any event, Frank and I must get home. There is a rumor we have some bike riding to look forward to this afternoon."

"Of course," Carissa said, and drifted off.

"Bike riding! Can we ride on the boardwalk again?" Frank jumped up and down several times.

"Well"—I took his hand—"I can't promise the boardwalk, but if one of your parents has the time to drive us to the ramp, I don't see why not."

Grady helped us load the bicycles into the trunk of his SUV. As we were getting into the car, he said, "Aunt Jess, I'm so happy you are here. The boardwalk is such a great place for bicycle riding and Frank loves to ride. Unfortunately, I had another top-priority audit, files and all, pop up on my laptop about an hour ago. One of Mr. Hargreaves's 'hush hush, rush rush' jobs. On top of that, Donna has been summoned to Tyler Young's house for what he called a strategy session. Several of her work colleagues are bringing special files from the office so they can, as Tyler put it, 'outline the future of global.' Sometimes I think these Wall Street guys are cuckoo."

"Just remember you are one of them," I said as he pulled out of the parking lot.

It was a beautiful day for a ride on the boardwalk. Frank and I had slathered on sunscreen before we left the house, and I was happy to note that he had gotten into the habit of setting the alarm on his smart watch for a redo in two hours. There were just enough clouds to give us brief periods of shade so that the afternoon sun wasn't as damaging as it could have been. As we rode along, I admired the miles and miles of blue ocean with white-foam waves cresting and rolling.

We sat on a bench for a short water break and were about to remount our bicycles when I felt a tap on my shoulder. Agent Josh Keppler.

"Good afternoon, Mrs. Fletcher. Great day for a bike ride."

"It is. I am beginning to think that every day is a great day for some activity or another here in the Rockaways," I said.

"I know the feeling. When I was assigned this case, I groaned, 'Not another boss who can't keep his hands out of the till.' Then when I found out that the person I was investigating spent most of the summer here at the beach, I was psyched."

Frank had found a paper cup filled with seashells near the staircase that led down to the sand and he was busy examining the contents, shell by shell. I took Keppler's arm and moved us a couple of feet away so Frank wouldn't overhear us. Then I told the agent where Donna was spending the afternoon and why.

"And since I know how easy it is to get to Wall Street from here, I have to wonder why Tyler is having files brought out to the beach house when it surely would have been easier for him to travel into Manhattan. And why involve Donna?"

"Mrs. Fletcher, I could kiss you. But I won't because your young escort is giving me the evil eye." Keppler laughed.

It was the happiest I'd ever seen him.

"Don't worry." I laughed. "You are only getting the evil eye because Frank is now bored with the seashells and anxious to ride away. And so am I. Have a great day, Agent Keppler."

"Thanks to our conversation, I definitely will. Now, if you'll excuse me, I have to call my office."

And he began jogging intensely toward the nearest off-ramp.

About an hour later, Grady was waiting for us right where he'd dropped us off. He loaded the bikes into the car with the muscular assistance of his son, and as he pulled away from the curb, I casually asked if Donna was home from her meeting.

"Not when I left, she wasn't," Grady said. "And I tell you, Aunt Jess, I didn't like the sound of it. Why involve her in a meeting that has nothing to do with her direct line of supervision? I've worked in a lot of money firms, but Courtland is by far the strangest one I've ever seen."

Detectives Tieri and Kelly were getting into their car just as we pulled into the parking lot. I had a lot of ideas swirling around in my mind. I knew I had people to call and questions to ask, but since the two detectives were standing in front of me, I thought, *What better place to start?*

I told Grady and Frank I'd catch up with them at the bungalow and then I stopped to ask the detectives if they had heard from Agent Keppler. When they said they hadn't, I told them that they might well hear something soon and repeated the conversation he and I had.

Aisha Kelly winked while she gave me a broad smile. "You do keep your finger on the pulse of things, don't you, Jessica?"

"I certainly try." I laughed. "But there are a lot of things that are still tumbling around in my mind. I wonder if you could help me get access to some old police files."

Vinny Tieri gave me a long appraising look. "You know Mort Metzger advised me to always go with your hunches no matter how crazy they might seem. Tell me, Jessica, do you have a hunch about who our killer might be?"

"I wouldn't say a hunch, exactly. It's more like I have some unanswered questions that, quite honestly, may have nothing at all to do with Jason Courtland's murder, but I'd—"

"But you'd like to have the answers just the same," Vinny said, finishing my sentence. "We'll see what we can do to help."

"I appreciate it." I told him which files I thought would be helpful and I ended with "And if I can render any assistance . . ."

"You could tell us what you know about the widow," Vinny said. "She has enough doctors and lawyers at the barricades to prevent us from any type of formal interview. If there is nothing too suspicious going on, we might allow that as a courtesy for the first day or two, but this woman has pushed us far past the limit. I am ready to show up at the house with a warrant. The only problem is I'm still looking for cause and don't quite have it. Maybe you know of something?"

Aisha Kelly, always one to go for the gentler touch, said, "So tell us, Mrs. Fletcher, is there any way you think we might catch her off guard for a short, less-than-formal chat?"

"Well, I can't say for certain, of course, but I do know that Linda Courtland is an avid tennis player. Naturally her private court is off-limits and for her, emotionally, may never be usable again. I do know that she dislikes using the public courts, but it would not surprise me to find her on the schedule to play a set or two with a comforting and understanding friend at whichever posh tennis club lists her as a member."

"That is genius! After a tragic loss, many people try to burn off the depression and grief with their favorite exercise. Certainly worth a shot. Thank you." Vinny unlocked the car door. "And about what you asked, we'll see what we can do."

I waved my thanks and headed to the bungalow. Anya was sweeping the steps that led to Matilda's front porch.

Without looking up, she said, "Sand! As much as I love living here in the summer, the sand is everywhere. I've brought in loads of mulch, compost, even potting soil, and over the years created this entire garden."

Anya waved her arm, indicating the plants that were scattered around the lush seagrass. "Look at my daylilies. And my beautiful pink and white crinums will be in full bloom very soon. I did all that to tamp down the sand around the houses, and yet I'm out here sweeping the steps every day."

I started to commiserate but she cut me short.

"Jessica, I can't thank you enough. Since your visit Tilly is like a new person. She is up and dressed, even watched the news at lunchtime. I can't thank you enough," Anya repeated.

Although I wasn't sure why I deserved such praise, I started to thank Anya, but she brushed off my gratitude and continued. "Tilly reminded me that we owe your family a boat ride. I called Captain Craddock and gave him Donna's phone number. He's probably called her by now."

"If so, I do hope she was able to take the call. She has been tied up most of the day in a meeting with Tyler Young and some other people. I know Frank will be thrilled. Please thank Matilda on behalf of all the Fletchers."

A shadow crossed Anya's face as soon as I mentioned Tyler Young. She covered her mouth as if she was about to cough, or perhaps she was trying to keep words from escaping. I wasn't exactly sure.

Then she said slowly and carefully, "Now that Jason is out of his way, Tyler Young will most certainly try to take over leadership of the company. Edwina will drown herself in bourbon and pretend it is not happening. I am not sure that Dennis has the brains and the strength to fend him off. I am afraid both sides will hound Tilly, and she cannot take another upset so soon after losing her son. I will do everything I can to protect her from them. I only hope I am strong enough."

"From what I have seen, Tilly is blessed to have you as . . . What was it Dennis called you? Her gatekeeper—that was it. I believe she is in very good hands."

"I do my best. Now I suppose I should get back inside and see what Tilly is up to. If I am gone too long, what kind of a gatekeeper would I be?" Anya picked up her broom. "And please let me know if Donna and Captain Craddock don't connect."

"I will," I assured her, "but I have a quick question."

I asked, and she looked surprised, but she answered before hurrying into the house.

I walked slowly past Edwina's house, hoping to see her sitting on the porch with her ever-present iced tea, or perhaps I could overhear something from Tyler's staff meeting, but there were no signs of life. I headed to the bungalow and my iPad, which I was sure could give me more answers.

Chapter Twenty-Five

The Mets and the Giants were tied three all in the bottom of the seventh inning, which had Grady and Frank glued to the television when I got home.

Grady said, "Donna texted. She is still stuck at Tyler's house. I'm going to grill some burgers and hot dogs as soon as the game is over if that's okay with you? I checked the fridge; there's potato salad, and you know Donna always makes sure there are plenty of fresh veggies for salad."

The crowd on the television roared. Grady turned to follow the action and I slipped away to my room, glad to have some time alone with my iPad.

I took out my suspect list and read it carefully. I made notes here and there as I went along, crossing off some things and adding information that I'd recently collected.

I heard the crowd at the baseball game roar again and

Frank yelled, "Oh, no." I suspected things weren't going well for the Mets. Things simmered down in the living room.

I noted one last reminder of things I wanted to do tomorrow and went into the living room just as a bat cracked a ball and a Mets player broke the tie with a home run. Needless to say, the living room crowd went wild. Before I could find out the details, the front door opened, and Donna walked in, looking exhausted but happy to be home.

Frank jumped up and gave his mother a big hug, which turned into a happy dance while he outlined the last few minutes of the game.

Finally Grady snapped off the television and said, "I'll go start the grill."

Frank ran outside behind him, still talking about the game. Donna sat down and kicked off her sandals.

"Honestly, Aunt Jess, I am not sure how all this is going to work out. I am in so far over my head. Tyler reviewed a half dozen files that I never heard of and kept directing the staff to remember that I'm in charge of this procedure or that procedure. If they have any questions, he told them, 'Don't hesitate to consult Donna. She'll be your lead.' Lead on what, I'd like to know."

I glanced out the window. Grady and Frank were busy with the grill. I leaned close to Donna and said, "I can't go into it right now but I suspect that Tyler will not be able to cause you any more trouble at work. Just hold tight for a few more days."

Donna looked stricken. "Don't tell me. Are you saying that he . . . ?"

I stroked her head, brushing her hair back from her flushed face. "I am not saying anything other than I have a sense that things will get better in the next few days. Now, check your phone to see if you have a message from Captain Craddock. Anya tells me we are being invited for a boat ride."

Donna brightened instantly. "In Jamaica Bay? Frank will be thrilled. Let me go to my room and see if he's called and we can connect right now. I need some good news."

Don't we all, I thought.

After dinner Frank thumped me soundly at a game of chess. Then we each settled down with our books for a cozy last hour before bedtime. My phone rang. Vinny Tieri. I ran to my room as I answered.

"Jessica, I was able to get everything you wanted. I have to say it is quite an eclectic mix. Aisha and I are sitting here trying to make the connections. Anyway, all I need is your e-mail address and I'll send the files right over."

Even though I was sure of much of what I was about to read, my heart was pumping as if I'd jogged ten miles. I gave him my e-mail address and asked if he was working tomorrow.

"Aisha and I will be working day tours tomorrow. Are you planning anything special? Will we need bulletproof vests?"

"Don't even joke like that. No, at this point I'm not planning anything. I wanted to know if I could find you to thank you once I've had a chance to look over all the documents you're sending me," I said.

"Got it. I guarantee we're both anxious to have you clue us in on what connects all this rigmarole. As to thanks, all I need is for you to put in a good word for me with Metzger. When Aisha gets tired of putting up with me, I might want to retire to the boonies and become Mort's deputy." Vinny was still laughing when he hung up the phone.

Vinny's e-mail had more attachments than I'd expected. Grady saved the day when I asked if he or Donna could drive me to the library in the morning so that I could use the printer.

"No need to go anywhere. We have a printer in our bedroom. It was Donna's idea to bring it, which turned out to be lucky, because Mr. Hargreaves keeps sending work files to me." Grady opened his laptop. "Forward the files to me."

I sat on my bed and read every document carefully. I had hoped to narrow down my list of possible murderers to no more than two people, but in short order I realized there was only one, and that revelation was bound to cause Matilda Courtland even more heartache. I outlined a plan of action and then turned out my light, hoping for a good night's rest.

At breakfast, Frank was bubbly as he described the doorstop he was making in art school. "I have a pail of sand on the porch that I am ready to take with us to school this morning to use to fill my doorstop. I have extra in case someone forgets their sand."

"That's very thoughtful," I said, but I suspected everyone at the table could see that my mind was elsewhere.

Frank said, "You are coming to art class with me this morning, aren't you, Aunt Jess? You did promise."

"Of course. I wouldn't miss it. I have to make some phone calls before we leave, but then I promise I am all yours."

My first phone call was less difficult than I'd imagined it

would be. The person agreed to my request without hesitation. However, when I made the second call, I was bombarded with questions that I answered as tactfully as I could.

My final chore was to ask Grady for a favor. He agreed instantly.

I gave him a kiss on the cheek and said, "I can always count on you."

Then I sat on the porch enjoying the view of the ocean until it was time to leave for the community center.

Reggie Masterson brought several lavender plants to class, and we used them as models. The children were excited because they could use their newly honed skills to mix primary colors until they had the exact shade of secondary colors they wanted.

During the break I asked Jamie Ingram how her mother was doing. She seemed surprised by the question.

I said, "I understood that you left early yesterday to take her to the doctor."

"Oh, that." Jamie dismissed the doctor with a flap of her hand. "That was a routine checkup. My mom has a ton of illnesses, so she requires a lot of attention, but I make sure she gets all her tests and never misses a doctor's visit, so she'll probably outlive me."

She was immediately distracted by a little girl who needed help opening a water bottle, followed by another girl who needed help with a hair braid that had unraveled. Jamie gave me a "what are you going to do?" look, and I said I would talk with her later and went into the pottery class.

I was fascinated by the various shapes the children had

chosen for their doorstops. There were leaves, flowers, boats, and bells. Frank's design was a sailboat. After we carefully poured sand into the hole in the rear of the boat, Frank plugged it very carefully. Carissa came around with sealant to secure the closures, and there was a lot of passing the doorstops around the room. The children were lavish with praise for one another's work and were taken by surprise when the bell rang. While the little artists scurried around the room, gathering up their artwork and their belongings, I found Jamie and asked her to help me hurry along the stragglers in Carissa's class. Grady was already in the doorway, and he gave me a thumbs-up so that I knew he would walk Frank home.

When the last of the children left the room, I said to Carissa, "I understand your real name is Carrie Stockly."

Carissa laughed. "Well, that's nearly true. Carissa is my actual first name, but my father thought it was a heavy burden for such a tiny baby and he began calling me Carrie the minute I was born. In fact, I didn't discover that Carissa was my real name until I started school. When I opened my studio, I thought Carissa sounded more professional and I added Potter as a catchy, career-prone surname."

I nodded. "Well, that is certainly true, plus, anyone from the North Fork would probably recognize the name Stockly. I understand that your father was quite a prominent attorney in the community before his terrible accident."

Carissa began to nibble on her lower lip. "Please don't bring that up. The pain is still with me."

I hoped I sounded sympathetic. "I'm sure it is. Tell me, exactly how did you find out where your father was going when the accident happened?"

Carissa stared at me, trying to decide how much I knew. I kept my eyes directly on hers and she began to realize I knew everything. Her shoulders slumped and a single tear trickled down her cheek.

"He left a letter for my mother telling her he was leaving for that wicked woman. Leaving my mother. Leaving me. Mom kept that piece of paper with those horrid words in her jewelry box all these years. I found it after she died."

"So you decided to connect with the Courtland family through this art school," I summarized.

Carissa nodded. "I researched the Courtland family until I knew everything about them. When Jason started the art project, I found my way in. At first I was happy just to be able to watch them, to laugh at how dysfunctional they all were: Edwina with her drinking, Dennis with his womanizing, and Jason, a grown man who could not keep his life or his company on track without running to Mommy every few minutes. Matilda the matriarch couldn't function without having that link to Jason. His neediness gave her purpose."

"I can understand your anger at Matilda, but why kill Jason?"

Carissa threw back her shoulders and smiled. "I was a small child with no means of taking care of myself and she took away the man I could rely on—my father. Now she is old and infirm, so it was time for me to take away the man she relied on to give her life meaning—her oldest son."

"How did you get him to stand in front of the TeachTennis and be pummeled to death?" I hadn't quite figured that out.

"That was the easy part. I spread a rumor that Linda had

her eye on the tennis pro at the private tennis club in Wood-mere. And I made sure the rumor reached Edwina. Getting it from her to Jason took a matter of seconds. Then, while we were having a staff meeting with Jason, I asked Reggie if he played, which I knew he did not. I pretended to have championship skills and said I was afraid of getting rusty. Surprise, surprise! Jason offered to play with me, provided I show him a few pointers and we kept it a secret from Linda. He wanted to surprise her by improving his skills."

"And you set up the TeachTennis?"

"Not right away. We met for lessons a few times, and when I was sure he would do as I directed, I dragged the TeachTennis out from its corner. The first time, I stayed on his side of the net and set the machine slow and easy. It batted balls across the net and we both hit them. Jason was heading toward his own death and enjoying himself while doing so. Kinda cool, don't you think?"

I couldn't comprehend how Carissa could see it that way. I moved on. "And it was you who shaved the tennis balls?"

"Of course. That was simple. The gate to the court is never locked. Anyone could come and go as they pleased," Carissa said. "Actually, the whole thing was simple. The day it happened, I got to the court extra early and set the TeachTennis to pitch a ball every second at a hundred miles an hour. I took the remote and stood outside the court behind those trees on the far side. When Jason arrived, I came along as if I was running late. He was standing on the court and I laughingly suggested that he get into position opposite the machine because it was ready to really challenge him. Not knowing that I had the remote control in my hand, he laughed good-naturedly and moved to the perfect spot. I pushed the remote's power button."

She paused and her eyes took on a look of satisfaction at the memory. "The first ball was a lucky shot. It hit Jason on his forehead. He reeled backward but managed to stay on his feet. Before he could fully recover, two more balls landed. One thumped against his chest and the other hit him square on the chin. That's when he went down. And he never got up again. I ran down to the ocean, jogged about ten blocks to the east, and flung the remote as far into the water as I could. I was on my way back to my apartment to shower and change when I met you and Frank. The rest is history."

I glanced at the doorway. Detectives Tieri and Kelly had two uniformed police officers with them. Aisha Kelly walked over and told Carissa her legal rights in a strong, clear voice. Then the uniformed officers led her away.

Vinny said, "Boy, Mort Metzger was right about you, but I do have questions. You asked for all records associated with Edward Ingram's arrest and you asked us to get the records of Arthur Stockly's car accident, which happened decades ago, from Suffolk County. Were you thinking that Carissa Stockly and Ingram's wife were somehow in cahoots?"

I chuckled. "Oh, Vinny, I wish it were that simple. The reason I asked for both sets of records is that I wasn't sure if someone connected to Edward Ingram had reason to want Jason dead. His wife was the logical choice, but Jason had been kind enough to offer her work so she wouldn't starve, plus, as I just learned, she is the caretaker for her aged mother. So I couldn't see it."

I brought up another thing that had puzzled me. "And we never answered the question of why Jason was on the court so early in the morning, dressed in tennis whites and carrying a racket. Who was he meeting? I remembered reading that Carissa was a tennis player in college. She'd be a natural for a tennis date with Jason. I wasn't sure why he wanted to play with her, but now we know. She set a trap. He fell for it."

"When you called this morning and told me about this setup, I'm sorry I asked so many questions. Next time, I'll trust you. Easier that way," Vinny said.

We were both chuckling at that thought when one of the uniformed officers came in and told Vinny that a Ms. Wiggins was outside asking to speak to Mrs. Fletcher.

Vinny nodded his head toward the door. "So I guess I wasn't the only phone call you made this morning. Go ahead. The family deserves to know."

I walked slowly out of the building, trying to find the words to tell Anya the reason why Jason had been senselessly killed.

Chapter Twenty-Six

It took a few days until I finally felt like we were on a family vacation. Grady parked the car and grabbed the cooler Donna had filled with juice boxes and assorted snacks from out of the trunk. We were each carrying hats and waterproof jackets, which belied the sunshine of the day.

Frank was beside himself with excitement. "Which boat is ours, Dad? Where is *Getaway*?"

"Anya said it was docked in slip twenty-eight. Over there. That looks like a directory. Let's check."

He and Frank ran to the weather-beaten sign.

Donna said, "Aunt Jessica, this is so exciting. We finally get the boat ride in Jamaica Bay that Mrs. Courtland promised. I am so glad you could join us. I hope this trip wasn't too stressful for you, what with the murder and all. I still can't believe Carissa—"

"Donna, that is behind us. We've been able to spend time together and that's what counts the most."

I put my arm around her and gave her a squeeze.

"Still, it's a shame about the art program. I guess Reggie will have to carry on by himself until summer's end," Donna said.

"Maybe not. I happen to know that Jamie Ingram has a talent for papier-mâché art. Perhaps she could step up," I said.

Grady waved at us and pointed left. "Slip twenty-eight is down this dock."

While watching Grady trying to keep Frank from running ahead, I said to Donna, "These are the moments that count. The trials and tribulations will always come along, but family time, ah, that's what matters."

Grady stopped next to a supermodern Sea Ray. It was at least a thirty-footer, stylishly white with navy trim on the hull.

"Oh, my," I said to Donna. "Matilda did say the family had a couple of 'smallish' boats docked here, didn't she?"

"She sure did," Donna said. "You have to wonder what size it would have to be before she would consider the boat to be large."

A man, hair and whiskers a matched set of gray, waved to us from the cockpit, adjusted the peak of his nautical captain's hat, and hollered, "If you be the Fletchers, welcome aboard! Come ahead aft"—he pointed to the rear of the boat—"and I'll give you a hand."

As we clambered aboard, he said, "I'm Benjamin Craddock, skipper of the *Getaway*. You can call me Captain Ben.

Anya Wiggins said I was to treat you like royalty, and believe me, she says that about absolutely nobody. You must be pretty special."

He looked at the cooler Grady had set on the floor. "What have you hoisted aboard, laddie?"

Donna said, "I packed a few snacks and some juice boxes. If eating on the boat isn't permitted, we understand perfectly. It'll keep until we get home."

"Eating on board is fine. In fact, it's recommended. Anya's local caterer dropped off a picnic lunch a while ago. I stowed it below. It'll be ready whenever you are. Now, if you folks will get settled in, we'll be off."

I raised my hand. "Captain Ben, I was wondering where the fishing gear is stored."

"Aye, there she be, a gal after my own heart."

He took two steps to a long bench covered with plump pillows and popped a latch. The storage case contained rods, reels, nets, and two tackle boxes.

"Help yourself to whatever you need. Let's get these life jackets strapped around you, and then I was wondering if this young man and his dad would like to climb up into the cockpit with me for a bit of time."

Captain Ben laughed heartily at Frank's ecstatic response.

Donna and I made ourselves comfortable in the stern, where we sat on luxurious plush pillows covered with marine-grade vinyl as Ben drove us out of the slip.

Captain Ben spoke through a microphone so everyone on the boat could hear whatever he had to say. "Here we are in Dead Horse Bay."

Frank's head snapped up and I thought he was going to say

something about this being the wrong bay. Grady apparently got the same notion and gave the universal parent gesture by holding up his hand to signal Frank that he should listen and not speak.

Captain Ben continued. "On our left is Floyd Bennett Field, namesake of the naval aviator who, along with Richard Byrd, is said to have made the first flight to the North Pole in 1926. Be mindful, though, there are folks who dispute that fact. In a few more miles, we'll make a left turn under the Marine Parkway Bridge entryway to Jamaica Bay."

Frank clapped gleefully. "Captain Ben, if it wouldn't be too much trouble . . . Are we going to see the wildlife refuge?"

"Say no more, sonny. Anya told me you are a big fan of the refuge, but only hand-powered boats—you know, canoes, rowboats, kayaks, and the like—are allowed to land on any national park wetlands, but we can get in pretty close and take a good long look. And I'll make it up to you by sharing my secret fishing spot, where I guarantee you'll have no trouble catching a nice fluke or bluefish."

Frank's excitement was contagious, so I began searching through one of the tackle boxes, looking for the equipment I was sure we'd need when the fishing started.

Behind me I heard bell tones that sounded like the Beatles tune "With a Little Help from My Friends."

Donna was digging through her purse. "Darn, I forgot to turn off my phone. And that's Carole's ringtone, so I'd better get it."

I went on searching the tackle box, but I couldn't help listening to Donna's chorus of exclamations.

"Seriously? This morning!" followed by "How could that be?" and then "The world's gone mad."

At that point I went back to my seat and waited for her to finish the conversation and tell me whatever had gotten her so flushed with excitement.

"Aunt Jess, you won't believe it. Early this morning a slew of FBI and SEC agents marched into Courtland Finance with warrants. Then Dennis Courtland arrived, demanding to know what was going on. He spent an hour locked in his office with two agents, and when Carole described them, well, I'm sure the one in charge was Josh Keppler."

"Oh, that wouldn't be surprising at all. He's been working on whatever this case may be for the longest time. Tell me, Donna, would there be a way for the office records to show which files were brought to Tyler's house the other day and whether or not they were returned?"

"Of course, Aunt Jessica. Everything is computerized. If there is something special you want to know about, I can call Carole back and have an answer for you in under two minutes."

"Oh, that won't be at all necessary. The important thing is that, thanks to you, Agent Keppler knows that files were removed and who ordered the removal. I'm sure he already had a strong idea as to why."

The boat was slowing to a stop. Captain Ben reached up and tugged on the rope tied to the clapper of the brass ship's bell that hung behind his shoulder. As the ringing faded away, he said, "Hear ye, hear ye, ladies and gentlemen. We have entered the sacred fishing ground of Captain Benjamin Craddock. Please raise your right hand. Do you swear to keep this location a secret from any encroaching fishermen who want to find this magical spot? Now please say, 'I do.'"

Naturally we all said "I do," but Frank was by far the loudest. Donna and I exchanged a joyful look. After all the stress, it was wonderful to relax and watch the boy have fun.

Grady, Frank, and I all put on our waterproof jackets and sun hats. Then we picked out rods and reels from the storage bin. I put odds and ends of equipment in a creel and set it at my feet.

Grady did a terrific job of helping Frank bait and cast off. Once Frank's hook was in the water, I followed suit. Frank kept asking how long we thought it would take for him to catch his first fish. Grady cautioned him, saying that fish liked to take their time and that they liked quiet.

With that, the Beatles ringtone from Donna's phone sounded off loud and clear. Mercifully she found her phone quickly this time, because Frank's look of reproach was something to see.

Donna whispered to Carole, and I could tell by Donna's face that the news was staggering. When she hung up, I lifted my line out of the water and walked to the starboard side of the boat and dropped it in again.

Donna came over and whispered, "You won't believe it!"

"Try me, especially if it is about Tyler Young."

Donna's eyes widened. "Aunt Jess, you are a marvel. Catch a killer, save a company—it's all in a day's work for you."

"Oh, no, my dear. You are the one that saved Courtland Finance by being forthright with Agent Keppler, and that phone call you made to Anthony Barlowe was paramount in getting Keppler to trust us. Now, tell me what has happened." I was dying of curiosity.

"Well, Tyler Young marched into the office a while ago,

ranting and raving, demanding to know what was going on. He went into Dennis's office for a closed-door meeting, and five minutes later, he came out, walked to the elevators, and hit the down button. When the elevator arrived, he held the door open with his hand and yelled as loud as he could, 'You have my resignation. You will hear from my lawyer.'"

I nodded. "That's not surprising."

Donna said, "Perhaps not to you, but the staff in the global division is floored. And Carole said that within twenty minutes the rumor began to circulate that Dennis was going to ask Anthony Barlowe to step in and run the division on a temporary basis until all of the records within the division could be scrutinized."

"Well, that would be sensible—"

Frank's line started to jump. "Dad, Aunt Jess, I think I caught a fish. What do I do?"

"Hold on to your pole. It's always surprising how strong a fish can become when he feels trapped. He'll fight you every inch of the way."

I set my pole firmly in a rod holder mounted on the boat's rail, stepped behind Frank, and put my hands on his fishing rod.

"Here, let me give you a hand. Now, point your rod toward the fish. That's good. Slant it down. Now reel him in. Slowly. Slowly. Good job."

And that was exactly when the fish gave a hard yank and Frank's line unraveled. Frank looked at me in a panic.

"Don't worry," I said. "He's pulling away. That's what fish do. Tip your rod down and reel him in again. We'll win this fight. You wait and see."

There was more back-and-forth, and all at once it seemed as though the fish surrendered and we reeled in a beautiful, healthy-sized bluefish.

I corralled him in the fishing net, disconnected Frank's line, and said, "Here comes the best part."

I pushed the fish down into a bucket of seawater and grabbed the fishing pliers out of the creel. I held the fish's mouth open with one hand, and once I straightened the hook, we eased it out of the fish's mouth.

Then I handed the bucket to Frank. "Your fish is in excellent shape. Do you want to toss him back, or shall I?"

"Please, I'd like to do it, but first we have to give him a name."

I clapped my hands. "That is a great idea. Do you have a name in mind?"

Frank nodded. "Well, he was a strong fighter, don't you think?"

"Oh, yes, a worthy adversary. Absolutely," I agreed.

"So"—Frank bent his head down until his nose was nearly in the bucket with the fish, which was flapping his tail, eager to get back home—"I want to give him a name worthy of a fighter. We'll call him Marquis, after that great warrior, the Marquis de Lafayette."

Frank struggled to lift the bucket until Grady lent his muscles to the job. Together they were able to drop Marquis over the side and watch him swim until he disappeared into the depths of his lifelong home—Jamaica Bay.